# COUP D'TWELVE

## The Enterprise that
## Bought the Presidency

By David E. Martin

*David E. Martin*

COUP D'TWELVE: The Enterprise that Bought the Presidency

Fifth Estate, Post Office Box 116,

Blountsville, AL 35031

First Edition

Cover Designed by An Quigley

Printed on acid-free paper

Library of Congress Control No: 2011939556

ISBN: 9781936533152

Fifth Estate, 2011

## Table of Contents

**Dedicated to**
My Lady
Spud & Zuke

and

*The families and memories of those who have suffered and died in the stories rendered herein. That they neither died in vain nor suffer for the clandestine interests of those who breach their public duty.*

# CHAPTER 1 - THE ASSASSINATION

"Give him Osama."

"You're shitting me. Why would we do that before we know who the Repubs are going to run? After all, if they're seriously going to let Trump take a shot, the least we could do is keep everybody guessing until October 2012 and then pull a Reagan – hell maybe even with Iran again!"

"Listen, he's kept us covered and God knows the economy isn't getting any better. No chance that unemployment is going to improve. And, let's face it, the marketing of 'Change' and 'Hope' doesn't have a prayer of working again…"

Staring out the 38th floor window overlooking Central Park, the balding gentleman crushed out his second cigarette. It seemed like such a good idea when Steve pitched the idea in 2000 – so avant garde, so next millennium. Pick the perfectly marketable candidate, run him for President in 2008 and have him finish the job.

"You know," he mumbled, "I still don't trust your smooth talking focus group wizards," his voice dripping with contempt. "Your slithering marketing geniuses wouldn't stand a chance next to one of my quants."

"Listen, Carey," his voice lowered, "you know that ISI is telling us that Dr. Khan is in and out of the compound several times a day since late March. Having a dead mastermind who died in a diabetic coma isn't going do us a damn bit of good. Let's see, how would the headlines go? 'Arch Enemy of the Free World Dies in Exclusive Hospital Compound'. Oh, yeah, that will do us all a shit load of nothing!"

"You see, that's the problem with you neocon pretty boys. You can't think two steps ahead of your own damn feet," growled Keith. "You actually think that you can keep a corpse propped up and use him as a card-board cut out. There was a time when we could do that but that was before that little Scandinavian shit started leaking our material. Hell, by now he's probably got intercepts in a file somewhere with reports of the mysterious termination of dialysis a few days ago. If the world doesn't have a corpse with a bullet in it, there's no way we'll ever sell the story that we finally got him. Bottom line, the bastard didn't wait for the elections and so we've got to stage a killing."

"What does the Circle think about pulling the trigger?" Carey asked, his tone suitably deferential.

"Who gives a damn what they think. We'll tell them that we had to get it done and that there was no way in hell that they could keep selling the deal if they didn't get the public to swallow a dead Terrorist-in-Chief killed by our boys."

The smoke rising from the cigarette butt in the Waterford bowl stopped coiling for a moment and just rose. This was a crazy Spring in New York. A few days when you'd think it was June and then, bam, rain, cold, wind – something to grind La Guardia and Kennedy to a halt. It just felt like things were askew – imperceptibly most of the time but, then, when you just stood long enough on Madison or Fifth, you could even see it. People were walking a bit differently. Yes, there were more Asians this year but it wasn't just that. There were moments when it felt like somebody had their finger poised just above the giant red reset button. But you couldn't quite tell what that button would do. The only thing for sure was..., well, come to think of it, that was the problem. Nothing was certain except that gnawing.

"Alright, I'll call Pinocchio and let him know that he's got green on OBL," mumbled Carey in a tone so low that nobody really heard what he said.

There was a time when he would have given up his own mother just to be in the same stadium as the President of the United States. Back when, aspiring to serve the cause of freedom, he knew that the Commander-in-Chief actually really meant something. Now, it was his job to report orders to the President. What kind of world had it become or was it always this way and he was just finally seeing it from inside the matrix? He was going to give the President an order from the Twelve and they hadn't really even given the order. In fact, they were going to find out that Osama was erased this way the same way everybody else would – on the news.

"We got naval assets in position off the coast. It's got to look legit so let's give CNN the bait to sell the story. Make sure that we lose one bird in the Op – no 'Blackhawk Down' bullshit but, you know the drill. The more people know that it was dangerous, the less they'll look for any other leads."

The voice at the other end of the phone, this time not reading from a teleprompter in that methodical, Max Headroom syncopation, paused for a moment.

"Isn't he already dead?" asked the President.

"He's not dead until we have Navy SEALs back on deck with a body bag and with a bullet in the corpse."

"Who gets to run the Op?"

"Get Panetta to make sure it's clean. We need our boys to be around the compound to make sure that any ISI operative is taken out before they can tell a different story. Let me be clear – you'll get to get up in front of all the cameras and announce the deal. You know, it must be nice to know that on this story, you're not just kicking across tornado damage all weekend with governors who aren't looking very happy to be standing next to you in the photo ops. Liz is working on your speech and we'll give you a couple slots to ad lib. We want the Agency coordinating and we need to make sure that the world gets the official story – Navy assets, surgical strike, minimal shock and awe – you get the picture."

"When do I bring people into the Situation Room?"

"They're already on their way."

"On their way? I thought you said…"

He couldn't finish. The line was dead.

The first guest showed up at the White House seven minutes later.

"Mr. President," he stopped to shake his hand.

"Looks like we're going to have one helluva an evening, Sir," he continued. "We've arranged for a front row seat. You should have some decent images off the birds and we'll have enough footage to make sure that this thing can't ever leak."

"So you're saying that we'll have the Operation streaming," the President mused off-hand.

"Well, yes – all but the part when we…"

Another visitor arrived.

"Sir," continued the first guest, "you understand that we can't record the actual shooting. If that signal were intercepted, and God knows somebody would, we'd have a tough time dealing with shooting at a corpse and calling it a Navy SEAL Op."

"Evening, Robert."

Ever since the briefing, the President marveled at how people who allegedly lived in the United Kingdom, Russia, Cyprus, Kazakhstan, and God knows where all else, could just show up at the White House like they had just been strolling through the Rose Garden.

"How the hell do they get here this fast and how long ago did this all go down?" he mused.

He didn't need to be reminded. When he and the First Lady-to-be were visited on the night of the election back in 2008, it took a solid twenty minutes to actually let the message sink in.

"So what you're saying is that you *bought* the Presidency and I'm who you *bought*?" he stammered, incapable of comprehending what he was hearing.

"Let's see," replied the man introduced only as Silas, "yes."

"You can't honestly believe that you won a fair fight. McCain's a great guy, war hero and all, but Palin, are you kidding? You can't seriously believe that you and Joe ran against a real ticket. You see, we bought both sides and, let's face it; you better believe it was tough to tell McCain that he was playing to lose. He didn't take it so well but, soldier to the end, we set him up so he could be one of those candidates who never was the guy who lost."

"Are you saying that the first black President elected in the history of the United States was *bought*?"

He still couldn't get his head around what was being said. Michelle wanted to leave the room in the worst way but was frozen – unable to consider what rabbit hole she'd just fallen through.

"This is America!!! You don't buy the Presidency and you sure as hell don't buy a black man. That's… that's…."

"No, this is America and, based on all of our focus groups since the Spring of 2001, we found that America was sympathetic to a black President. For awhile, we thought that Colin would fly but, let's face it; he cratered when the world saw him lying to the UN. No, we needed somebody with no real background – somebody who would appeal to the majority but somebody we knew we could get along with. And, you're the man. Articulate. Black. From Chicago. Hell, you even have a middle name that will appeal to the other side. You, Mr. President, are OUR man!"

The words hung in the air.

When something had to get done around elections, Silas was the man. His Octobers and Novembers started getting interesting back in the Carter days and, this day in 2008 was no different. As long as he got paid and was immune by order of the Twelve, he was the man. You need Iran to play ball on the hostages – he's your man. It was a bummer that real people had to die in that boondoggle but the money was good and Ollie was clean cut enough that the Bible Belt would exonerate him. So when he had to fall on the sword, well, that's what a Marine does. Hell, he'd be the patron saint of Religious Right and he'd give Jerry Falwell a run for his money in speaking fees. Funny how Lynchburg, Little Rock, and Bloomington would all get suckered by a patriot who sold out his country to the Iranians as long as he did it in defense of Christianity. But that story is as old as the Crusades. Most of the nobility that made it back were probably turncoats. But since they were the ones telling the story, the Church would believe it. And if the message comes across the pulpit with a bleeding savior serving as the backdrop, it's gotta be true.

"Can you please tell me what this means?" whispered Michelle.

"Not really – at least, not now. What I can tell you is that Twelve investors have a lot riding on you and you are not going to fuck – excuse me – I mean disappoint them."

"Who knows about this?" asked Barack, still recoiling from what was supposed to be the happiest night of his career.

"Everyone who needs to. Goodnight."

"Mr. President, Sir," his thoughts were interrupted.

"Yes."

"The video feed is back online. The communications are up if you'd like to thank the SEAL who actually set up the shot."

"Why yes."

"This is the President."

"Yessir," came the voice from the dimly lit face.

"Your Country is indebted to you for your service. I would like to find a time when I can invite you and your beautiful wife and daughters to the White House to extend my thanks when you get home."

"Thank you Sir," came the voice.

"What are we going to do with the body?"

"We'll take it back to the USS Carl Vinson and arrange a burial at sea."

"I think I need to go upstairs and get ready for the address to the nation. Hell, I might have to have a cigarette just to get my game face on."

"I don't think the First Lady will fall for that excuse, Sir."

"No."

He walked past the camera crews as they were setting up. Frank, one of the producers from NBC, stopped what he was doing long enough to notice the President walking by.

"Mr. President."

"Good evening, Frank."

"I just want to let you know that you're going to make a bunch of my sister's family happy with the news tonight. Ever since that September, they've been hoping that somebody would get him and

I'm sure proud it was you, Sir. I mean, no disrespect but things would have been a lot different if President Bush had done it."

Things sure would have been different. Two and half years into what was not the Presidency he thought he was running for, he had plenty of opportunities to reflect just how different things would have been. W's successor would have been able to preside over the bank payoffs; would have been the puppet for the Twelve; would have watched as the largest wealth transfer in the history of the country insured that this Presidency would be more Hoover than Reagan. Sure, they have all been beholden to the few but, seriously, having every single day dictated by twelve shareholders was starting to drive him nuts.

"Thanks, Frank. I'll see you in a bit."

"Thank you, Mr. President."

📠

"Where are we going to watch the President's speech?" Keith asked amused at how quickly this had all gone down.

"I feel like a cigar on the rooftop of the Peninsula," Jonas replied.

Three black Suburbans were idling out front when they reached the street. Each man paused at the elevators. One by one they would leave. One man would get in the back vehicle and all three

Suburbans would drive away. Only one of them would drive tonight. Keith would wear a hat, set low enough to insure that, with his aviators, you couldn't get any facial ID. Jonas would shuffle out 10 minutes later walking that infernal terrier and would go south into the Park. One of the Operators would pick up the dog under the bridge next to the Balto statute and he'd exit the Park near the Apple store. He hated Apple – hated the lunatics who lined up outside the glass cube at 5th and 59th for every new release of every new product but there was something about the corner – maybe it was the irony that we just have changed our toys from FAO to Apple – didn't much matter. A creature of habit, he'd walk west on 59th, head south on 6th and come back on 55th. Those damn security cameras on 5th made him nervous and with so many tourists, God knows who could be taking pictures. Carey would go around back, hop on his Ducati and take it for a quick spin through the park looking for any of the joggers who decided that a late afternoon run in their tiny shorts and unimaginative jog bras would give him enough fantasy to last another night in this city. Sun would be the last to leave. He'd make sure that every cigarette butt, every bottle of Evian, everything that any one had touched would find its way in the trash pick up next to the Trump Tower just north of Columbus Circle. Not necessary as they were using the sheik's apartment but, you know, you can never drop the habit of being careful.

As he walked down Central Park West, just as he was crossing 61st, a bicycle courier came from out of nowhere. The bag filled with the afternoon's trash dropped as he put up his arms to shield his left side from the near collision.

"Watch where you're going, asshole," he growled as the courier hit the breaks.

"Go to hell."

He picked up the bag and continued on. On days like today, you just don't need more stress on your nerves. He was fine but his brain was swirling.

*Damn, I'm on edge,* he thought as he tossed the trash into an overflowing receptacle. *Nothing that a good drink won't help. And hopefully Cindy will be there tonight. God I could use another night with her.*

The wind came down 60th Street and lifted some of the garbage from the side of the road into the air. It floated a bit, just 15 feet off the ground and then a gust blew it into the Park.

Salon De Ning was buzzing tonight. Despite the economy being on the verge of more carnage, it sure seemed like nobody here had a care in the world. The same overpaid Goldman wannabes were wooing their girlfriends like they had been doing before the bubble. The same 50+ year old guy was buying drinks for the Asian date young enough to be his daughter. The rooftop scene was a great vibe

– good drinks, warm weather inspiring scantily-clad clientele – a perfect place to let the news of the day chill. Sitting on the corner couch inside the glassed lounge was an Asian man in his mid-50s. A partially emptied cranberry juice had just a hint of condensation on the glass. He liked his juice without ice but the bar always served it chilled.

Carey got there first. Walking past the bar, his head whipped around not believing who was sitting on the couch.

"Good... good.... Evening, Sir," he managed to whisper not sure whether to turn around and walk away or stay.

He'd seldom been invited to socialize with the international members of the Twelve and yet here in front of him was Chan Siew himself!

"Assalamu alaikum, my friend," was the silken voice. "Come, have a seat. You're drinking Bombay Sapphire, yes?"

"Sir, no, I will have a juice with you," not wishing to offend the sensibilities of his Muslim unexpected host.

"The others are coming, yes?" he went on.

Carey didn't know what to do or say. He'd never imagined a day when he'd be sitting with one of the Shareholders on such a momentous occasion. In all his years in the Agency, he could lie like the best of them. But he didn't know what the Twelve thought about such practices. No one had ever briefed him. Hell, nobody had ever told him that he'd ever be sitting in New York with one of the most illusive men on Earth. Erring on the side of caution, he deflected a response.

"We've had a busy day today, Sir."

"Oh come now, my friend. Why do you think I'm over here? Several of the gentlemen took the offer to have a front row seat at the White House but, no, I knew that the real play was here," he chuckled. "Come, sit close. Do you think he's going to make the announcement tonight or tomorrow morning?"

"Well," Carey cleared his voice to speak lower, "I've heard that he's going to stick it to Trump and interrupt The Apprentice."

"You're Fired!" squealed Chan Siew, doing his best Malay impression of Trump.

"Oh no, not you Carey. You know, Mister Trump says, 'You're Fired'."

They shared a laugh. The kind of courtesy laugh when strangers from different cultures know that nothing really was funny save the attempt at cross cultural humor. They fell into distracted pleasantries and didn't see Keith or Sun come in and walk out to the open air patio unseen and unseeing. Jonas shuffled in, one corner of his shirt nearly fully untucked. To a stranger, he could have appeared disheveled – that is until you realized that every article of clothing he was wearing cost more than most peoples' entire wardrobes. He saw Keith and Sun and was on his way out with a, "The Usual," to Alfonso who was behind the bar when he saw Carey and then him. Jonas, long mastering the cloak and dagger world of his early days in cryptography and espionage, was unphased.

"I should have known to expect you. How are things in Jahor Baru my friend?" he asked taking a seat beside Chan Siew.

"We're getting by. Palm oil's been a little less reliable of late with the Singaporeans running their investments into our territory. And, we figure that rubber will be slow in the wake of the Japanese tsunami although the Chinese will pick up the inventory. It's not been a good spring but, my friend, the sun is shining and so I'm o.k."

"You came from Brussels when you got word from Cecil?" Jonas asked.

Cecil, also known as Control, had never been seen by any of the Operators – at least they never knew it if they had. None of them knew whether 'he' was one of the Shareholders, above them – whatever that meant – or precisely who 'he' was or where 'he' was stationed. While the name was always at the other end of the phone when a Requirement – or Req – came down, the level of sophistication on masking the voice inferred that 'he' was a man but, who knew? There was one day back in 2008 when, during a communication disruption thought to be linked to a solar anomaly, the voice seemed unscrambled for a moment and Sun thought he heard what sounded like a woman's voice. But, celibate not by desire but out of profound respect for his father's morality, Sun heard and saw more estrogen – including women who found his cluelessness intoxicating just making his life more miserable – than anyone else so his report that he heard a woman's voice was not entirely reliable.

"When we heard about Dr. Khan, we knew what you gentlemen would do," Chan Siew dismissively said. "It's like we're an old married couple. Ever since this started in Athens back in 2004, we know what you Americans think. We knew that you couldn't deal with him dead unless you could write the cover-story that you killed him. If the world ever found out how we've been keeping him alive to keep Americans running into debt with the wars, they'd be most disappointed."

The Operator who had been the one that drew the motorcade straw was the last to arrive showing up at 9:10pm. This time, the evasion route involved three drops – one at 70 Pine St where the narrowness of the road made a tail easily tagged and dropped. They continued to Battery Park for some tourist photos and to pick up a decoy while any observer was distracted. A quick switch of cars at the light in front of Trinity Church and then a cab back up to The Peninsula. She was good. This Operator – only known as Emma – had a sixth sense. She never needed to be reminded about vigilance. God knows that if you tried to remind her, she'd get dangerously close to ripping off your head. Nobody knew where the anger came from. During her HC clearance interrogation at the Farm, they tried to work out what happened back in 1986 – the only time where she had 'disappeared' in Mexico for six months. Emma wouldn't talk about the time at all, claiming to have no recollection of events after being struck by a car. She thought she'd spent quite a bit of time in the hospital but she had no scars, no records, nothing. Just a blank 6 months.

She hated sitting with the team in public. She knew that one day, this cavalier practice – make it look like you're an exclusive group of traders or quants had been the instructions – would one day link her to one of the Operators who would undue the Enterprise. And with all she knew about what the team had done, she knew that if this ever happened, water-boarding would be a walk in the park. However, when she walked in and saw the team sitting with Chan Siew, she knew that she had to join them. After all, this was the first time she had seen Chan Siew in the flesh and, the more you can profile a target, the better.

"How much have the Pakis kept out of the last payment?" Keith asked.

"They've upped their commission to close to 40%. It's really pissing off the Serbs who were getting used to pulling in close to $2 billion each year out of the allocation," Jonas volunteered.

"Yes," confirmed Chan Siew. "We have been hearing that shipments have been a bit slower but, with Israel preoccupied with Egypt and Syria, the pressure is off a bit. Hamas has been meeting with the Brotherhood to determine who is going to take leadership. The Suez is the sticking point as everyone wants to control Choke Point 2. They know that we're the ones that actually control what happens but everybody wants to be the hero when we execute Scorpion Strike."

There it was. 'Scorpion Strike' was a name that all the Operators had heard but they had no idea what it meant. When the Shareholders were planning something big, they'd start socializing a code name weeks – sometimes months in advance – but you'd never know what the plan was until it happened and, even then, only what your role had been. It seemed that no one ever knew all of the plan. Obviously somebody did. None of them. Did the Shareholders know? What difference did it make?

"It is funny," he continued. "None of the Contractors seem to want to fight over Hormuz, Malacca or Zone 59 but the Suez is an emotional one."

Carey, sitting quietly since the team had arrived didn't need another invitation.

"I just visited the Rabbit Hole and got a massive briefing from Lightning. He showed us the latest traffic data on the Choke Points and who was running metals lately."

He went on for 30 minutes on all of the intelligence about the platinum trades using so many codes for Contractors and codes for Ops that anyone listening would have thought they were listening to Walt Disney on acid after Fantasia. One of the great things about the media obsession with Bourne Identity and Eagle Eye is that you could talk about covert plans in public and everyone would mistakenly believe that you were discussing a movie that they'd seen. The more you made names sound like novels, the more you could hide activities in plain sight.

None of the team had looked at the clock but Chan Siew had the view of the television screen behind the bar.

"There's what-do-you-call-him – oh yes, Pinocchio – walking to the podium," he said, pointing to the screen.

"Alfonso, please turn up the TV. It looks like the President is getting ready for a press conference."

"Tonight I can report to the American people and the world, the United States has conducted an operation that killed Osama bin Laden, the leader of al-Qaeda and a terrorist who's responsible for the murder of thousands of innocent men, women, and children," the President started.

They all wondered the same thing at the same time.

"I wonder how many Americans can detect how tired he is. He's not holding up very well after close to 2 ½ years of being a puppet."

He really wasn't holding up well. You could hear it in his voice. Like a caged bird who is fed to sing while being kept on a damn wooden dowel instead of flying free in a rainforest, the President was starting to show the effects of being smothered. In the first two years, he couldn't use his electoral mandate for 'Change'. While he had the majority – yes, the majority – in both houses of Congress and the Oval Office, he had been forced to talk about being in the minority because he didn't have a veto override majority. Imagine that, the President with a majority aligned in Congress having to always be reminding America that he couldn't deliver on promises. He'd done year one in moderate success but going into the mid-terms, his anger would boil after every public appearance. Having to hand the Republicans the House was bad enough. Having the Tea Party phase of the Enterprise kick in made him long for the simple stupidity of Sarah. She was so pathologically idiotic that he could dismiss her the way you dismiss a mosquito in a tent when you're camping. But some of these Tea Partiers were legitimately annoying.

Minutes later, cameras panned to Time Square, Ground Zero and Washington Park where chants of "USA! USA! USA!" confirmed that anesthetized Americans had taken the bait.

"Well done, lady and gentlemen," Chan Siew raised his third glass of cranberry juice. "It looks like the bait has been taken. By tomorrow, we'll have the mop up and we'll move to Phase 4."

A homeless guy shuffled past Trump Tower. There was a cigarette butt half smoked. He picked it up, lit it and wandered towards the Park.

"Damn cheap cigarettes," he muttered. "Can't believe somebody this cheap would have thrown away a perfectly good cigarette without smoking the whole damn thing. New York smoking laws have made everybody stupid."

## *CHAPTER 2 - THE ENTERPRISE*

Inside of every good conspiracy is an even better idea. Inside such an idea would be a Herculean opportunity. What if you could combine every conspiracy – say since the Egyptian-inspired Jewish Messiah – through the Crusades, through the Nazca and Maya, through the Chinese Fleet of 1432, all the way up to the mother of all conspiracies and form the perfect global coup? Yes, in a way it's about the money but only insofar as money is the scorecard. The Rothschild's have gotten so much traction courtesy of the heist of the Bank of England and the rest of Europe's treasuries at the dawn of the 19th century. Wouldn't it be amazing to see if you could actually steal all of the G-7 assets right out from under the noses of the world's self-proclaimed elite? And wouldn't it be a blast to end the show with all of the current conspirators – including all the names like Rockefeller, Morgan, Kennedy, Rothschild, Oppenheimer, Blankfein, Goldman, the list goes on – scratching their heads wondering who in the hell had the audacity to actually use their hubris as the fulcrum to empty their collective pockets. Best of all, wouldn't it be fun to use the media – novelists like Dan Brown; networks like CNN, FOX, al-Jazeera; and BBC; and Hollywood films – to leak just enough of the truth to insure that the actual operation wouldn't require secrecy? Because, if you could convince people that what was really happening was an illusion created by the media, than the truth could unfold and no one would believe it.

The Summer of 1999 was a scorcher. Walking past the lawn beside the lake on the way to the Spugenschloss, he had to take his jacket off. Of course, this seemed downright monastic compared to the throngs of topless young ladies who were soaking in the sun's rays bathing in the reckless stares of every male in the vicinity. Save, of course the gay foursome sitting half in the shade. The more flesh they saw, the more public they seemed to need a lewd demonstration that they were not seduced by the firm young breasts blooming in the grass. The fountain in the lake was jetting water 20 meters in the air and, with no wind, the spray hovered over the glassy surface as if, for a moment, to defy gravity in deference to one short moment of suspended physics. He had no idea that he was being watched from an office building four blocks away. If you would have walked up to him that day, you would have encountered an optimist – no, an idealist – who had a pretty good idea that the world was going to change and that he was going to play a role in that change.

*If Emilie was here,* he thought, *I wonder if I could get her to go topless?*

He had met Emilie in the Fall of 1989 and for the past 10 years, they had vainly attempted to fake a textbook illusion of a marriage. Yes, there were moments where it was passionate but those moments would pass quickly. But for his nauseating sense of loyalty to an ideal which had long ago been replaced by the pragmatism of realizing that marital discord was the norm, the thought of ending it was more offensive than tolerating it. However, when he walked by the lake this afternoon, he did pause long enough to buy an Orangina from the vendor who managed the booth with the best view of raw flesh. The bottle was emptied slowly.

"We can't figure him out, Steve," Karen said as she scrawled a note in the folder laying open on the desk. "We know that Emilie hates his travel; so many trips out of the country; but, we've never seen him do anything but look. When he was in Amsterdam, we had a driver take him to the Red Light District and, sure he looked out the window but he went back to reading a book for Christ's sake. Same thing in Bangkok and Tokyo. Funny thing is she doesn't trust him one bit. She's sure that he must have cheated on her at some point but, as far as we can see, he seems to defy gravity."

"What does get his attention if it's not women, money, or fame?" Hans asked.

"You know, this is going to sound weird, but the only thing that we seem to know is that he'll disappear for hours in libraries, churches or empty cafes, write like the Devil, and come out with a look on his face like he just figured something out," Steve remarked.

"Words?" Hans asked incredulously.

"Yeah, crazy as it sounds, this guy consumes more information – everything from papers to books to God knows what all – and then, if you ever hear him talk, you'll see that damned if he doesn't remember everything he's touched."

"We've never seen an Asset with his profile and I'm not sure we can use him," cautioned Karen. "If you can't control him through something; if you don't have some angle on him where you can damage his reputation with something he's hiding, well, we just don't know how to figure this one."

"Sounds like the perfect Control," Steve responded.

"I know that we wouldn't want him," Karen replied. "If we can't control you, you're dangerous. And we control everyone. But ever since we first saw him in Nicaragua back in the 80's, he's been a puzzle. Our files are as wide as your ass and still we can't find a stitch. Hell, most of us in the Agency wonder if he's human."

"He's checked in and he's in the room we've prepped. The video is coming up."

"You've got his phone monitored?"

"Yes."

The monitors lit up to show Cyrus walking past the bathroom door shedding his shirt on the way by.

"Looks like he's going to head out for a run," Emma said from behind her monitor. "It sure is paying off. Look at his..." her voice drifted off.

Three minutes later, he was back out for a run around the lake. Not surprisingly, his route took him past the lawn again. There were a few moments where his head was distracted but it looked like today was another one of those days when he would be faithful to a woman thousands of miles away.

"I wonder what goes on in his head when he ignores so much of the world?" Emma mused.

"Why don't you ask him?" Karen said downing the last of her espresso. "You could bump into him at one of the cafes off the Paradaplatz and see if you could talk him into anything."

"I just might do that," Emma replied.

She left the monitor on while Cyrus showered, officially so she could make sure she identified the clothes he would wear out tonight.

"Guten abend," he greeted the waiter when he sat down in view of the tram station.

In a few moments, Emma walked up. A light summer dress barely moved over her body as she came and sat down at the table closer to the street. She had a stack of folders with Zurich Re logos on the front.

Cyrus looked over just as his wine came.

"Do you work for them?" he inquired.

"Yes," Emma replied doing her best to contain her enthusiasm.

Maybe this was going to be easy. Maybe she would be the one to break the record of so many field officers before.

"Would you care to join me? I haven't ordered yet?" Cyrus asked.

"Are you sure it wouldn't be an intrusion?" Emma feigned.

"Not at all. It looks like you're new in town and, from the boarding pass still in your purse, it looks like you haven't been here long."

*Damn,* she thought, *why didn't I leave that at the hotel?*

"Yes, I just flew in from Washington DC today," she said.

"DC," Cyrus repeated. "That's interesting. I live in Bethesda. Where do you live?"

"I just graduated from GW and I live in the District," she lied.

She was beautiful. Not the Italian or Persian model untouchable, but rather that almost-accessible beauty. Cyrus knew better. Since his first memory, he had told himself that there was an inapproachable quality to beauty and Emma was right on that line. Slim but elegantly proportioned. If he was ever going to fall for someone, this would be the type that would lead him astray. But he was never going to fall. Ever.

"What are you doing for Zurich Re?" he inquired.

"We're working on a new initiative launched by one of the leadership team – a real game changer. I don't know if you know much about them but if our project gets off the ground, it will change the face of business."

"Really, that's interesting," he added. "Turns out I'm in town having a similar conversation."

"He's IMPOSSIBLE!" Emma said when she fell through the command center door at 1 am. "We stayed out until 11pm. He said that he would walk me back to my hotel – some sort of 'gentleman' bullshit. I invited him in for a drink and the little shit turned me down and walked off to his hotel – not before taking a long walk back to the lake. He called Emilie – I couldn't hear much of the call but I'm sure we've got the tape. And then back to the hotel and his light was off in 4 minutes."

"He's our man," Steve declared. "Invite him to New York but don't make it obvious. Make sure you use someone he knows to make the invitation. If you do it directly, he'll do his diligence on you and on us and we can't afford that at this point. God knows it will come but the less he's on to us, the better."

"Yessir," Emma replied.

She turned the camera back on and there he was, sleeping with the window wide open with nothing on.

"That bastard," she mumbled. "He's got no clue what he could be doing right now instead of sleeping."

She was wrong.

"Cyrus, I've been asked to invite you to New York for a meeting with some private equity guys who are interested in what you're doing over at Horus."

The voice at the other end of the line was John Michael, a former Congressional aide turned lobbyist.

"I'm in Zurich and heading back to DC tomorrow," Cyrus replied.

"Oh, well then in that case, can you make it next week when you're up there for the Citibank meeting?"

"Sure. Can you tell me about who I'm meeting?" Cyrus asked.

"Yes, an old friend of mine – Steve Donner – who's putting together a $500 million venture capital fund. He's heard about you and thinks that you're exactly the kind of person he'd like to support out of the gate. He used to work for some of the big European banks – made a ton of money and has come to New York to ride the wave."

"Do you trust him or is he just another one of the dot com groupies?" Cyrus asked.

"Trust him?" John Michael paused. "I don't know that I trust anybody, Cyrus. After all, 10 years on the Hill, what's to trust?"

They shared a laugh for different reasons. Cyrus didn't trust anyone. John Michael knew that playing the iconoclast card seemed to work with Cyrus and he hoped that he knew what he was doing.

"See you on Wednesday – just send me directions and I'll get a cab and meet you there."

"We'll have the meeting in the rooftop lounge at the Gramercy Park Hotel."

"Got it."

"In the event of a water landing, your seat cushion will serve as an approved floatation device. Simply pull up, place your arms through the straps and hold the cushion to your chest..."

*Really? The USAir shuttle is going to be filled with a bunch of businessmen hugging their seat cushions when they crash into the Potomac or the Hudson,* he thought. *Could air travel get any more ridiculous?*

At the morning meeting, he was surprised to see Kozo Nakahara, one of the former vice-presidents at Mitsubishi Bank – Tokyo who now was in the Special Assets division at Citi. Kozo had been around when Cyrus had assisted in the analysis of distressed credits during the collapse last year and he'd bailed to New York just as Tokyo was awash in crisis.

"Where are you going now Cyrus-san?" he asked at the end of the meeting.

"Downtown."

Cyrus didn't have any interest in bringing any more attention to his next meeting than absolutely necessary.

He flagged a cab and was relieved that the traffic was light. Arriving at the Park 25 minutes early, he found a coffee shop and got an iced latte. Just a week ago he was sitting by the lake in Zurich – now the concrete jungle and the noises of New York City.

The room was full of people when he got up to the interior seating area on the top floor of the hotel. John Michael wasn't there.

*That's strange*, Cyrus thought. *I would have expected him to be early.*

"Cyrus," a portly man who looked to be in his early 50's came striding over.

"Yes?"

"I'm Steve Donner – great to meet you. I've heard so much about you. Fact, some of my friends in Zurich said you were over there last week."

"Yes, I had some meetings there – hottest time I've spent in Switzerland."

"You into the ladies over there this time of year?" he asked.

"My wife wasn't with me though I'm sure she would have enjoyed the lake and the cafes," he deflected.

"Come and have a drink. I hear that you don't drink but you'll have a gin and tonic won't you?"

"No thanks, I'll just have grapefruit juice if they have it," Cyrus replied.

"Can do."

"I'd like you to meet a few of my colleagues, Cyrus," Steve proceeded without pausing. "Robert Haverford, Henri Giroud, and the beautiful Gabriela – don't even think about it – ha, you already were...," he continued around the room.

They all shook hands. Several people were not introduced. There was a young man in his early 30's, clean-cut, looked a bit like Jim Carey, sitting near the window. A slightly younger man of Middle Eastern or Mediterranean descent sat next to him dressed impeccably, tie perfectly coordinated with his heavily starched blue shirt. An older gentleman sat outside the room smoking. Cyrus didn't know if he was with the group or just a guest in the hotel.

"Let's get down to business shall we?" Steve began.

"Robert, can you hand me the folder?" he continued.

"Now Cyrus, this is highly unusual. We're going to dispense with the formalities. We notice that you have been doing a lot of creative things for years; traveling a ton. You've been a bunch of places of great interest to us. You're married and we see you have a daughter and a son. That's the part that everybody knows, right?" he paused.

Cyrus could see that the file sitting in front of Steve had pictures of his home, what looked like his college transcripts and something that he couldn't make out save the airport codes which were familiar.

"We've been interested in you for quite some time. Not just in you but in what you do. Now, let's face it, none of us can figure you out but what we know is that if we're going to do our business, we're going to need you. And if you're ever going to get rich off your ideas, you're going to need us. So, we figured we'd sit down with you today and lay out our plan. Mind you, we can do it without you but it will be better for all of us if we're on the same team. And, you can never breathe a word of this meeting to anyone, ever. I'm sure you are smart enough to know that we'd all deny it and we'd make you look like a delusional conspiracy wacko. Jonas, would you do the honors?"

Jonas – now he knew that the man was part of the group – entered the room crushing out his last cigarette just inside the door and exhaling the smoke in the room.

"We are going to buy the Presidency in 2008," he started. "The way we figure, we've got eight years to put this plan together. Ten, maybe twelve investors are each going to put up $500 million and we're going to buy the White House. We're going to find the perfectly electable candidate – hell, by then he may be gay, black, or even a she, who knows – run them, insure that they win and then we'll own the son-of-a-bitch. We've already covered this election and we've got the Dynasty in place to make sure that '08 falls our way. Those bastards were cheap. W is a puppet – nowhere near the man his father was – but Cheney will pull the strings and W will dance to whatever tune we play. You'll see soon after they're in office, we'll get a war going – even have planned a biological terror attack which will throw the country into a panic. Everybody will think that this is another bite at the military industrial complex apple. Just you watch, Bayer will make more money on drugs out of this thing than Boeing will make out of planes."

Cyrus just sat.

"We call it the Enterprise – like it?" Jonas continued.

"And here's where you come in," Henri chimed in. "We need two things from you. First, we need your access. You can get into and out of more places more easily than anyone we've ever seen. We need you to help us put all the chess pieces on the board, oui?" he continued. "Next, we need your technology because we need the crème de le crème of data crunching capabilities because to make this work, we need to know – not just guess, but really know – what will push buttons in the U.S., Europe, hell, the whole world. And nobody can do that like you."

"Isn't there a tiny problem like the Constitution?" Cyrus blurted.

"Wait to see what W and Dick do with that inconvenience over the next few years and watch to see if any American gives a shit. Once you scare people enough, they'll give up anything – including an old rag that none of them have read and even fewer understand," came a voice with a distinctly Southern drawl. "The Constitution's like the Bible, son. The more people holler about it the more unlikely it is that they've ever cracked it open."

"Ladies and Gentlemen," Cyrus started, his voice cool and measured, "I can assure you that I have no interest in your little plan and, more importantly, I can assure you that this meeting was one of the biggest mistakes you've made in your lives. Clearly missing from your files is any clarity on who I am and what motivates me. Also missing from your little scheme is the fact that, having had this meeting, I will be your worst nightmare. Good day."

"Hold on there," came the Southern voice again. "You have no clue who you're dealing with. You can't say 'no' because we're doin' what we're goin' to do and you're in this whether you like it or not. Bottom line, son, you can't turn us down and you sure as hell can't threaten the likes of us."

"You know," Cyrus dropped into a near monotone – the voice that found its way to his mouth when he was enraged, "some of us don't threaten. No, I suspect the reason I'm standing here is because you know that I deliver! And, before you think that for a few million dollars you can change your own lives, much less the world, I know that at least one of you would have given everything you had so that the heir you wanted to be your immortality would have been the one that survived the avalanche in Davos. I wonder how much money it would be worth to be able to get the snow to bury the son that was an embarrassment?"

One of the guests who had not been introduced shifted in his chair.

"How the hell does he know about Alex and Nathan?" he whispered to Connie sitting to his left.

"Why do you think we've been tracking him for so long?" came the breathless reply. "No one knows how he does it but what we do know is that he knows a hell of a lot more than we do. In fact, he's probably picked you out of a file somewhere in his brain from a document he read years ago.... God knows."

"Mr. Cyrus," Connie began. "I think that you are very good at what you do – maybe very smart, yes? I would like to remind you of all the many people who respect your work and would appreciate your consideration of our offer."

"Offer?" Cyrus responded. "I guess I didn't hear an offer. I heard a reckless plan described here suggesting that you're going to fulfill some pathetic fantasy by lying to hundreds of millions of people and preying on their stupidity, trust, or both."

"It's no different than what the World Bank and American investors have done on a smaller scale in my country," came a comment from a tall, well-dressed African man sitting comfortably near the door. "It's been happening here since 1980 and all we're doing is opening it up to investors rather than the heirs of wealth created close to a century ago who don't use their power efficiently."

"With respect, Sir," Cyrus replied, "you'll find that I can walk out this door, fly home, and go about my life. You'll also find that one day, you'll wish you had gotten to know me a bit better because you won't be in my dreams but I will always be gnawing at the edges of your nightmares. Thanks for the grapefruit juice. Ladies. Gentlemen."

And with that, he walked out to the elevators. He had to urinate but forced himself to walk past the bathrooms and get out of the place as quickly as possible.

"US Airways, please," he instructed the cab driver.

"Hope you get out before the thunderstorm," said the driver whose Medallion tag simply said 'Berhanu'.

"Your family's from Ethiopia?" Cyrus commented.

"Yes sir," came the reply.

"Do you see them often?"

"No sir, I haven't been back for 5 years. But I love America. This is a good country. Are you going home?"

"Yes."

Forty-five minutes later and the ground hold at LaGuardia would have meant he wouldn't get home until 11pm with the traffic on the inner loop of the Beltway. But the storms stretching from Connecticut down to Virginia held off just long enough for him to get to his car.

*What a day,* he thought as he turned on NPR.

# CHAPTER 3 - THE SHAREHOLDERS

You have to pick people who missed the internet bubble. Yes, they all needed to be rich. But they had to have staying power and the last thing you wanted was people who were suckered into fads. No, to be a Shareholder, you need to have a particular profile. It goes without saying that you needed to have access – not bought but earned. In addition, Control needed to have plenty of access to data on your every move. That meant that, albeit wealthy, you had to still move commercial enough to use SABRE, to charge things to cards in your name, and to have enough insurable risk to have a decent insurance disclosure – all vital, leaky data streams which are rich with what you want people to know and what you wished they didn't. Political donations were o.k. but you had to be one of those who would fund a local Republican congressional race but still send a big check to a homeless shelter or children's hospital.

"Fiscal conservatives with either a heart or a guilty conscience – don't matter much which one of those," Steve said to Karen as they were drafting the short list.

Steve called Fabrizio in Zurich.

"We got your first cut. Thanks for that."

"Bitte schön," came the young man's voice.

"Could you please do another cut? We'd like to have people with no more than two children – make sure they've traveled together within the past three years. Also, if you could confirm cause of death of at least two generations preceding. We want to make sure we're not soliciting heart attacks, aneurysms, or cancer. After all, we can't execute this plan if we've got someone who's going to be in surgery during the first three phases. Anesthesia is a bitch."

"Meine freude!"

Unlike any of his deals before, Steve had an interesting challenge. He'd have to pick twelve people. The right 12. You can't get anything about the profile wrong. God knows what would happen if you solicited an investor and they decided to out the project to the press. Loose lips, predisposed to indiscretion when under the influence, any of these would be lethal. He'd keep the pitch simple. For too long, people – not just the illusive private sector, but real flesh and blood – have not controlled the world. Sure, it's made a few people rich, even the prospective investors. But, there's so much more that could be done if governments and systems ran like a company answerable to shareholders. You could make decisions – not try to shape opinions. One thing that the last 20 years had shown the world is that every form of government was equally corrupt and corruptible.

Doesn't matter if its communism in China, a delusional autocrat in Zimbabwe, or the military industrial complex that hijacked the U.S.

back in the 50's, they've all pulled up the ladder and nobody else can get up into the tree house. It would be so much better if you could buy your way into control and – when you got what you needed done done, you could monetize the interest to the next guy. It's not about dynasties – just efficiency.

The principle of the Enterprise was simple enough. Twelve founding Shareholders, organized by Steve, would be selected for an investment lock-up period of ten years. They'd each put up $500 million and would agree to source one Operator and one Critical Path – a utility, as it were – for the execution of the first three phases. During Phase 1, structural instability and privacy erosion would be critical to gain access to 'market data'. How various demographics respond to fear, government intrusion, and exogenous, asymmetric impulses would be profiled as widely as globally possible. During Phase 2 – also known as WH08 – the selection of the perfect Presidential candidate would be defined, selected and run. Suitable distractions deflecting domestic scrutiny would be maximized – war and terror were to be maintained at a rolling boil – so that nobody would have the ability to focus attention on the realignments required for Phase 3. Phase 3 would be the systematic termination of Phase 2 distractors once all the variables were aligned. And Phase 4 would be the complete asset reallocation into The Enterprise. No Shareholder would be free to liquidate during the first three Phases. If anyone elected to exit at Phase 4, they'd get their principal plus a carry of Treasury plus ten percent. Through the completion of Phase 4, only existing Shareholders could buy interests; afterward, the shares could be distributed to individual outside investors approved by the remaining Shareholders. No family dynasties would be allowed in the Enterprise including transfers of interests in estates. Titled families had presented the world enough headaches and while there was no problem having off-spring influential in a new paradigm, the Enterprise needed activists, not lazy progeny, harvesting the wisdom of previous generations.

Each Shareholder would make their real returns off of their respective 'Critical Path'. A Critical Path represented one of the required constituent utilities to effectuate the Enterprise. It may be a technology to operationalize part of the plan. It may be a corporation which was suitably diffuse to facilitate opaque financial or logistics transactions. It may be a management consulting agency with a global reach to infiltrate, both for accessing intelligence and disseminating influence. And each Shareholder's Critical Path would be given carte blanche to engage in the Enterprise plan at whatever fare the market would bear. No collusive pricing – just no competition.

⊟◀

Steve and Karen sat in the lobby bar of the Pan Pacific Hotel near the sprawling mall complex in Singapore. Outside, neatly placed excavators were beginning to dig ground for one of the most amazing consumer labyrinths in the world – an underground temple to the consumer – where on any given day an immense number of families, couples and youth would congregate to escape the tropical heat.

"You know," Karen mused over her sweating Tiger Beer, "I can't help but wonder what would happen if the ventilation system would ever be compromised in the maze of shops and food stalls."

"Yeah," Steve replied. "Thank God the Singaporeans have the security apparatus that every sovereign dreams of," he continued.

"God knows that the Japanese subway would be child's play next to what would happen on a hot weekend afternoon," Karen replied.

Momentarily, a man in his late fifties walked through the door, the graceful doorman bowing gently as he passed. He flashed a glance toward the bar but was immediately greeted by three guests in the lobby.

"Patrick," one warmly opened.

"Well, my dear friends," he replied, "what brings you to the Pan Pac on this afternoon."

"We're here for Vincent's wedding."

"Oh," he replied, "please pass along my warmest regards and best wishes. You know Vincent and my son King Poon served together."

"Were they together when the First Commando Battalion won the honors in 1997?"

Patrick beamed. He was so proud of his son. Now fully engaged in the Ministry of Foreign Affairs, he had turned out to be every Singaporean father's dream. A patriot, a public servant, and soon to be the father of Patrick's first grandson.

"So good to see you all and please convey my congratulations," he said as he shook their hands. "Now I must attend to other matters."

"So good to see you and we will indeed," they replied and resumed their conversations.

He walked away. Rather than walking straight over, he walked around the crisscrossing escalators, went up to the second floor so he could take the measure of the two Americans at the bar. He disappeared into the bathroom for a moment double checking his tie and making sure that the perspiration from the afternoon had not become too visible through his shirt. Confident, he feigned an entrance from the escalator and walked up to the low table where Steve and Karen were sitting.

"Mr. Donner and Ms. Wilson, so good to have you in Singapore," he addressed the duo as they rose to meet their new guest.

"Mr. Cheong, Chris was quite accurate in his description of you. So good to meet you. Won't you join us?" Steve responded.

As the three sat, a willowy waitress attired in a crimson Singaporean traditional dress slit up to her upper thighs glided over.

"Good afternoon, sir," she started. "May I take your order?"

"Indeed," Patrick replied. "Make it a pineapple juice with light ice, please."

"Certainly, sir," she drifted away.

"So Chris tells me that you're interested in RFTrax," he began.

"You know, we were Titan's first investment in Singapore. With the growth of the transshipment business here over the past few years, there's no better place to perfect RFID technology than right here. We're beginning to discuss the possibility of setting up a technology incubator of sorts here in Singapore and we think that we'll be able to get in front of the market. Having the public sector support for monitoring," he paused and chuckled, "well, monitoring everything and everyone, we're getting a lot of support."

"Yes, we heard," Karen said falling into the charm of a refined, soft-spoken businessman.

Without missing a beat, Patrick recounted the statistics on how many containers pass through Singapore, the nature of their contents, their origins and destinations. He described the regional dynamics with the growth planned in Malaysia and while clearly dismissive of their ability to compete at scale, was careful not to diminish the efforts being made in Kuala Lumpur. There was no question that Steve and Karen had found their perfect, first candidate for the Enterprise shareholding. With visibility on the movements of what seemed to be nearly everything, Patrick would be invaluable. And who couldn't love this guy? He was refined, good-looking, respected.

"Chris didn't give me a lot of information about your business, Mr. Donner," Patrick concluded his monologue. "He just said that I would find it very auspicious to take the meeting and, given that his money has been invaluable to us, I thought that I should follow his recommendation."

"Yes," started Steve, "part of that is not necessarily Chris' fault. While we've known each other for years – we were classmates at Wharton – his business and ours are quite different."

"I've taken the liberty of chartering a boat to carry on our conversation. Is that o.k.?" Karen chimed in.

"Certainly," Patrick and Steve responded in unison.

As the three rose to exit the lobby a slightly over-weight Greek gentleman and his date hurried to take an impulsive self-portrait. You know the kind. Two heads close together with one person's arm outstretched holding the camera and blindly snapping a photo. Their two faces would be in the foreground. Who knows what would be somewhat blurred in the background?

Six hours later, Steve and Karen were waiting in the Silver Kris lounge at the Singapore airport. They were not traveling together. Steve would be heading north to Beijing while Karen was off to Dubai. It's always difficult to know when a team can operate as individual components and when it needs to stay together. But, if today was any indication, the Enterprise pitch made sense and, judging by the outcome, one or two more times and they'd have the proposition nailed. Patrick's soft commitment pending at least three others equally on-board was a godsend. Of course, with the intel that they had on each candidate, a 'no' was unlikely. That said you always like to know that the value proposition connects and that someone gets it without too much resistance.

⊟

The stench of sulfur and chemicals was enough to burn your eyes. As he walked through the airport, Steve noticed the proliferation of security cameras. Some on the ceiling, some on walls and support posts. He was not a big fan of in-your-face security. Even more unsettling was the obvious camera placement behind the immigration officers where you could tell that surveillance included watching citizens performing their duties – not just the inbound visitors.

"Thank God," he muttered to himself, "we'll never have this type of insane conspiratorial fear in the U.S."

In the expansive reception hall outside Customs, Steve saw a short, white-gloved driver standing with a sign which simply read 'S. Donner'. Before he could advance toward the man, the driver was coming to take his luggage from him.

"Mr. Donor," he stammered. "So sorry, Mr. Donner," the driver valiantly greeted his charge emphasizing each syllable the way he'd practiced it a dozen times on the way to the airport. "Ms. Zhang is waiting for you at der office. She is very sad not to greet you."

"Not at all, thank you," Steve replied.

The drive from the airport was too long. Punctuated by pathetic tree plantings that were hopelessly losing the battle with dust and pollution, the landscape all had a non-descript brownish tinge accented in subtle grays. The closer they got to the city, the more densely packed the chaotic buildings. No architectural theme. Aesthetics, it seemed, were an enemy of the State. Did anyone in this place actually know what blue sky looked like? Did anyone know what green trees or grass looked like? Did anyone care?

As the car pulled up to the office building, Steve noticed that this was no ordinary office. The building itself was painted a dull gray green. Its six stories covered about a half of a city block. The entrance to the left of the building had armed security and a wall with impregnable razor wire fence surrounding what looked like the entire compound. Once through the gate, the driveway circled around a small fountain pond – the rusty stream barely trickling down on the large koi swimming in the dank water. Four more armed guards flanked the doorway and a sign, all in Chinese characters was emblazoned left of the entrance. Steve couldn't decipher what this was but it was clearly not a commercial enterprise. A single fluorescent tube flickered on in the late afternoon light somewhat pointlessly adding an industrial glow to the sun still adequately lighting the foyer.

Then she appeared. Connie was, to say the least, as stunning an Asian woman as Steve had ever laid eyes upon. She wore a white shell dress so tightly and perfectly fitted as to leave no room for any inquiry as to how well she'd cared for herself. He had several pictures in her portfolio but nothing remotely resembled the experience of seeing her in person. In his briefing with a member of the International Cooperation Council staff, he had been told that Wei was considered one of the luckiest members of the State Council for having married her – family connections, influence, and looks – but she'd been undersold.

"Steven, so good to see you. So sorry to leave you alone at the airport. You are most welcome," came the effusive greeting. "You must be exhausted," she continued before he could respond.

"No, I got great sleep on the flight up here," he replied.

"We've arranged a dinner for you this evening – Peking duck," she said. "Come, come in and we'll speak for a few minutes."

She waved to the security guard sitting at a small metal desk inside the door and they walked up two flights of stairs. In the late afternoon light, there was a notable darkness in all of the stairwells and halls while fluorescent light poured out of one or two open doors. When they arrived at the conference room, he noted that the table and chairs were well worn – not unusable – but clearly not what you'd expect in any conference room anywhere else.

"The Information Ministry," she began, "has been a partner in our venture and they are very generous with our use of their space," she said.

Connie and a team of engineers and programmers from Shenzeng and Tsinghua universities were launching a concept they called VirtualUS. She described the idea of a website where people could share personal information with each other – maybe pictures, resumes, and other interests. The International Cooperation Council arm of the State Council Organization for the Restructuring of

Economic Systems – ICC-SCORES – thought it would be very helpful for foreign businessmen, for example, to be able to share their information with their Chinese business partners.

"VirtualUS gives us an ability to share information between business partners so much more easily," she gushed. "We think that maybe we can have maybe 10 million users. What do you think, Steve?"

Her words hung in the air for a moment.

"I have heard some people back in the States talking about the idea of creating communities on-line," he began. "There's some thought that you could have such a platform be interactive so that people could indicate who else they like, or how they're affiliated with each other."

"Oh, that would be wonderful," Connie chirped. "Wouldn't it be a good idea to have people find each other on such a website? Maybe even they could form groups. Oh, that would be very nice."

"I wouldn't be surprised to see universities or alumni groups build something like that," Steve said dismissively. "You know, put a Stanford or MIT team up to it and I'm sure they'd love to create ways to socialize after they graduate."

"Here in China, I'm sure that we will have much support from our friends in the government," Connie said.

As the evening was approaching, she made a short phone call and, in three minutes, they left the room and returned to the foyer. They rode together to dinner.

There were eleven guests around the table at dinner. Steve didn't understand their names as they were being introduced. And it didn't help that they would be introduced with their given and family names but then they'd finish by saying, 'but you can call me' followed by an English name that didn't even come close to their real name.

You-can-call-me-Julie was the only one he remembered because she sat next to him at dinner and was a wonderful conversationalist. She worked at one of the Ministries though he couldn't even remember which one it was nor did he much care. Her lilting voice had a hypnotic effect on him as the evening wore on. She spoke about her growing interest in being a part of the new China and how important it had been for her parents to insure that she had a great education – including excellent English language skills. Her tutor had been a college student from Indiana who had returned to China after a brief stint in college to teach English in Tianjin.

"Mr. Donner," she began.

"Please, Julie, call me Steve," he interrupted.

"Mr. Steve, if you need anything at all during your stay in China, please take my handy phone number and call me – anything at all."

"Thank you, Julie," he replied, adding, "I think the only thing I need now is a bed."

As if he had given an order, the dinner abruptly ended and he was whisked away to the Jade Dragon hotel and within minutes, was escorted to his room. The décor was modest but adequately appointed. Walking into the bathroom, he stripped off his clothes and turned the shower on full strength. He had no idea how hot the water would run and in an instant, the bathroom was filled with steam. Backing the temperature down from scalding to damn hot, he stepped in and felt the dust melt off his body. He stood under the water for a solid five minutes, first in a mindless haze and then, reflecting on the Enterprise.

"This may work after all, dammit," he spoke into the darkness.

Pulling back the shower curtain he reached for the plush white towels perched above the toilet. He started drying off, still lost in thought. It wasn't until he stepped out of the shower that something peculiar caught his attention. Two sections of the mirrors, one just over the sink and the other up in the upper right hand corner of the mirror were clear while the rest of the mirror was totally fogged.

"I don't suppose there's any place in this country where there's not a camera," he muttered. "But do they have to have surveillance in the bathroom for Christ's sakes?"

With water still rolling down his back, he was startled by the phone ringing in the room. Wrapping his towel loosely around his waste, he stumbled into the darkness of the room.

"Mr. Donner, would you like a massage tonight?" came a melodic voice at the other end of the line.

"No thank you," he replied.

"O.K., then sleep well."

"Thank you. Goodnight," he replied.

He was just rinsing his mouth when the phone rang again.

"Good God," he thought, "don't they have the good sense to let me rest?"

"I'm fine," he started before he could hear the caller.

"Oh, Steve, this is Connie. So sorry to bother you. A car will be waiting for you at 8:30 in the morning. We are going to the only place we can speak freely."

"Connie, I'm sorry. I didn't mean to be disrespectful."

"Oh no problem, Steve," she replied. "Sometimes Chinese hospitality for foreigners is misunderstood. Goodnight."

He laid down on a firm mattress and adjusted the rice husk filled pillow under his head.

*I don't know if I can sleep on this pillow*, was the last thought that went through his head until the phone rang in the morning.

"Good morning, Mr. Donner," was the cheerful greeting. "Your car is here."

"I'll be down in five minutes," he said collecting himself.

"I've decided that we should visit the Ming Tombs on the way to Badaling this morning," Connie said as he stepped into the car. "After all, the underground tombs of the emperors are one of the few places where we can speak freely."

"Very well."

☒

Karen awoke in her opulent suite in Shangri La on Sheikh Zayed Road. The call to prayer from the mosque two blocks behind the hotel had reminded her that she was not in Manhattan. Today, she needed to be at her best. A lunch meeting scheduled for 1:30 pm with Darius Sanati, a senior member of the Iranian Academy of Sciences and one of the top biochemical engineers in the entire region. From his academic and corporate posts, he'd managed to become an iconic symbol of the Revolution – a consummate master of navigating the tenuous line between the hardliners surrounding the Ayatollah and the more moderate reformists.

That meeting had to end by 5:30 pm to accommodate the evening entertainment with the cosmopolitan 38-year old rock star of Dubai, Ayman Akbari. Ayman's reputation in structured financial products – clearly far from anything remotely resembling Shari' ah compliance – had ingratiated him to Sheikh Mohammad's inner circle. And his choice in lifestyles was, well, not something that was mentioned often. He maintained a suitable wife and two children in an opulent villa on the Dubai Creek but they were props in the theater of his life – not lead actors. In fact, come to think of it, Ayman was savant in his structured finance world. And the rest of his world was one giant party.

The gym for women was on the third floor and was brimming with largely unused pristine equipment. Karen managed her crazy travel schedule across multiple time zones each week by sticking to a regimen. Up by 6:30 local time and immediately in the gym for a minimum of 90 minutes. This gave her enough time to get a great workout and still be ready to launch into 9:00 am meetings wherever she was. But today, she had the luxury of stretching the workout to two hours with another 30 minutes in the steam room as she didn't have to be suited up until midday. She couldn't know that on a separate floor, and in a separate gym, a stunning, muscular blonde Scandinavian man was keeping the same routine. Modesty, after all, dictated that single women staying at the hotel were confined to women's floors and single men to single men's floors. Elevators weren't shared and the keycards to access floors and gyms insured that no indiscretion would be convenient.

At 9:10, drenched to the core, Karen returned to her room. The marble bathroom with its exquisite features had every appointment imaginable – complete with a cosmetics kit, toiletry ensemble and perfume that put her signature Chanel to shame. Opulence was wasted on her, though. Try as she might, her routine in the Agency as a field officer conditioned her to a 90 second shave and a two minute shower, max. No pampering. Three doors down from her, Elizabeth Petrusson slipped out of her jog bra and running shorts and filled the tub to brimming. Glancing into the mirror, she took a moment to celebrate her beauty. Her tanned skin perfectly contoured over a body that would make the Creator blush. She reached up and tossed her hair thrilling in her nude profile. After a killer workout, she was going to indulge herself with a long bath. This day was unlike any in her life. Her first day anywhere in the Gulf. And, posing as a journalist from the *Financial Times*, she was going to get the inside scoop on one Mr. Akbari's business. Her employer was eager to find out whether derivatives trading would serve as an ideal instrument to move vast amounts of money and, knowing Ayman's proclivity for beautiful women, she was the bait for this mission. No fish could resist. No one.

At 1:26 pm, the hotel staff knocked on Karen's door. They escorted her to what looked like another room at the end of the hall. Inside, all that was there was a tiny foyer and an elevator. A guard sat inside the elevator as the doors silently, yet abruptly opened. Once inside, the elevator sprang to life and ascended as if catapulting out of the building. When the doors opened, they were greeted with the blazing morning light on the roof top. A Heli-Dubai chopper sat silently awaiting its duty. The helicopter passenger door opened and out stepped the most elegantly dressed man Karen had ever seen. His three piece suit was tailored to perfection. He wore an impeccably starched white shirt without a tie. In his right hand, a strand of beads slowly clicked as he moved each bead across his thumb and forefinger.

"Ms. Wilson," his voice resonated like waves hitting the sea wall. "Shall we insure that our conversation is, what is your word? Discrete?"

"Certainly," Karen replied stepping into the chopper.

The two sat alone in the private passenger compartment and two minutes later they were effortlessly soaring across the waters of the Persian Gulf. Below them, the landscape was dotted with construction cranes and holes into which the foundations for the aspiration of Dubai would be poured.

"You see," Dr. Sanati continued, "we feel that our work in genetic engineering will have vast implications for vaccine production in the years to come. As you know, in America, tobacco was repurposed as a manufacturing plant for numerous compounds. In our labs in Tehran, we know that we can express *Bacillus anthrasis* and, in partnership with our collaborators in Pakistan and Europe, we believe we're less than two years away from having an anthrax vaccine. Imagine, a tomato plant actually serving as a biochemical laboratory. Now that's Persian science!" he exclaimed.

Karen knew that, of all the Shareholder prospects, it had been more difficult to verify the true net worth of Darius Sanati. Somehow, he had become ingratiated to the Iranian Revolutionaries in the early 80s and they had found him an invaluable asset when U.S. interests were arming the conflict with Iraq. The file contained the Baumgart and North transactions and so they were confident that he met the capital qualifications but the extent of his commercial ventures beyond the ones they found were opaque to say the least. That said, when you're 7,000 feet over a body of water which separates the Emirates from the Islamic Republic of Iran, discretion suggests that you probe cautiously.

"Now, Ms. Wilson, what is your proposition?" Darius inquired earnestly.

"We're forming an Enterprise…"

The Ming Tombs are an exquisite testimony to Chinese engineering. Vaulted ceilings over 20 feet in height are formed with giant blocks of cut marble. The chambers are laid out to represent the cosmology of the emperor's life and destiny; empty on entry and removed from artifacts of life at death. The giant doors and chambers enjoy a balanced symmetry unrivaled in any modern architecture and there's something quite astounding about being inside the Earth on a day when no one else, save Steve and Connie, were there. Steve wondered just how much clout someone had to arrange private access to these engineering marvels. However, it mattered little. Connie clearly had more than enough influence.

"Steven," she whispered, "I'm honored to accept your offer. However, there is one small problem. You know that I will need to insure that my interests stay within the Council's reach, even after I choose to disengage. If this presents a problem, than I am afraid I cannot participate."

"I'm sure we'll find a path to resolve this," he whispered in reply.

"I am sure that you, no we, will enjoy great success, Steven."

"Would you like to join me for drinks at my majoles?" Ayman concluded his prolonged lunch with Elizabeth. "Maybe we can discuss arranging a meeting in London to continue our acquaintance."

"I didn't know that we could drink," she protested, "here in Dubai."

"Oh, nonsense," he retorted. "I have the best liquor in the world here as do all the rest of the movers and shakers. You know, when they leave Dubai, some of them wait to leave the Emirates airspace before they lose their abayas and trade them in for Gucci and Armani but I can assure you that you won't find any of these guys who don't cut loose the minute they are out of sight of...," he didn't finish his sentence.

His phone rang. She only heard fragments of conversation. Something about home prices in the U.S. Another quip about AIG. She couldn't make it out.

Returning to the table he sat closer to her. It was clear that the siren was working its magic. Not that this was difficult for a man who had, or could buy, anything he wanted. Little doubt that in the moment, all he wanted was her. His mind had already played out a million scenarios and every one of them included being far away from Dubai, his trophy wife, his kids and the watchful eyes of this place and involved the things he'd love to do with Elizabeth.

"I'm sure I can arrange something with my editor to do a full feature on your efforts to open up the region to Western capital."

All he could think about is the regions he'd like to open on her. For Ayman, sex did not warrant a distraction from his frenetic life. With the cash that he could use in the foreplay, he never found a climax out of reach. But he knew that his greatest weakness would be if he ever encountered a woman who was as intelligent as him. After all, easy prey make meals but illusive prey are the real game. He would not lose the scent of this quarry for a long time. No, she was a rare specimen and he would one day mount her on his wall.

"My editor insists that I pick up the check," Elizabeth broke into the awkward silence.

"There is no check to pick up, my dear," he replied. "This lunch is on the house."

Karen was beaming when she stepped out of the Mercedes limousine that had been arranged as a departing courtesy by Darius. This was her first solo close and damn, it felt good. However, she quickly snapped back into the present as she saw Ayman emerging from the restaurant in the company of a goddess. This guy had a reputation and, if this lunch companion was any indication, he had a connoisseur's taste. She'd never seen such perfect form: beautiful hair, regal neckline, breasts as elegantly proportioned and a stomach so tightly contoured – and that was with her clothes on! She darted into an alcove inside the door and picked up a copy of the morning's Gulf News. She knew where Ayman's eyes would be focused so there was no chance she'd been seen. Her back to the door, she had no idea that the blonde had not left with her lunch companion but had, instead crossed the lobby towards her. As she turned to put down the newspaper she swung right into Elizabeth who was standing just behind her. In an instant, she felt the fiber of what she'd idolized just moments before. And what came next just deepened the spell.

"Hell of a way to say hi," Elizabeth did her best to sound indignant.

"I'm so sorry, ma'am," Karen stammered. "I didn't mean to…"

"Grope me?" she laughed.

Before she could come to her senses, she blurted out, "I'd love to."

What the hell was she thinking? The high rollers can get away with blurring lines of appropriateness all the time. She was not in that class. Not that she wouldn't want to be. And, after all, she had just seen $500,000,000 in cash get transferred into an account she'd set up for Darius' commitment! That made her…

"Where you from?" Elizabeth asked nonchalantly rubbing her hand slowly across her abdomen.

"Most recently from New York."

"You don't sound like you're from New York."

"No, I live there now. I've lived all over. Five years in Zurich right out of college. Originally I'm from Omaha, Nebraska."

"That's a long way from Dubai, don't you think?" she said. "What brings you to this part of the world?"

"Just another American trying to take over the world," Karen replied pretending to amuse herself with the truth in the statement.

"I love a woman who sets her sights high," Elizabeth mused. "Married?"

"Oh no. There's not a soul who would put up with my travel schedule. Hardly a romantic catch when you spend 45 weeks out of every year traveling all around the world."

"I wouldn't be so sure," she shot back. "I'd love to be a fly catcher for somebody who sees the world. In fact, I'd love to know that I could keep a distracted person..., well, distracted," she added striking a pose that she'd clearly refined to achieve precisely the effect she was having. "Of course, a woman like you probably has a sailor in every port."

"No. Not that I haven't fooled around now and then. But lately, I've been so damn busy that I haven't spent much time with anyone or anything. Now if that guy," she said pointing to her anonymous work-out partner from the gym below this morning, "threw himself at me…"

"That's a shame," Elizabeth said, "letting a perfectly charming asset like you go to waste. And to think that you're straight, in great shape and clearly in need of a good f…," she stopped herself. "You probably can't say that here can you?"

"How long are you in Dubai," she tried to change the subject.

"I'm flying to London tomorrow night," Karen was entranced with this woman and had not even indulged the glance from the Scandinavian man who was still looking at her through the plate glass window.

"Seriously? So am I. Would you like to share a car to the airport?" Elizabeth volunteered knowing that she'd get turned down by someone who clearly didn't fall for pick ups easily.

"I'd love to."

75

There's something quite interesting about men who are smitten with delusions of conquest of a woman. They are predisposed to acting impulsively. Fifteen minutes into Karen's presentation, Ayman Akbari was in. The rest of the night the two of them bent all the rules. If she had preconceptions about the Arab world and austere conservatism, they were all blown away that night. However, the haunting presence of Elizabeth seemed to chill the fires that were being lit through the night and she stumbled back to the hotel at 3am with nothing but relentless passion flaming for her. She was straight, she thought, but the raw sexuality of this stunning goddess was so arousing that, in that moment, she wasn't sure. She wondered how many men were capping off their lonely night with the same porn playing in their heads with a vision too untouchable for words. Six thirty came early and the work-out was more intense than it had been in months. She was a woman! And tonight, she'd fly on a magic carpet with the most gorgeous woman she'd ever seen. She would be in her company and, for now, that would be enough. She needed to stay focused and this bizarre Greek drama was off script.

Per their agreement, she sent an e-mail with a single line:

"Patrick: two fish caught and on ice."

"Transferring," was the immediate response.

# CHAPTER 4 - THE CLOSE

"I can't believe that Americans are going to fall for an idiot who can't make it through a single thought without a brain fart," Carey said as he turned off CNN's coverage of the final debate.

"Let's see," began Dan with his characteristic bristly tone refined during his years in Israel's elite special forces. "You're shocked that Americans will fall for someone who reminds them of themselves? Oh, forgive me but, in a world where NASCAR is a sport, the real surprise would be a President who actually can read and tie his own shoe laces. If it were possible to do simultaneously it would be downright genius!"

"An inauguration catered by Hardees and the Inaugural Ball with line-dancing...read it and weep, my friend," came the voice from behind the double screens on the desk.

"How are we coming with the logistics for the Gathering?" Dan was changing the subject.

"It looks like we've got all eleven confirmed and, when Steve gets back from Dallas, we should have the whole posse," another mumble from the desk.

"Thank God he took that one," Sun blurted out from his repose on the couch. "I had a hard enough time with Giroud when I had to get that pretentious son-of-a-bitch to focus during our meeting in Brussels. Fucking management consultants are worthless pieces of shit and he runs the nuthouse. If it weren't for the incompetence of Harvard Business School management training, the whole lot would suffocate under the weight of their own bullshit. I can't imagine how Steve is going to close the Reverend when he tells him that we've got an Iranian in the fold."

"Oh, he's got the juice," responded Dan. "You're going to love this one. In a few short hours we're going to find out if God or money is trump – I'm going long money on this one."

Keith walked through the office door. You know that there are tall kids who, groomed by over-achieving parents, wind up being super-star athletes. They are basketball players, quarterbacks or pitchers. They get some decent muscles on them and they achieve a bit of the Adonis look. In college, they go Division III, are the toast of the fraternity, date a few cheerleaders and wind up owning a car dealership or working as a vice president at a bank unless they join the Army in which case they become lobbyists. Keith was not that kid. He was tall, lanky and wore prescription lenses that would have been last fashionable in the mid 80s – which, by the way, was the last time he held out hope that his appearance would end his draught with women.

"Steve got all the files he needed," Keith announced. "This one is going to be fun. Kind of reminds me of the Devil tempting Christ in the desert. Just wish I could be a fly on the wall to watch the master work his magic."

American Family Network – AFN – was a media empire built by Dr. Jerry Robertson. A graduate of Liberty University, Dr. Robertson rose from his humble beginnings as a pastor of a Southern Baptist church in Little Rock, Arkansas to a media tycoon. His empire included AFN which had recently acquired a 24-hour 'news' show filled with well-dressed, perfectly coiffed talking heads who could mindlessly drivel over marriage and recoil in horror with everything that smacked of a threat to American values.

There was that one weekend at the Republican National Convention in 1979 when Jerry had been caught in a photo coming out of a strip club but, after a tearful repentance, televised on his fledgling network, his star vaulted into the constellation of fallen yet redeemed celebrity pool. His size 2 wife sat next to him and tearfully took 'some responsibility for not being a help-mete for him' and vowed that she would work to model what all good Christian wives should be in service to their husbands. And when the city of Jacksonville was getting ready to tear down its arena to bring more sports revenue to the city, he stepped into 'God's blessing' and bought the building forming a mega-church boasting 50,000 American Values Christians. Success dripped out of every pore and no Republican stood a chance in any election without appearing on AFN and attending a prayer breakfast at AFN Ministries.

"Michael has tried to talk some sense into me about what you're proposing, Steven, but you'll have to forgive this servant of the Lord," he greeted Steve in his lavish offices overlooking downtown Atlanta where he and Suzanne shared a modest 22,000 square foot second home on the north side of Buckhead. He found that folks in Georgia made better neighbors and, in his private plane, commuting to Jacksonville gave him time with the Lord before events.

"Thank you for taking the meeting Dr. Robertson," Steve began.

"Call me Jerry," Dr. Robertson interrupted.

"Jerry," Steve resumed his introduction, "what we're doing is the only way we see to insure that the Left doesn't overwhelm our nation. You undoubtedly know that I'm not religiously inclined but I certainly know how important morality is to you and to most Americans and we feel that your influence could, well, be quite influential in our Enterprise."

They fell into conversation about moral decay, business and the need to cut taxes, shrink government, and limit social spending.

"You know, our ministry provides afterschool lunches to nearly 400 inner city kids," Jerry said, waiting for Steve to be impressed.

"We firmly believe that private citizens, like you, are the key to solving most of the country's challenges," he said deflecting the pathetic generosity of his host.

"I've arranged dinner on my yacht so we should head to the airport," Jerry changed the subject.

"Wonderful."

Thirty minutes later, the Gulfstream shot off the runway and rose to 41,000 feet.

"Not a lot of ears up here, just the Lord," Jerry chuckled.

Steve knew that there was one possible fly in the sacred ointment. A former African dignitary turned Ambassador who happened to be in the defense business would be seen as expedient. No worries there. The middle aged Brazilian heiress who happened to become the largest shareholder of Sony and Nintendo would appeal to his exotic taste. A British Lord would serve to add a certain cache to the club. The fact that said Lord was in on-line gaming sounded like it might be a great synergy to AFN's little disclosed positions in pornography and gaming interests in the U.S. After all, Jerry had rationalized, if you're going to convince sinners to part with money, best to insure that there's a healthy arbitrage on guilt. He could brush past Kate O'Connor's real role by letting Jerry know that she was the only heiress in the group selected because of her public renunciation of her family's wealth and name. And since nobody ever understood Jonas, saying that he was a former cryptographer turned equities trader was sufficient. The only risk was an Islamic Iranian. He had an angle on that one but he didn't know how it would fly.

"Darius Sanati!" Jerry exclaimed. "How is that sumovbitch?"

Steve was dumbstruck. He wasn't sure whether he should be more concerned at the fact that intel had not picked up this association or that a Southern Baptist, conservative Christian minister had any connection to one of Iran's most colorful characters.

"I haven't seen him since Santa Rosa," Jerry continued.

Then all the pieces came together. Towards the midpoint in the Iran-Contra negotiations, the DEA, CIA and other interested parties had coordinated a meeting at Samosa's former estate just south of the Nicaraguan border. The identities of attendees were all classified so, unless you were there and knew someone from another venue, you could have been sitting next to a saint or sinner and not known who was who. There had been a delegation from Virginia arranged by General Dynamics and apparently, this young aspiring minister had been part of the team.

"We were at dinner down at Playa del Coco when we met – had one hell of a night!" he continued. "You know Steve, back in those days, covert ops were so much more fun. That's when we learned that keeping bad guys alive was far more valuable than shootin' them. Hell, whether it was the Jackal, Noriega, or any other two bit hustler on one of our payrolls, once they went rogue, turning them into public enemies was great for business. None of the Beltway would have any of its pretty buildings if we didn't come up with a way to turn assets into public villains and God knows, the public will gobble up any line of shit we feed them."

Steve noticed Jerry getting visibly excited, his face flushing and his eyes squinting.

"You know," he continued, "putting Nancy up to the 'War on Drugs' was my idea. I got ministers across the country to pray to put an end to the scourge of drugs while we went on and cashed the checks. That's the same playbook we're running at AFN. We know that men are all sinners and so might as well give them something to sin with – makes preaching so much more interesting when you come armed with the stats on how much porn your flock has flogged last week. Great business model."

For a moment, Steve actually found himself genuinely despising this guy. *What a shit,* he thought to himself.

But the thought was quickly replaced with the recognition that, if the Enterprise was going to be successful, operating in plain sight with every God-fearing American suckling from the pendulous tit of the AFN network would be a homerun. After all, if you want to get people to suspend all critical thinking and roll over to plans as audacious as his, the utility of AFN was a necessity. The fact that Jerry was a hypocrite was just a necessary evil and *necessary* was far more important than *evil*. He didn't have to like the guy. He just needed to use him until the Enterprise was fully operational.

"Brilliant," Steve punctuated his thoughts misleading Jerry to hear an accolade. Jerry was good at hearing praise.

The *Genesis 2:25* was tied up at the end of the exclusive moorings at the San Diego Yacht Club. This 130ft shrine to the blessings of God was already bustling with activity when they pulled up in Jerry's white Land Rover. Young crew, equal numbers of men and women under the age of 25 and all of them torn from the pages of a Polo advertisement, were readying the boat for casting off. They were greeted at the gangway by a picturesque couple, Sam and Melissa, who were thrilled to welcome Steve to the *Genesis 2:25*. Sam, formerly a Marine was tanned and had muscles that were quite evident under his one size too small polo shirt. Melissa was equally tanned and wore a khaki skirt that was more painted on than fitted. They were a lovely couple and set the tone for a lovely evening.

"Have you met Congressman Conway?" Jerry pulled Steve's shoulder to introduce a portly man standing on the aft deck just beyond the heli-pad.

"No I don't believe we've met," Steve said extending his hand for a hearty handshake.

"Which kind of night is this?" Conway inquired of Steve, "business or pleasure?" He took a long, slow draught of his cigar.

"Well Sir," Jerry replied, "I believe that Steve is someone you should meet. And more than that, a little birdie tells me that you may be coming into some serious blessings, if you know what I mean. I just talked with Brewster up at the club and it seems that with Steve's plans, we might have a couple years of plenty a comin'"

"So it's business tonight, Reverend," Conway said with a sigh. "Alright, what are we up to now?"

The engines hummed to life as they cruised out of the harbor and headed for Catalina Island. Dinner tonight would be Chilean sea bass with a chipotle chutney, roasted potatoes and mashed – Conway wouldn't have dinner if it didn't include mashed potatoes – and creamed spinach. Jerry had the crew load an extra case of '79 *La Chapelle* and they'd have Melissa's apple cobbler – a decadent, oozing orgy as cliché as they come but good nonetheless. When Melissa served it, nobody was thinking about the 'mom' but, oh, the apple pie! The service was impeccable and the weather cooperated. Light winds, clear skies, and monogrammed jackets to match the crew when the sun set.

This was going to work.

⊟

"We'd like you to testify for a hearing we're having on Defense procurement," Dean said after Cyrus picked up the phone. "We hear that you have some ideas about how we could streamline the process to get a little more bang for the buck and the Navy says that they like your ideas."

"When's the hearing?" Cyrus inquired.

"Well, we've got to make sure we can get the right appropriators in D.C. so we'll need to get back to you on that one," Dean replied.

"Who else is going to be testifying?" Cyrus asked.

"The usual suspects. We'll have some folks from the Pentagon and they'll bring some of the Lockheed and Northrop senior team," Dean added. "You know we're just starting to socialize some reform so we need you to be, well, you know, your normal contrarian self."

"Emilie and I were thinking about heading off for a long-weekend in the next few weeks. Any chance you know whether it will be on a Monday or Friday?"

"Oh, not a chance. With the elections and all, getting anybody to actually work a full week is going to be impossible. We'll shoot for a Wednesday or Thursday in one of the next three weeks," Dean said.

"Great, I might drag her along – it's been a while since she's seen me on the Hill. She seems to like it when she does and I don't mind over-nighting downtown. A night away from the kids always puts a smile on her face," Cyrus remarked.

"I'd love to invite Sara and the four of us could do dinner after the hearing if you're up for it. If you guys want an evening alone, we can take a rain check but I know Sara would love to see Emilie again," Dean added.

"Let's do it. When you know the date, I'll get a sitter and we'll make an evening of it. Great talking to you," and with that, Cyrus hung up.

"Thanks, man..." Dean tried to say but the line was already dead.

"Fried green tomatoes? I don't think so," Emilie said scrunching up her face at the thought.

"No, you really have to try them," Sara said half-laughing. "The breadcrumbs they use are a bit spicy and there's a dressing to die for that you dip them in."

"You had me at fried bread," Emilie smiled her endearing smile.

Georgia Brown's was one of their favorite spots in the city. The food was always good – not necessarily great – but you could be assured that you'd walk away satisfied and with a smile on your face. The wine list was not anything to write home about but still serviceable. But there was something about the place that just fit them. The foodies in the D.C. scene may not rave about the cooking but if it were up to them, they'd pick it for a dinner or date the majority of the time.

Cyrus had picked his customary seat. Compulsively, he'd ask for a table – never a booth – and he'd sit facing the door. They were just finishing up a banana caramel vanilla ice cream extravaganza when Cyrus froze just for an instant. Walking in the door was a face he hadn't seen for over a decade. The other three men in his company were not familiar but Cyrus could never forget the face of none other than Darius Sanati.

"Is everything o.k., babe?" probed Emilie always capable of picking up when Cyrus was drawn into *that* space.

"Sorry," he replied so absorbed in his recollections as to barely perceive her question.

"What's wrong?" she probed.

Back in 1987 he had been working in San Jose with the Costa Rican Red Cross and, during a trip up to Guanacaste to work in refugee camps, he had taken a weekend trip to the beach. That his choice of a beach resort happened to match the selection by a delegation from the multi-agency task force responsible for laundering democracy support through drug cartels was an unfortunate coincidence. The fact that he was on the beach when Darius was discussing the consortium of Saudis', Iranians', and Syrians' appreciation for generous U.S. funds supporting the arming of assets in the region was a conversation not meant for his ears. But Cyrus had a bad habit of forgetting neither face nor conversation and here, at Georgia Brown's, was the same man.

Immediately, he went into the mode that Emilie found most irritating; that moment when it was clear that Cyrus would rather be eavesdropping on a conversation half a restaurant away rather than the social banter at the table where he found himself sitting.

"Those two guys look like spies," she said playfully as she followed his gaze to the group of four as they sat down.

"That wouldn't surprise me," he began, his voice lowering to nearly a whisper.

"I'm going to freshen up in the Ladies' room. Care to join me?" Sara interrupted.

"Yes, the iced tea, wine, and coffee have all conspired at the moment," Emilie rose to follow Sara off.

When they had cleared earshot, Cyrus leaned over to Dean.

"Why the hell would an Iranian delegation be in D.C. this week?" Cyrus asked.

"No idea, exactly," Dean began, "but we did get word that there were some VIPs coming in and Capitol Police were placed on high alert."

"They wouldn't do that for one guy, would they?" Cyrus persisted.

"Unlikely, why?" Dean replied.

"Well, the fellow over at that table is one of the Iranian assets that the CIA and DEA were using for Ollie's folly with the Contras. And the fact that he's here in town would suggest that something's brewing. Could Bush and Cheney being pulling a reprise to destabilize Gore?" Cyrus mused.

"Who would we pay off this time?" Dean chuckled. "The Balkans have settled, the Palestinians are not too unsteady at the moment, and Iraq has become less interesting than the Afghanistan drug racket. We've already got the Afghanis in a partnership with the

Brits and they're cooperating with our financial expediency – funny how drug cartels are so vital to national security ever since…" his voice tailed off as the ladies returned to the table.

"Solve the world's problems, Cyrus?" Sara said as she sat back down giving Dean a gentle peck on the cheek.

"No, just making more," he said pulling out the chair for Emilie. "Looks like we've got another interesting election on the horizon."

The four fell back into conversation and talked about the kids. Sorin was playing basketball and hating every minute of being on a losing team. Anna was playing soccer and was coasting in school. Dean and Sara's kids were still in pre-school but Francine was doing so well with the cello that several schools were already looking at offering her a music tutor.

"I can't believe it," Sara started. "When I was her age I was still learning how to ride a bike and she's already a legitimate musician."

"Don't know where that comes from but I'd sure like to meet the father," Dean laughed reaching over and giving Sara a gentle kiss on the hand.

"It must have been the concerto we were listening to back in Munich that night…" she drifted off to a memory that they clearly shared.

"And on that note," Emilie blurted, "I think the night needs a bit more *Eine Kleine Nachmusik* and I've got a concerto planned for Cyrus."

"You bring the strings and I'll bring the bow, my Lady," he said signing the check and rising from the table.

"Actually my dear, I believe you brought me the strings from a little shop in London a few weeks ago," she flirted.

⌗

Whenever the Agency wanted to have a meeting, they'd rent a hotel suite at one of the mid-level Hyatts or Sheratons on the way out to Dulles just off the toll road. The fact that they did it so often seemed to defy any sense of security as anyone who cared to do so would just sit in the lobby and watch who was checking in without baggage. Observe a group of six people arrive sans luggage and go to the same floor and, voila, you would have your IDs. Keith had suggested that the Gathering take place at the Hyatt but the plan was scuttled when at least three of the Shareholders vetoed the location. He was not pleased that his recommendation was dismissed so quickly but this was Steve's call and so he'd go along with the plan.

The decision was made that they'd all convene at the Greenbrier in West Virginia for a long weekend. The setting was perfect. Limited controlled access, plenty of discretion in meeting locations and ample support for security if and when it would be required. Logistics

92

would be coordinated so that they could all assemble without anyone knowing the real purpose of the meeting. The gathering would be officially billed as a private security conference. They settled on the theme, 'From Bombs to Bytes – Warfare in A Digital Age'. Promoted as a watershed conference to discuss the only relevant security risk facing the developed world – namely cyber threats – the attendees would include mid-level military and government contractors and the speakers would be a few appropriators, a couple military brass from the Navy and Air Force, and one conservative CEO from Silicon Valley if such a person still existed. Keep it intimate – invitation only. No media. And the special event of the weekend: falconry. This would allow 'random' groups of 12 to 14 to disappear into the meadows and hills for several hours at a time in absolutely plausible intervals.

"As you are all aware, we've assembled without much time before the elections," Steve began as he turned up the collar on his riding jacket. "And, we're assured that the Bush-Cheney ticket is going to win. What we all know is that our job would be much more difficult with Monotone-in-Chief on Pennsylvania Avenue. So, I've asked Dr. Robertson to introduce you to a little favor he's agreed to do to kick things off… Jerry," he turned to his hypocrite turned consigliore.

"Well, folks, the way we see it, this is going to come down to the wire. Anyone with a college education knows that W's got the intellect of a fence post" – an illusion lost on most of the Shareholders – "but our bet is that Florida may very well be where the race is won or lost. And we're not going to lose it. AFN has insured that every Christian in the country gets a voting guide at their church on the Sunday before elections, you know, make sure they know that a vote for a Democrat is a vote for homosexuals and big government. And then, we've hosted a prayer breakfast with a couple judges. We've got two who are regulars in my congregation in Florida and they've come into some blessing lately just in case they need to be called upon to do the Lord's work."

"Thank god the EU's atheist," Henri Giroud sighed. "I'm not sure I could handle the idea of a god in the mix. We've got enough trouble with the Greens. We've already got so many special interests that adding religion would be, well, Islamist!" he said shaking his head disapprovingly.

"Indeed," chimed Lord Haverford. "We formed a church to endorse our monarchs, not to choose them. Bloody reprehensible that the colonies would off and let freedom of religion be turned round about and let religion dictate freedom!"

Chan Siew and Patrick Cheong glanced at each other immediately knowing that mixing religion and geopolitics in their part of the world was a powder keg best left alone.

"So," sang the deep voice of the Ambassador, "what you are saying is that you have judges who will assure that a close call falls our way? Splendid! I like this Enterprise already."

"That's correct compadre," Jerry bellowed, pleased that his contribution was the first impression any of the twelve saw tangibly expressed.

Gabriela was the first one to be fitted with the falconer's glove. Her arm disappeared inside as the guide gently coaxed the giant bird from his hand to hers. In one of her early video games, she had falcons as one of the weapons warriors could use in their period battles and she'd always wondered what it would be like to manipulate one in real life.

"Gently lower your hand and then lift it quickly," came the voice of the guide.

With a gentle dip and toss, the mighty bird rose from her hand escorted by a subtle shriek of delight.

"Oh my god, this is so beautiful," her voice sounded reverent.

Suddenly, the giant bird hurtled towards the ground to catch a piece of rabbit flesh lofted into the air by the guide. The group gasped in amazement as this giant flying machine hurtled into its prey with a precision none had ever witnessed.

"We spend a fortune trying to make technology which can fly with such precision," Connie quipped. "Wouldn't it be amazing to see a plane find a target like that?"

Kate O'Connor and Jonas exchanged glances. They hadn't had their conversation with Ambassador Olusimibo but that was scheduled for this meeting.

"Warfare, since the cold war has ended, will no longer be about missiles, planes, ships, and soldiers on a battlefield. No, the soldier of the future will defend freedom in cyberspace. The Marine of yesterday will be replaced with an 18 year old who has grown up with computers. The Special Forces of yesterday will be replaced by engineers who know how to design RF-shielded data and communications centers," proclaimed Hugh McGrath, Deputy Chief of the White House Cybersecurity Task Force. "Unmanned vehicles in the air and sea and on the ground will replace the M-16 as the soldier's primary weapon and he'll manipulate them with a joystick and a video monitor far from harm's reach."

At the end of the speech, Jerry couldn't restrain his impulse to walk up to Hugh and offer him a position as a National Security Expert for AFN.

"Pleased to help in any way I can," Hugh replied. "Of course, while I'm employed by the government, you know I can't get compensation, however, if you ever need an expert in unmanned air vehicles – UAVs you know – well, Sir, I'm your man," he hastened to add.

"You think they're going to be a credible weapon?" he interrupted himself and changed the subject. "Hey, enough business, I'll have my office send you an agreement and we'll sort out compensation when you're a free agent." Jerry replied. "Rules are rules. I like a government man who has high integrity."

"Thank you, Sir," Hugh replied.

After coffee was served by white-gloved staff, the mingling guests – some with their wives, some with their lovers, and some alone – disappeared into the cavernous halls and lounges throughout the Greenbrier's lavish, nostalgic grandeur. Steve had selected a room perched above the main entrance with elegant windows looking out towards the mountains now punctuated with a few oaks who had not yet succumbed to the freezing night air. The Operators were not at the compound – just some of Steve's long-time allies from security details he'd used when executives needed extraction from hotspots in the early 80s. These guys were masters of discretion. Each one of them chiseled with hours in the gym each day – real Spartans. And, as long as the pay was good, they'd do anything asked of them. Anything.

The Shareholders all meandered their way through the halls and struck up casual conversations with invited guests. They were to convene at the lounge at 10:05pm at which time there would be a fire drill. Everyone but the Shareholders and Steve would evacuate the building and for one minute, all the lights would go to emergency back up power. During this time, the Enterprise would enter a room behind the bookcase on the left-hand side of the room and the real business would begin. After 4 minutes in the cold, the lights would come back on and the house staff would offer everyone an open bar for the inconvenience. Best way to distract this crowd, they figured, was to get them drunk enough that they wouldn't remember much of the night.

"10:05pm?" Henri had inquired.

"A time selected by Lord Haverford I'm afraid," Steve had replied earlier in the afternoon. "It seems he likes to do everything he does at times and on dates that reflect his near pathologic obsession with Lord Nelson. He's asked to share one of Nelson's gems of wisdom at our opening tonight."

"In my line of business, you can find a gentlemen repugnant but, providing he is paying for your wine cellar and your August holidays, you learn to swallow indignation," Henri sighed. "Let the British bugger have his way," he added miserably faking an English accent.

On cue, the fire alarms resounded through the vaunted establishment and guests scurried to exits aided by beguiling, calm staff. Behind the bookcase, the elevator was at the ready and lowered the Shareholders to the sub-basement in which a state-of-the-art conference room had been readied.

"Good God," exclaimed Chan Siew as they walked into what looked like the set of a futuristic science fiction fantasy.

Glowing, Steve turned to his guests and began.

"If you would please take your seats you will find a small monitor mounted into the table exclusively for your use. Please take a moment to read it carefully as this will be the only time you'll see any of the information regarding your role and the project phase in which you will be operational. There will be no further communication on these matters and you are to commit every detail to memory. For operational security, once we leave this room, all hardware in this room will be exposed to an EMF pulse and then incinerated and with it any chance to retrieve the slightest evidence of the meeting."

"Sounds like I am in a Mission Impossible episode... this disc will self-destruct...," Ayman quipped.

"Oh to the contrary my good man," Lord Haverford injected, "Mission Inevitable."

Connie, Jonas, Gabriela, Darius and Ambassador Olusimibo exchanged knowing glances. Kate sat emotionless. Something on her screen had obviously been unexpected.

"With that vote of confidence," Steve continued, "I nearly forgot, Lord Haverford, what was it that you wanted to share with the group – a Nelson quote, I recall?"

Filling his chest and clearly doing all he could to conjure his Horatio Nelson inspiration, he enunciated, "I laid before them the plan I had previously arranged for attacking the enemy...when I came to explain to them the Nelson Touch it was like an electric shock. Some shed tears, all approved – it was new – it was singular – it was simple!"

He paused to see if his delivery had impressed the room and then continued.

"Steven, since October, 1805 – 10-05, a more clever, comprehensive plan has not re-emerged. The floor, my good man, is yours."

Steve was good. When it came to taking a complex 10 year plan and boiling it down into a few bite-sized morsels, he did it with the best of them. Assuming that everything went well, Dr. Robertson's first contribution would insure that George and Dick restored morality to the Office of the President. And given his close association with

George H. W. Bush, he'd insure that the White House was friendly with the Enterprise. He would be Vice President Cheney's 'Pastor-in-Chief' and would get direct access to the Naval Observatory residence. While Dick would have little need of pastoral guidance given his disdain for all creation – both actual and imagined – the role would serve as pretext for unlimited access.

"Within two years, we must be operational and, for Phase I, we're going to plan two simultaneous strategies. It's going to be challenging but we've got all the winds in our favor. It seems that a group of our assets in Afghanistan and northern Pakistan are making our business relationship much more difficult. As long as they cooperated with the Agency's need to move cash through opium and heroin, we had them by the balls – sorry ladies," he hurried.

"But now, they've got it in their turbans that we need them more than they need us and we're going to use the government's vindictive impulses to create an enemy we can all fear. We've confirmed with our friends in Europe, thanks to Lord Haverford and Henri Giroud – thank you gentlemen," he nodded, "that they're equally concerned with some of the more radical fringe and we've also confirmed that, so long as we give the State Council access to the region's oil and metals, our friends in China will not intervene – thank you Connie."

She glowed in the light of the praise.

"Chan Siew, Ayman, and Darius have been invaluable at giving me a crash course in Islamic factions and, while I never thought I'd want to know most of it, what we have confirmed is that there's one nut job who's vilification will cause the least possible collateral damage – an asset that has become unmanageable and has few friends – Osama bin Laden. If we're going to implement our Enterprise, we've got less than two years to get Phase I executed and, as of this evening, you now know what you've got to do."

There was a long pause as everyone looked around the room at each other. Each one of them knew that they had $500 million apiece on the line. None of them had anything to go on save Steve's compelling presentation on the synergies that the group represented. And each of them knew that half the funds were placed in strategic investments in Mongolian metals and strategic oil operations far from harm's way and from the inquisitive eyes of conspiracy theory purveyors. Steve had shown each of them where their individual business interests for their individual contributions to the Enterprise would more than offset the committed capital. It was, to quote Lord Nelson, singular and simple.

"From here on out, the only authorized messages you'll receive regarding the Enterprise will come from Cecil," Steve said.

*Cecil?* they all thought at once, *who's Cecil?*

No one breathed a word. They sat in silence for three minutes, each one re-examining the text on the screens set into the table. And then, a single message appeared on each screen:

"Let everyone do their part."

The screens flickered twice, flashed and then went dark.

As they entered the elevator, there was no speaking – they knew what would happen next and they weren't looking forward to it. Waiting up in the lounge through which they passed to enter the meeting would be an armed escort. Each one would be taken from the facility and distributed to locations throughout the world and would be without any form of communication for two weeks. No phones, no credit cards to trace, no knowledge of where they were. Just a jet, a guard, and hospitality on the ground. Their families would be advised of a delay in their return from the States.

# CHAPTER 5 - PHASE I – THE DISTRACTION

On July 10, 2000 a few hundred people died in a pipeline explosion in Nigeria. Six days later, a hundred more were killed. Every year a few dozen miners are killed in Chile and, when you're buried a few thousand feet underground in a Chilean mine, who's going to go down there and see what actually caused the explosion. Given the demolition skills that were preserved with places like Colonia Dignidad in Chile, the idea of human casualties in the pursuit of a more pure humanity was the perfect place to refine explosives and unprecedented demolition capabilities. And, so long as the tests could be explained away under the dismissive guise of careless working conditions and rogue mining operations, who would know that what was being developed was an explosive which could be used to detonate charges that would vaporize structural steel, and, in the blast, render its existence untraceable? Pipelines and mines were the perfect combination. Once perfected, positioning the materials was going to be a challenge but that's where Steve's experience kicked in.

The Port Authority of New York bought its property and casualty insurance from Miller Insurance, a Lloyds broker in London. As the policy was coming up for renewal, competing bids would demand the ability to do physical inspections of the property in and around the World Trade Center. Structural engineers would pour over building specifications, maintenance records, materials tests and, at some point they'd have to bring in engineers to independently assess the integrity of the buildings. This was no light task and hundreds of contractors from Lloyds members, along with competing bidders like AIG, would need to be given access to plans, integrity reports and the like. Clearly, all of them would want to pull the records of post bombing inspections after the attempt in February 1993. Since its construction, this would be the one time in decades where the complex would be littered with people and equipment. This would be the perfect distraction. And how ironic that, something as simple as an insurance renewal or replacement would be so fortuitously timed. The Lloyds policy would either renew or expire on September 10, 2001 and someone – Lloyds or otherwise – would go 'on risk' on September 11.

Dan Goldstein was the only one of the Operators to object.

"How the hell are we going to take down a few icons in Manhattan without killing thousands, hell maybe tens of thousands?" he had protested.

"We're not going to, my friend," Carey replied. "All we're going to do is send detailed maps and images to a team who is working on a new video game that we're planning to release in June. Some random bunch of gamers are going to be flying planes and none of them will know that, at the right moment, they're going to be going from virtual to reality. There's not going to be one goddam piece of evidence anyone will find because there will be none."

"We've arranged a virtual gamers conference for the launch of pre-holiday betas. They'll be some actual video gaming conferences running from September 9 – 12 in Singapore, Xian, Rio, Johannesburg, and Tel Aviv and we'll have hot links into consoles in each location," Sun explained.

Sun was, without question, the scariest of the Operators. He appeared to be about 30 but nobody was interested enough to engage in conversation with him to actually ask. He was either Pacific Islander or Asian but, again, he had one of those ubiquitous physiques that he could have been from anywhere. He had worked for MI-6, for the CIA, and for the Singaporean intelligence service for quite sometime. They had heard rumors that he had been recruited out of third or fourth grade when he was identified as being 'gifted'. He didn't volunteer any details about his life, his family, or even what he did when he'd vanish from the control room. But what everyone did know is that the digital world was his absolute domain and if he had a keyboard at his fingertips, there was nothing that he couldn't do.

"The coolest thing we've done," Sun continued, "is we've got a team of real crazies – kids that have exhibited ridiculous skills at multi-player games like Commando Grit and Shock & Awe III – who've agreed to play out scenarios with us. We'll have them see if they can simulate a variety of attacks on critical infrastructure in cities around the world. We've wired in what we call 'pin ball machine' which gives extra points if you can take out more than one target with the same assault. For example, could you crash a plane into one of two neighboring towers and have the fuselage strike a second one in a kill location."

"That's some messed up shit," Carey exclaimed. "What you're saying is that we're going to hit these buildings with planes being flown by a bunch of video games?"

"Yep," Sun chirped without missing a beat.

"And the best part about this deal is that we've got Jonas and Ayman cued up to short the hell out of the market so Steve's pretty sure that we'll close to double our money," Dan seemed to get over his moral aversion. "I'm going to make sure that we contain the casualties and I've got a few ideas on how to pull that off."

"Oh, isn't that touching," Carey scoffed. "A hardened killer going soft in his old age."

"Listen you piece of shit," Dan retorted, "I've got friends who work downtown and I didn't sign up for this gig to kill them."

"Show off," Carey shot back, "you've at least got friends – you should share some with Keith."

"I'd like to arrange of shipment of zeolite," came a voice at the other end of the Ambassador's phone. "This is Cecil."

The line went dead. He knew what to do. Back in his early days with Bart Ivanhoe, they'd worked out the perfect way to ship materials, money, hell, even people, without detection. Put contraband in a shipment of zeolite – the grainy substance used in the processing of petrochemicals – and not a single customs inspector in any port on the planet will even look past the first few thousand cubic feet. They'd moved platinum that way on numerous occasions. They had designed a pod in which a person could be self-sufficient for up to 45 days buried under tons of this stuff – a device that had come in quite handy when war criminals from the Balkans were smuggled out of Turkey through the Bosporus. From time to time, governments who needed weapons moved without a trace contracted with Midway Logistics, one of their many shell corporations, to provide services this way. The Ambassador would put the chemicals in containers and get them to New Jersey. From there, the engineering team would know what to do.

⊠

"So what you're saying, Director McGrath, is that you can reasonably expect to have these drones or, what do you call them, UAVs, actually replace the Air Force?" Tim Simpson, anchor for AFN's Security Watch, asked incredulously.

"No, it's not a replacement, Tim. It's really more an adjunct to conventional tactical assets. The big difference is we can put a lot more of them in the air and minimize loss of our servicemen by limiting the number of brave men and women that have to go into harm's way," Hugh clarified.

"What's the risk that this type of technology could fall into the hands of our enemies?" Tim continued knowing that around the country at least 8 million viewers would eat up another excuse to be afraid.

"With America's technical superiority we're quite confident that there's more risk of being struck by lightning than to have any of our enemies use unmanned vehicles against us. No, there's more chance for hijackings and bus bombings like our friends in Israel face each day than there is for unmanned aircraft to threaten our security," Hugh reassured his rapt listeners.

"Tell me about the rumors that North Korea and Iranian missile technology may be used by Saddam Hussein," Tim changed the subject to an 'Axis of Evil' theme that always aided ratings.

"Well," Hugh started, "we've got credible intelligence suggesting that several Pakistani nuclear engineers have been sharing technical knowledge about nuclear weapons with Saddam Hussein's regime." He smiled at the thought of his growing status as an expert for the generous and lucrative empire of Dr. Robertson. "As a matter of fact, we believe that there is a potential link between Iraq's interest in nuclear weapons, weapons of mass destruction and uranium sources in Africa," he added.

"Wow, that's really scary stuff," Tim did his best to hold his patronizing tone. "You really have to wonder whether George Bush Senior should have gone all the way to Baghdad before this threat could become so serious."

"A decade later," Hugh began, "we're in a superior position to surgically strike key targets with far less threat to our forces or civilian populations. Any mission in Iraq should be accomplished in ninety days."

"Thank you, Director McGrath, as always, America is fortunate to have experts like you who help keep us safe. God bless you and...," looking straight into the camera, "God bless America." Tim signed off with AFN's mandatory benediction on every guest deemed one of Jerry's elite.

Sun's 'crazies' were starting to get eerily proficient. In one scenario, they flew an A-320 into the Sears Tower in Chicago and managed to have a wing take out several key train platforms. In another, they had a competition to see how many fragments of sufficient mass could take out multiple targets – their favorite targets including the World Trade Center, the CN Tower in Toronto and the towers looming over Shinjuku Station in Tokyo. The fact that they loved to fly planes into the Microsoft logo above Shinjuku Station had more to do with their adherence to anarchist predilections than collateral damage but, who would give a shit? By the time they'd been a week into the scenarios, they'd been drinking more Mountain Dew than a human kidney could tolerate and they were convincing themselves that there'd be no target that they couldn't take on. Each flight of fancy by the crazies was analyzed in the basement of the Trinity Building operations center for its viability, collateral damage, and simulation feasibility. After all, if the gamer conferences were going to take the controls of real aircraft, they would have to believe that the games were plausible.

"I think we'll need three UAVs if we're going to tag the WTC complex," Keith said as he poured over the simulations. "From everything that we're seeing, it appears that our African supplier is moving along quite nicely with the explosives and he's got a doozy planned for an October 'dry run'," chuckling to himself with the irony only he could get at the time.

"What if we don't get all the birds into their respective nests?" Carey inquired.

"As long as we get the majors – which should be the easiest targets – we'll have enough chaos that people won't be too concerned with a collapse that doesn't seem to have a cause," Keith said. "After all, they'll be so much pandemonium that the whole scene will just be a blur."

"I still don't like the collateral cost of this whole operation," Dan protested.

"What if we could throw in a freebie for you mate?" Carey offered.

"What do you mean?" Dan responded.

"Well, if we could make sure that Deutsche Bank's building is part of the impact zone, wouldn't that appeal to some of your team's zeal to inflict a bit of pain on German interests? After all, you seem to think they've still got some of your gold, don't you?" Carey goaded his colleague where he knew he'd get a rise.

"Are you kidding? If you were targeting that Bank, I could get some of our folks to take the controls," Dan replied falling into his comfortable Israeli accent.

"Then, for the sake of your conscience, let's make sure that they pay, shall we?" Keith added. "And, if you need to discretely warn a few folks to stay away when this all goes down, well, we can arrange for that."

⚐

The *Gulf Crescent* was completely loaded to capacity and was scheduled to make a few stops en route to Newark. To insure that all the material was in place by no later than January 2001 – the target dates that they'd arranged to have an insurance inspection allegedly on behalf of AIG – they'd make just a few stops. After Doha, the first one would be operational. They'd do a final QC run using an autonomous vehicle strike in Yemen where they'd test out the game-controller and explosive interface. The goal was to insure that the charges would perform to specification on steel construction and they'd definitely have a few targets from which to select. As the ship disappeared into the Gulf, the Ambassador stood at an office window overlooking the harbor. Turning to Henri and Darius who had elected to come down to christen the Phase I inauguration, he said,

"Gentlemen, I believe my task is largely completed." His tone was low and serious actually conscious of the fact that what had now been put in motion would have grave and lasting consequences. "Henri, thank you for getting your team at Resilience Global to assist us with the paperwork. I had no idea how helpful it would be to have your team embedded in the Customs and Trade ministries."

"It is my pleasure," Henri gushed.

"And Darius, I never thought a biological engineer could move so much sand so quickly. Kind of ironic that Iranian zeolite is hiding some of the most sophisticated explosives we've ever developed," the Ambassador continued. "Now gentlemen, if you don't mind, I must excuse myself as I'm needed in Dubai. My family has been enjoying some shopping there and we're scheduled to head on to Nairobi before heading home."

Sun contacted Yuri Drovic and Salman Bashir, system engineer contractors assigned to SAS, to pick any continental Africa flight to test the override module. He didn't want to know which plane they'd pick or which route. They'd be traveling onboard and be able to report any interruptions to the flight as the Operators assumed control of the aircraft. The more data they could detect in flight, the better the planning for the Distraction. He'd communicate with Cecil to make sure that none of the Shareholders or any Enterprise assets were in the region. The good news is the plane they picked was an Airbus 310 so they'd get some good data on system control functions and operability. The bad news is that they could never have known that the winds blowing across the Sahara would close the airport in Lagos forcing the plane onwards to Abidjan, Côte d'Ivoire. And worse than that, they had no clue that, sitting on board this plane, comfortably in the first class cabin, would be Ambassador Olusimibo and his entire family. For some reason, the Ambassador's phone was malfunctioning in Dubai. He could make outbound calls but wasn't receiving any inbound. He was so distracted with his family that it didn't occur to him to check messages.

After sitting an interminable three hours on the tarmac, the plane took off to the west into the darkening African sunset.

"Nose up." The text lit up the screen of Sun's console.

"Going live in 30 seconds," came the text response.

The plane appeared to veer to the left in a sudden violent turn.

"Is that you....?" the text trailed on Sun's console precisely as he realized that something was terribly wrong. He switched his controller unit off to allow the crew to fly the plane themselves but, in the frenzied cockpit, the pilots had already found the controls unresponsive and were unable to intervene. The plane dove into the Atlantic just after 9pm GMT taking with it all 168 passengers and crew. The official crash report would conclude that a combination of electrical system failure and pilot error doomed the flight. But, twenty-four hours later, there'd be bigger headaches all around. One of the Shareholders was dead and, to add insult to injury, he'd been killed by the Enterprise.

Steve showed up in the dimly lit room where Sun, Dan, Keith and Carey were pouring over data. From the looks of things, the failure had not been at their end. It looked like Yuri and Salman had failed to upload the entire operating system. Since they'd been given access to a service pack sent out by Airbus, they had more than a month to get the override coded but, looking at the system commands, it appeared that several signals from Sun never activated the onboard systems.

"Gentlemen," Steve began, "how did it go?"

He saw the look on the faces of the Operators and knew that something had not gone to plan.

"From the looks of things," Sun began methodically, "it would appear that our operating service upgrade failed to operationalize fully, Sir." He did his best to stay stoic.

"And, what you're saying is that we didn't take control of the plane?" Steve pushed on.

"I believe, Sir, it maybe a bit more complicated. I wouldn't be surprised to find out that the plane..., well, went down, Sir."

"Well, should be containable," Steve started with a callousness finely honed in his years of dealing with insured losses. "I can't imagine we can't find the bug and fix..."

The phone rang.

"Steve, Cecil here," the masked voice spoke through their speakerphone. "We've just received word from Nigeria that 84 nationals were on a flight out of Côte d'Ivoire this evening and, it appears that the Ambassador and his family were on board."

Steve stood dumbfounded. In an instant, he was overwhelmed with the knowledge that his operational insulation strategy, an absolute necessity to preserve anonymity, had just proven costly. He hung up the phone without a word.

"Gentlemen, the official report will identify the cause of the crash as electrical malfunctions and pilot error. I'll contact the insurers and make sure that we cover their loss in exchange for an expedient review of the service file. This afternoon never happened."

"Yes Sir," Sun replied, his voice for the first time showing a sense of gravity for what had, to that point, been a technical glitch.

Three days later, the *Gulf Crescent* entered the port in Aden, Yemen. It was October 9, 2000 and they'd spend two days in port. Shortly after midnight, they'd fit an unmanned undersea vehicle – provided courtesy of Connie's PLA engineering friends in 'Attack 86' (the special unmanned vehicle research program for the People's Liberation Army) – with special sensors to record the blast damage assessment of 'Dry Run'. Carey was to meet up with Amal Abdulfattah and his cousins, the ones who were going to actually conduct the operations.

"Assalamu alaikum," he greeted them as he walked into the café two blocks from his hotel.

"Wa alaikum salam," they rose and each greeted him with an embrace.

"It's been a long time, my friend, Carey, since we've seen you," Amal began. "While I would love to tell you that we miss you, what we really miss is the money that you carried for us."

They all laughed. Amal had been one of the CIA assets in the region and had worked to identify resources for field officers who needed access from Yemen to Northern Pakistan. With family members infiltrating and employed legitimately by intelligence services throughout the region, he could access anyone or anything that was required. His only objection was any project directly involving the Agency's use of the Afghan opium and heroin producers and dealers. He didn't mind religious and ideological conflicts but he drew the line at drugs. In his Sunni up-bringing, any form of substance abuse was anathema and he wasn't about to violate his family's principles.

"We've got a package that we need delivered to the *USS Cole* after we sail out on the night of the 11th. It's not going to be big enough to sink any of your boats like the one that some of your friends tried back in January," he said referring to the attempt on the *USS The Sullivans* in which the explosives were so heavy that they sank the missile boat. "Best guess is that it will be a total weight of about 250 kilos so all you need to do is throw three guys off the boat and no one will ever know the difference."

"I've received word on the Kuala Lumpur meetings from Khalid al-Mihdhar and he says that he's got a few Saudis who are ready to serve. I think some of your bosses met him in San Diego a few months ago, yes?" Amal offered.

"I don't know about any meeting," Carey replied. "But I know that the operational tasks won't take much effort. We've already put the Chinese UUVs in the water and they're swimming around the *Cole* getting all the final details we need for the operation. And we've got Mak Kayani working on the remote controls for the boat. After all, once we're live, we don't want anyone trying to get cold feet once the *Cole* starts firing... if they start firing."

"You underestimate how effective some of our imams have been lately, my friend," Amal directed his serious tone to Carey. "We have some true dedicated resources – remember like we used to help you guys during the conflict with Iran?"

"Yes, Amal," Carey hastened to clarify, "I don't mean to suggest that you're not capable of operations at all. We're just testing some remote technology that we'd like to share with you in the future. We'll test the detonators on the water and you can have the technology for any devices you may wish to improvise on land or at sea, my friend."

"I love it," Amal exclaimed. "We'll get American technology from an American for blowing up an American ship! This is too good to be true. Your President must be as foolish as he sounds on CNN."

"Remember, this is an operational test," Carey continued. "We're not using this as an Act of Aggression, per se. No, this is more of an opportunity for us to tag some of those radical groups in East Africa as enemies of the U.S. If they can be Islamic militants, all the better, but, please use your sensitivities. We're fine if you fill the boat with Saudis, Sudanese, Somalis – whatever. Just make sure that we've got enough diversity to be effective."

"Will do," Amal confirmed. "I'll have the volunteers here tomorrow."

"Oh, and by the way, this may sound strange but one of my bosses would like to have the explosion happen at 8:18 GMT – some crazy Brit who loves to have events occurring at times that remind him of memorable moments in history," Carey added.

"I will never understand you English people," Amal said, shaking his head.

⌨

The TV in the Operators' office was interrupted with a Breaking News report on CNN and AFN within seconds of each other.

"The *USS Cole* has been the target of an attack in Aden just moments ago," reported the anchors clearly reading from the same script. "A small craft carrying what are thought to be Islamic militants approached the port side of the vessel and exploded a device. No reports of casualties are available but, from these early images, you can see that the explosion has ripped open a massive area on the ship's hull..."

"Well team," Steve began, "sure beats the hell out of the Ivory Coast experiment. It's a shame that the Ambassador wasn't around to see the steel melt. He worked a long time to get that perfected. You guys made sure Amal blanked out all the security tapes, right? We don't want to make it easy for anyone to reconstruct the events and I've been assured from our assets that, with delays and general uncooperative sources, the FAST teams won't get much access to any intelligence."

"Early reports suggest that the attackers are affiliated with an extremist Islamic group – possibly a group called al-Qaeda – operating out of Sudan," the news reports continued to flow in.

"Looks like we've got what we need – an operational test, perpetrators that nobody in the U.S. can find on a map, and a free option for any whack-job to use to take credit and recruit more crazies. Should make September all the easier if we can just have the right guy raise his hand to take credit for all this nonsense. Let's cut out and go to dinner. My treat."

As long as they walked different paths to the restaurant, they'd make observation difficult if not impossible. They called Jonas who had reportedly just returned from nearly six months in China.

"Any chance you'd be up for dinner at Tao?" Steve asked.

"As long as I can have the, what's that fish? Oh yes, the Chilean sea bass."

"8 o'clock?"

"Sure thing," Jonas hung up.

Cyrus had finished his meetings in the City. He was meeting with Citigroup's distressed asset team reviewing some recent data on some structured finance deals and some of the more esoteric credit insurance exposure in the portfolio. A few of them had decided to wander down 58th and, following two limousine-fulls of young men and women coming from a fashion show, they walked in to Tao.

"Do you have reservations?" inquired the young man who seemed to have enough gel in his hair to be a fire hazard with the candles lit next to him.

"No, but we could take that table back next to the Buddha and clear out by 8 since we're all exhausted."

"O.K., let me check," as he discretely whispered into a microphone clipped to his collar. "It looks like you can have the table as long as you're done by 7:45pm, o.k.?"

"Great," replied Francis. "Cyrus, you're going to love this place. Ian and I love to bring clients here – the later the better. It seems that the later the hour, the shorter the skirts on the women in this joint," he mused.

"I've heard great things about his place – can't wait to try the fish."

The foursome sat down at the table and fell into a conversation that spanned the globe. News of the *USS Cole* had flashed across everyone's Bloomberg terminals. They wondered if there'd be any short term spike in oil prices. While entirely irrelevant, investors seemed to quake every time anything went boom in the Middle East. No trader in New York or Chicago would need to know where Aden was or how irrelevant it would be on any part of the oil supply chain. No, all they would need is some scary news and they'd jack up prices for a quick gouge. The geographic and geopolitical ignorance of American investors always gave informed traders a 3-5% edge on the worst of days. This would be a great time to invest in defense contractors as any event like this would certainly amp up the Axis of Evil rhetoric.

"With any luck, a few more events like this and we'd have ourselves a war," Ian commented. "Only shame is that it wasn't an Iraqi payload so that George could settle his dad's score."

"Oh," Cyrus began, "you give the American public too much credit. All they need is something in the region to flare up and they'll follow their Patriot in Chief into war."

"Well, I'm already long General Dynamics and Boeing. Looks like I need to get some Navy coverage now too," Francis added.

They ordered the chocolate Buddhas for dessert finished off with coffees all around. As they got up, Cyrus looked towards the entrance and saw an older gentleman walk in the door. In a moment, he realized that it would be best if he didn't walk out while the man and his companions were standing in the lounge waiting for their table. He excused himself and went downstairs to the bathroom. Emerging four minutes later, the five new guests were sitting at the table he'd just left. Jonas' back was facing the exit and, as he hurried towards the entrance, he got a great look at the other four gentlemen around the table.

"Amazing how quickly they turn tables here," Cyrus said joining the others on the street. "Just bumped into someone I knew."

⊠

"How are you coming with the tomatoes?" Steve asked Darius as they sat together finishing a light dinner in Geneva on a pleasant May 2001 evening.

"Well, we've got the anthrax expressing across generations and we've done a nice job of getting an attenuation strategy for the vaccine production," Darius replied. "My colleagues at the Biotechnology Research Institute have been working with some colleagues in New Delhi and we're feeling quite confident that we can have some preliminary production by this summer."

"Are you going to present any of your findings at this week's conference?" Steve inquired.

"No, we don't want to attract attention yet – we'll let our Indian friends report on our collective progress. You know that if an Iranian gets up and talks about biologics, everyone in the U.S. will be told that we're working on weapons. The White House thinks we're developing nuclear weapons, after all. How silly of them. If we want to have a nuclear warhead, all we have to do is borrow one from our friends in Pakistan. Our numbers in their ranks are more than adequate to get whatever technology we need from them – no need to waste time and effort to replicate what is already at our finger tips," Darius expounded.

"I've invited one of our team from China to the conference and she'll be testing the waters to see who is doing interesting work," Steve went on. "Her name is Fengming Xu and she comes highly recommended from Connie."

"Very well, should I arrange to see her?" Darius inquired.

"Probably best if we don't have any meetings in public. However, I'll try to arrange something where we can chance into each other in town," Steve said.

"We've matched the samples that you got from the AFIP in Maryland and, at a minimum, will have enough material to effectuate Distraction part B," Darius went on. "In our tests, we're certain that we can provide a strain that no one will want to trace too far. After all, if they actually release the information about the source, they'll have to admit that they have a program that they've denied for decades."

"Does the AFIP know that the samples have been removed?" Steve asked incredulously, the thought of U.S. biologic weapons material in a lab in Tehran slightly bending his mind.

"Well," Darius replied, "I don't know for sure but I know one thing. The U.S. Department of Defense has just placed an enormous order of Ciprofloxicin from Bayer and, well, let's just say, I timed my investment nicely. Bayer's sales have been sleepy at best but, somebody knows something or they wouldn't have suddenly decided to order hundreds of thousands of doses."

"You should have told me," Steve chided. "I could have used a bit of lift in my portfolio this spring."

"Oh, not to worry, my friend," Darius reassured him, "the check will be in the mail..., get it?" he chuckled.

         ✉

On September 9, 2001 two switchboards started dialing numbers in the New York and Connecticut region. The switchboards were owned by a construction engineering firm who had done a significant amount of steel work for the Canary Wharf rejuvenation in London and the Petronas Towers in Kuala Lumpur. The pleasant, recorded voice said,

"Due to inspections associated with building operations scheduled for Tuesday morning, we encourage you to arrive after 11am."

Dan had arranged these calls with a little help from Fengming and Connie. Not everyone got the call and no messages were left. They'd count on 'survivors guilt' to keep the calls a secret.

The simulators worked perfectly. Ironic that the first impact hit at about 440 mph around the 95th floor of the North Tower and the second was almost exactly 100 mph faster when it hit the 80th floor of the South Tower. The explosives were concentrated around the 80th floor in both buildings with structural failure compromising charges between the 80th and 90th floor in both buildings. The thermal triggers took a bit longer than expected in the North Tower – heat rising and all. Keith had to use the remote on Tower 7 because the detonators weren't getting hot enough. In fact, in the whole operation, besides the Tower 7 malfunction, the only miscue was a 13 year old who was flying bird three when he walked away from the controller over some non-descript farmland.

"This game sucks," he said as he slurped down Coke. "The flight simulator totally rocks but the visual effects are boring – I mean who flies over farmland?"

"Do we go ahead with Part B," Dan asked after everybody had calmed down.

The day's events were masterfully choreographed. Getting the packages on the planes so that there'd be no question as to the culpability of al-Qaeda worked perfectly. Having anonymous video game players, like executioners given blanks and only one live round, fly the planes oblivious to their participation in the Distraction. The plan was brilliant. And each of the flyers, at the appropriate time, would be invited into lucrative careers in the security apparatus of either governments or government contractors and would be richly rewarded for what they never fully knew they had done.

"Senator, we just received a package…"

Plan B for good measure. Make sure the public is entirely distracted.

# CHAPTER 6 - OLYMPIAN PLANS

People would forget the President's insane apathy when, reading to a bunch of students – an oxymoron in and of itself – he was advised of the attack. They'd remember the constant images of towers falling. They'd remember the promise that we'll hunt these enemies to the ends of the Earth. And they'd embrace, as gospel, the vilification of terrorism.

Half a world away in New Zealand, an elite team of Special Forces and Agency operatives assembled and, just a few days after the attacks, were on the ground in Afghanistan. They knew that one of their past assets was responsible for inciting, if not actually pulling off, the attacks in New York and D.C. And, overwhelmed with patriotic zeal, they found Osama bin Laden within a few days.

"We have OBL in sight. Request authorization to neutralize."

"Authorization denied," came the response.

"What the fuck," Sam said still holding the AK-47 that he'd taken from the first combatant he'd killed just two hours before.

Sam was one of America's greatest assets. He had a distinguished military service and, following the unpleasantries in Somalia, had taken a particular interest in the radicalization of Islamic groups in East Africa and Southeast Asia. He'd been in the Pacific for some time and had developed the best intelligence network an American could hope for. With his relationships in Singapore, he could find out pretty much anything he wanted.

"Sir, with all due respect, we have the target and can neutralize," he repeated what he thought was a reasonable request.

"You will stand down, Sir. We need him alive," came the signal from JSOC.

"Sir, I've put 35 men's lives at risk with a mission to eliminate the enemy and we can achieve that objective," he insisted.

"Keep him in sight and we'll arrange support," was the reply.

Three days later, four MH-60 Black Hawks came in lower over the pass. Sam's attachment engaged the enemy taking out most of the ground-based threats. He lost most of his men. The extraction was successful and the choppers rose in the swirling sand and rocks and flew east. The Enterprise had its distraction, the President had his war – all was falling into place quite nicely.

One of the great lessons of modern economies is that war is a financial stimulus unmatched in scale or effectiveness. It took no time for Henri to make back his investment principal as his firm was selected to offer 'resilience and operational redundancy' advice to every major government in the G-7. Amazing what a remote enemy and mass hysteria at home can do for business. You can make all sorts of experts up over night and turn massive profits selling advice based on fear alone. Special commissions, investigations, international conferences on terror and asymmetric warfare – there would be more food in the trough than his firm could gobble, but, they'd gorge themselves as much as possible.

Ayman and Connie planned a meeting at the Tianjin University of Finance and Economics where they laid out plans to handle the economics of an America at war. The State Council had neither the appetite nor operational capacity to engage in the war effort. They would, however, agree to purchasing U.S. Treasuries provided that they would be given preferential access to oil in Iraq, oil and natural gas in Iran, metals in Afghanistan and assurance of little intervention in their Africa strategy. The President of the United States would announce that America's interest in Africa was AIDS and its eradication and would stay out of any resource deals required to feed the growth engine of China. In short, cooperative distraction and non-intervention would be the rule of the day and, Ayman's firm would be engaged to arrange structured finance product purchases using instruments that were unregulated and poorly understood. And, after all, when the country was focused on protecting itself from terror, nobody would dare expect the Treasury or SEC to question the necessity of the money.

As an act of patriotism, the President would ask Americans to go on a spending spree. Where war bonds and saving were the drumbeat of the World Wars, the patriotic response to religious-inspired terror was gluttony financed using consumer credit. Savings be damned, we needed to spend.

While all the Shareholders benefited, Gabriella was particularly pleased. It seemed that Dreamcast and Electronic Arts were ready to move from the cartoon world of Sonic the Hedgehog and Mario to more realistic titles with much more dynamic interfaces and virtual environments. Buoyed by the success of her remote operations and inspired by Sony's PlayStation2 success, she decided that the real money would be made in multi-player games – a world of virtual warriors fighting virtual terror was the mantra she recited to her design team.

"What if you would take Special Operations data and weave it into a video game – ideally one that multiple users could use at the same time in the same game?" she had suggested at a meeting in a hotel conference room overlooking Ipanema Beach in Rio. "While American youth will fall all over Madden's Football, they'd love to vent their fears of terror by shooting things even more."

"Why don't we use Bungie Studio's Mac platform shooter game, Halo, as our anchor architecture?" Eduardo asked.

"That would give us an immediate answer to Nintendo and Sony," Nathan responded. "Transitioning from the Mac platform over to ours shouldn't pose any significant challenges. We can do it in transition steps the way we've released all our products and we can have our users be engineering partners."

"You mean we'll let them debug it," Eduardo scoffed.

"Hey, it's a hell of a lot cheaper to have people pay for the privilege of debugging a program than to have it sit in our hands too long. Plus, if we're going to war, what better product could you want than to turn the combatants into Arabs?" Nathan added.

"Not to change the subject, or anything, but have we completed the WTC scrub?" Maurico asked from the back of the whiteboard-lined conference room. "We agreed that we wouldn't have any towers in our games for the next few years."

"Yes, that's already been done," Eduardo responded. "However it was interesting, when we were doing the scrub, our guys were kind of spooked with the fact that all of architecture coding in our games was far more detailed than we expected. That contracting team from Gray Fox was legit."

Gabriela was getting uncomfortable with the direction the conversation had taken.

"I hear there's a beach volleyball tournament tonight. If any of you want to go, I've arranged VIP passes."

Nothing like a bunch of tanned, bikini-clad volleyball players to break up a boring meeting in a conference room in Rio.

"They should out-law conference rooms in Rio on the principle of the idea. If you're at a beautiful beach, it should be illegal to be required to meet or do much of anything inside," Nathan protested as he walked out the conference room door.

"I'll look into it," Gabriela said pleased that her distraction had worked.

In nation-state conflicts, warfare typically pits well-equipped militaries against one another. The more equivalent the forces, the more protracted the potential for the war. And given the fact that the White House and Congress were both exceptionally pleased with the prospect of an undefined enemy and an amorphous military objective, Dr. Robertson was busy with his friends at the Vice President's dinner table while Lord Haverford was hosting similar conversations at Greydowns, his sprawling estate west of London. The reunions around these respective tables were filled with nostalgia – recollections of the ease with which Presidents from Kennedy to the present were malleable enough to insure that defense, communications and financial industry interests not only prevailed but thrived under ideological conflict. The "war on terror" was the mother lode as neither public nor private inquiry could ever access any legitimate information under the sweeping umbrella of national security and the brilliant 'Patriot Act'. Ever since Bush signed the Patriot Act into law, the ability for defense contractors, telephone companies and financial interests to eavesdrop on every citizen was unprecedented. "If only McCarthy would have had these toys," they'd whimsically muse, "we'd have crushed the liberal flower in the bud." With multi-strategy companies like SAIC, with interests ranging from electronic clearinghouse responsibilities for every check – paper and electronic in the U.S. that passes in any transaction in the country – to the ubiquitous airline ticketing and travel platform SABER, there was no movement made and no value exchanged that they couldn't see. It made Jerry's network seem almost prescient at times given the number of times that SAIC, Congressional, and Administration guests got a little too talkative after a few too many drinks on board the *Genesis 2:25*.

However, there was a tiny problem with the war on terror. While the Taliban and al-Qaeda had the zeal of a honey badger ripping into a cobra, they were not particularly well armed. In the protracted war with the Soviets, arming the Afghan 'Freedom Fighters' (now our enemies), was patriotic. Now that those weapons would be used against us, they reasoned, we're going to need a persistent threat to justify the business of war. And while everyone knew what weapons of mass destruction – a term which was the benchmark of ratings for AFN – were in the region given the fact that we'd sent them all there, there was the tiny problem of knowing precisely in whose hands they were at any given moment.

"What we need is a means to support the insurgency, my friends," General Simpson stated nonchalantly as he raised his fork to his mouth, a rare cooked bite of prime rib dripping au jus onto the table cloth.

"Precisely what do you have in mind?" the Vice President inquired.

"Well, we're not going to have an enemy with credible air or heavy artillery capacity so the nation won't believe that we need boots on the ground for any length of time," the General continued. "That means that we need to arm an enemy with weapons that are lethal, but random – something that can create persistent fear but inflict minor casualties."

"You mean like the mines we used in Nam?" Rumsfeld inquired.

"No, they're problematic. First, there's the terrain problem. When you're in a jungle or forest, mines are damn near impossible to find. But we're in a fucking sand box here and so they're not optimal. I've been advised that we've got some assets that the Reverend's friend from Singapore can help us with – some kind of tracking device. We can tag explosives with these radio devices – they call them RFID – so we can make sure that only expendables get hit," the General went on.

"I could have used them on my shotgun when I was dove hunting with one of my pals," the Vice President nearly choked on his own thoughtless humor. "Should have had a goddamn alarm that would have gone off before I shot his face."

"No Dick," Donald replied, "you would have needed a breathalyzer for that one."

"Gentlemen," Simpson tried to reclaim the agenda from the Vice President's tangent, "what we're thinking is that we'll tag some material from our friends in Eastern Europe and the Balkans and then insure that our old friends have the money to buy from our suppliers."

"How in the hell are we going to get money to the Taliban and al-Qaeda to buy shit from our suppliers?" Donald asked incredulously. "You really think we can do another Contra racket?"

"No sir," Simpson began, "we've got a much better plan. It has to do with the Olympic Games in Athens. You see, one of our firms was selected to provide electronic and physical security for the Games. Turns out that the contract was awarded with the approval of a group identified as 'The Enterprise' – don't really know who they are but, what the hell, our guys are in. Anyhow, what we're going to do is let the firm move the money – since they're private, no one will ever see their financials. And, we're already getting Iraqi insurgents all the help they need under the UN oil sale concessions."

Silas smiled. "Happy to be of service again, my friends," he slithered.

"Silas, there's got to be a special place in hell waiting for you," the Vice President slapped his friend's shoulder with a firm blow.

"Right next to you, compadre," Silas volleyed back.

"Well, brethren," Jerry cleared his throat, "as a man of the cloth I can assure you that we'll do our part in insuring that it's unpatriotic to ask any questions – hell, we'll make it downright sinful."

"Jer," the Vice President chimed, "with a sinner like you leading the flock, I suspect Silas and I will have some good company where we're going."

While they were enjoying some of Kentucky's finest Bourbon in the library, a slightly disheveled figure appeared with a Marine escort in the door.

"Sir," the guard began, "this gentleman had legitimate credentials and has told me that he's with Silas. He knew the code."

After hours, during what the Vice President referred to as 'commercial business', you needed to have a password to be admitted to the residence. If you were cleared into a meeting, you needed a code which happened to be the last closing bell price of one particular stock that was near and dear to his heart. This system insured that an eavesdropper wouldn't be able to decipher what would sound like a randomly generated numeric code.

Into the walnut paneled room with pomegranate and dogwood reliefs sculpted into the ominous shelves laden with volumes from antiquity came the travel weary visitor. His appearance belied his station as, in Athens, he would be altogether dripping with the latest fashion. He was a most intriguing character which went a long way to explain Silas' fascination and admiration for him. When they had been in Trieste several years earlier, Silas was entirely overwhelmed with Simon's lure with women. The two of them had shared an opulent suite overlooking the Adriatic with six tourists from Montenegro – wild college girls who had insatiable appetites for as much sex as they could muster for the weekend. While neither of them had visited a gym since college and they both knew that their pasty white, fat, hairy bellies were as offensive as gluttony could afford, for that weekend, their naked companions would be suitably distracted; nubile bodies covered only in oil applied in pornographic abundance. Simon, it seemed, was just pathetic enough to attract a certain sympathy from women who, when given luxurious accommodations for a weekend, would indulge the obligatory services for the few minutes that he and his companions could last.

"Mr. Voulgarakis," bellowed Silas, "you've finally made it."

Simon glanced around the room. He had heard about these gatherings but had never actually been invited into one before.

"Would you be kind enough to explain how we're going to arrange the arming of our enemies," Silas continued with a lilt suggesting that he was pleased with his masterful contrivance.

"Certainly," Simon stammered slightly, "Mr. Vice President and gentlemen," he began.

The plan was rather simple. A grainy video from one of Osama bin Laden's deputies had been prepared in which they would threaten terrorist acts in Athens during the Olympic Games. There would be enough specificity to expand the security contract to include complex 'system redesigns' which would include cost-overruns. Officially, the Greek government would put up an additional $200 million to an already half billion dollar security budget. Unofficially, this change order would be financed by friends of the Administration. No one would ever find out about this transaction. After all, a country can't go bankrupt like a company so who would ever look at the books? An arrangement would be made with 'security services' to provide protection for the Games – including the all important security of yachts and private aircraft. A deposit of $100 million would be paid to representatives of the 'enemy' as a good-faith deposit to insure that they inflict no damage at the Games. And upon the Games' successful completion and safe passage for all visitors, the second half payment of $100 million would be paid. These funds would be used for three authorized purchases. Material for Improvised Explosive Devices (or IEDs) for al-Qaeda and Taliban militia and armor-piercing rocket propelled grenades (RPGs) for Hezbollah. All supplies would be tagged with RFID devices supplied by RFTrak – a detail that would be known only to the Enterprise and the appropriate elite in the Coalition. Patrick had agreed to sell detectors to U.S. and U.K. chain of command for the tidy sum of $400 million all under the transparent lens of homeland security procurement.

The plan was brilliant. No one would dare argue with Olympic security. No one would ever see the books of the Greek government to find these payment anomalies. God knows that no one could track the money or the munitions. At least nobody that would matter.

"This is Director Ratcliff," began the voice as Cyrus was sitting down to dinner on Christmas eve. "I run the President's Office of Cybersecurity and I've been advised that you may be a person of interest."

"I'm sorry, Sir," Cyrus looked over at Emilie who had the kids at the table and was ready for a long overdue family meal, "I'm not sure what you're calling in reference to, but I'm about to sit down to dinner."

"Not a problem, we'll be sending someone to your office on Monday and we'd like you to listen to what he has to say," Ratcliff hurried his voice.

"Very well, goodnight," Cyrus put down the phone.

"Who was that?" Emilie looked up from the table pretending not to be perturbed.

"Someone from the White House," Cyrus said quietly.

"Daddy, did the President call you?" Sorin was beside himself with excitement.

"No duffus," Anna rebuked her brother, "Daddy is joking, it was just a courtesy call – I usually just hang up on them, right Mommy?"

"Actually, it really was a call from the White House but it wasn't the President," Cyrus sat down heavily in his chair.

"What do they want from you?" Anna assumed a serious, modulated tone.

"I don't know, sweetie, but it's time for dinner now."

Emilie had poured every ounce of Betty Crocker's gingham-checked cooking brilliance into this meal. The roast turkey fell off the bone yet was moist enough to absorb very little gravy. This didn't stop Cyrus and the kids from drenching every part of their plate with the oozing succulence. The mashed potatoes were transcendent. A fresh cranberry salad and green beans rounded out each plate. Looking into the dining room window across the blanket of light snow that had just fallen would have revealed a scene straight off a Norman Rockwell greeting card. Emilie loved Christmas and she'd done her best to insure that this year, for the first time since they were married, she would bring Christmas cheer to her bah-humbug husband who wasn't much for any holidays. She wore a short, Blackwatch plaid skirt, a white blouse cut low enough to remind him of some of their dating days. Save the interruption of the call, this night was perfect.

Tucked into their beds after begging mercilessly to open at least one present under the tree, the kids had finally succumbed to exhaustion aided by the sleeping agents in turkey. Emilie and Cyrus retired to their bedroom to put the finishing touches on the last packages. Emilie sent Cyrus into the kitchen to recover the roll of tape that the kids had left on the counter and, when he returned, he had a bouquet of red roses behind his back.

"For you, my Lady," he said holding the roses out for her inspection.

"Cyrus, they're beautiful," she exclaimed.

"You may want to smell them. And smell them all because one of them is particularly fragrant," he added.

She took the mass of crimson from his hand and closed her eyes as she took in the aroma thoughtfully.

"No silly, you have to open your eyes when you smell them," he insisted to her rather puzzled expression.

"Why? You know I like to sense things."

"O.K., because there might be something IN one of the flowers," Cyrus said, his voice slightly exasperated.

She looked at them and smelled them again. With all the movement, his ingenious plan had become dislodged. The ring that he'd put around the center of one bud had jostled down into the flower so that it was no longer visible.

"Smell this one, my Love," he finally relented.

Her eye caught a glimmer of the stones on the ring.

"Oh Cyrus," she said, "it's beautiful."

She pulled the ring from off the rose and he slipped it onto her finger. It fit perfectly.

"A little something to remind you that I'm still your man," he said pulling her close for a hug.

"Hold on," she interrupted. "I have something for you too."

She moved back the pillow on their bed to reveal a beautifully wrapped box. Inside it was a watch that Cyrus had wanted for months ever since he'd seen it advertised in a magazine.

"Put it on," she said, her voice dropping into a low, seductive register. "Now, I have an idea, why don't we wear our Christmas presents to bed? Just our presents!"

Somehow, they both managed to gouge each other – Cyrus scratched Emilie's back with the clasp of his watch while Emilie drew a little blood from his shoulder with her ring. All that did was add to the frenzy of their desire for each other. While the sheets had that crisp cool of winter nights, their lust was so complete that sweat rolled down between Emilie's breasts and dripped from Cyrus' forehead. Somewhere in the deepening hunger, they melted into each other finding a lush oasis into which they deeply plunged. They remained intertwined and together through the night and were jolted into consciousness in the morning with Sorin and Anna jumping onto the bed.

"Merry Christmas," the kids squealed in unison. "There are more gifts under the tree!"

They were beaming. This was the first year that they had gone shopping for presents and they had managed to keep their purchases a secret until this moment. Now they were bursting with delight. After a long embrace and his signature good morning kiss just on the back of her neck, they rolled from their bed, slipped on robes and were escorted by the children to the tree in the living room.

Sunday's news was horrific. Images of tourists being crushed by the tsunami waves, cars swirling into buildings, the echoes of 'Joy to the World' being drown by the shrieks of the dying.

He didn't want to leave for work on Monday morning. This was, quite possibly, the best Christmas he had ever had. The family had been as happy as he'd ever seen them. Emilie was as charming and sexy as she'd ever been. So, as he turned into his office parking lot he was too lost in thought to see the gray Lincoln sitting in the parking garage with its occupant barely noticeable through the tinted windows. He'd go in and review his e-mails, send out a few year end messages and, with any luck, get home before the light traffic that would be clogging the beltway for a shortened holiday rush.

He entered the office through the back door and was just sitting down when there was a knock on the front door.

Since no one else was in on the holiday week between Christmas and New Years, he went to the front and opened the door to find a young man about 30 years-old standing in the hallway.

"Dr. Alexander," the young, neatly dressed man began, "I've been sent by the Vice President of the United States to meet with you."

"I'm sorry, your name is…" Cyrus actually had put the Christmas Eve phone call in the back of his mind with a lot of help from Emilie and the kids.

"Carey," he said producing a black leather folio which he flipped open to reveal what appeared to be credentials. "I'm with the commercial resources program with the Central Intelligence Agency. You may not know that the CIA works with executives of many companies in the U.S. – all based entirely on their willingness to cooperate – to assist in its mission. We've become aware of some of your financial services and we believe that you may have information sources that we'd find most interesting in our efforts."

"What sort of information are you looking for?" Cyrus asked without hesitation.

"Well, before we could go into that, we'd need to know if you're willing to assist us," Carey continued. "After all, our sources and methods are classified – a closely guarded secret – and we need some assurances that you'll respect this."

"I would assume that if you wanted information from me or anybody else, you could just steal it," Cyrus added, not yet slowing himself enough to consider what was transpiring.

"Well, I suppose that's true," Carey responded. "However, sometimes we need people like you who have access to various sources of information and who look at the world in different ways to help us find things that we're unable to find. We've heard that you have the ability to track financial transactions and assets around the globe and we'd like to see just how deep your systems can penetrate."

"If you've got a particular interest, I can tell you what we can find," Cyrus volunteered still holding his noncommittal tone.

"Well, for example, there have been some planes that have been missing in Africa recently," Carey began. "Is that the sort of thing that you could help us find?"

"You mean the 767s that are registered to a shell corporation in Texas that has a mailing address in an empty warehouse in Brooklyn?" Cyrus shot back. "We found them long before March 8," he added, "and we helped some folks in Harare make sure that Equatorial Guinea wasn't another casualty in the long line of after-thought coups."

"Wow, they didn't undersell you," Carey recoiled. "How did you know about them?"

"Sources and methods," Cyrus smugly replied.

"Would you be able to help us on a project where we think a telephone distributor in Scandinavia is actually shipping munitions to enemies of this country?" Carey got to the point.

"Sure," Cyrus said, off-handedly.

"What information would you need from us?" Carey said.

"Nothing that you haven't already given me," Cyrus replied.

"If you would, early in January, we'd like you to come up to the Old Executive Office Building and meet with the Vice President's staff to discuss what you find," Carey concluded.

"Sure, let me know when and where and I'll be there," Cyrus said.

"Make sure you track every server call, every database, everything you can find coming out of his office over the next two weeks," Carey said to Keith and Jonas as he got back into his car. "We need to know how he finds what he does and who he's working with to get his information."

Sun had done his best to make sure every IP address was monitored so that Cyrus couldn't access a thing without their knowledge.

"How the hell did he know about Atlas Global? That's one of our best covers," Carey continued on this secure line.

"No fucking clue," Sun volunteered, "we can't find a single trace of him even looking at them before your visit – no searches, no inquiries, no client overlap – beats me!"

"This could complicate our plans for Zimbabwe," Keith mumbled.

"Bigger problem is for Rumsfeld's rendition plans. If he can trace the planes, he'll know that those planes at Dulles that we've erased are not just waiting to have their registration numbers repainted. It'll make moving trouble-makers a lot harder and we'll have to move our special assets to even more remote locations before extracting information from them."

"Why don't we send him overseas and see if we can find a human source that explains how the hell he finds his material?" Sun offered.

"That's a great idea. Let's have Jerry reach out to the Vice President and see who he'd like to do the invite. We'll send Elizabeth wherever they go so she can work on him the way only she can," commented Carey.

"Let's hope she's got better luck than when we tried getting Emma through to him a few years back in Zurich," Keith said.

"Would you be willing to give a speech on economic foresight at a conference in Tenerife?" Carey asked Cyrus when they met at a café near Tysons Corner.

"Who is hosting the conference?" Cyrus inquired.

"The National Intelligence Committee and some of our European Allies have teamed up with the Ministry of Defense in Singapore to host a conference on best practices in scenario planning and we'd love to have you there to talk about what you do," Carey said genuinely.

Ironically, Cyrus knew that field officers like Carey were trained to lie. However, with the passing months, he had actually come to like Carey and, while constantly aware of the fact that he was being used, Cyrus was having his own sport with his ability to offer critical facts and information which had clearly solidified his role as a vital source. He knew that Carey would, at the end of the day, be forced to choose between a relationship and his job and he knew that the choice had already been made but, for the time being, an awkward friendship would be possible.

"Can I bring Emilie?" he inquired.

"I don't see why not," Carey knew that this would undermine the utility of Elizabeth but, she was good and a ring hadn't stopped her before. "The conference will be the second week of April and, if you'd like, the taxpayers will be happy to extend your stay so that you can enjoy the weekend," Carey continued.

"Happy to oblige," Cyrus replied.

As the Iberian Air flight lifted off from Madrid, Emilie and Cyrus flipped through the in-flight magazine. There was a special on the hot-spots in Ibiza complete with glamorous photos of shirtless young Mediterranean men and bikini clad girls.

"When you die," Emilie leaned over and whispered in his ear, "I'm going to go here to grieve."

She pointed to a picture of a young man with deep Latin features – dark hair, bare tanned chest wearing nothing but white linen draw-string pants standing on a rock with the sea behind him.

"I hope you wait until I die," Cyrus teased back.

"You know," he said, changing the subject, "they believe that the eruption of the volcano on Tenerife was visible from the coast of Africa."

"Is it still active?" Emilie inquired.

"No, but if that guy is around, I'll do my best to make sure he's on the wrong side of the mountain when it blows again," he added, his voice holding a twinge of jealousy.

"Nothing to worry about, my dear," she took his hand.

"Dr. and Mrs. Alexander" read the placard held by a tall, statuesque woman wearing an immaculately white dress and dark red heels.

As they walked through the baggage claim area, they walked towards the woman holding the sign.

"About that volcano," Emilie whispered and squeezed Cyrus' hand, "she's not a magazine model – she's flesh and blood."

"Don't be silly," he said, "you've got nothing to worry about."

"Greetings Dr. Alexander," Elizabeth began, "welcome to Tenerife. How was your flight?"

"Wonderful," he replied.

"We've arranged for the two of you to have a suite at the hotel where we're holding the conference – right on the water. You enjoy the water, Emilie?" she added sizing up the two of them.

"Yes, I'm looking forward to some serious sun," Emilie replied.

✄

Simon had his camera with him at all times. At their first dinner, Emilie had fun trying to guess the nationalities of the various guests. When Simon spent the late evening pouring the fourth bottle of wine for the eight dinner guests, she told Cyrus that she thought he looked like a spy. As they got up from the table, Elizabeth came over to the table, sauntered up to Simon and planted a giant kiss on his lips. Still sitting at the table, he reached his hand up under her short dress and pinched her buttocks. She playfully slapped his hand away and moments later, the two of them excused themselves barely clearing the dining room before their intentions were quite evident. Cyrus and Emilie were just slipping into bed an hour later when the phone rang.

"Do you want to go out with us?" Simon said with Elizabeth giggling in the background.

"We just turned in for the night," Cyrus replied.

"Well, get up and meet us down on the street in 5 minutes," Simon insisted.

154

A few minutes later they met on the street. Down the beach three blocks a pub frequented by German tourists was filled with dancing and drinking. The foursome walked down the beach kicking their shoes off to feel the cool night sand.

"So, you work with the Vice President?" Simon inquired indiscreetly.

"Oh, darling," Elizabeth protested, "let's not talk about work tonight. Didn't I just fuck you enough to get your head out of your ass for at least a few minutes?" she winked at Cyrus and Emilie.

"Cyrus is in the circle, baby," Simon protested, "and I want to know if he and Silas have spoken recently."

Cyrus had no idea who Silas was but he'd make sure that he'd remember the name.

"You know I made the first payment that we ran through the Olympic security company a few weeks ago on a boat in Istanbul. Those animals are some crazy sons of bitches," Simon volunteered. "You wouldn't believe the boat that we used for the payment – huge yacht, owned by some porn producer and damn the women were hot."

The next day, Elizabeth plopped down on a beach towel less than 20 feet from where Emilie and Cyrus had posted up close to the high tide line. She slipped her cover-up off to reveal nothing but a fluorescent orange thong. A few minutes later she was joined by an olive skinned companion equally clad. The two of them lathered sunscreen on each others' bodies. Emilie watched the spectacle while Cyrus was lost in reading. She decided to let him stay focused on the book. There was a certain mysterious elegance to the fact that he could be surrounded with such hedonism and still focus on reading. She would do her best to distract him later.

At the conclusion of the Opening Ceremonies, Simon sent an SMS to Cyrus' Nokia phone. The texts were simple and replete with incomplete words to avoid intercepts.

"Have 2 say wtching athletes mks me feel lik all is wrthwhle."

"Snding $ to terrrsts?" Cyrus wrote back.

"Thyr fckrs but Firm is 2." Simon texted. And then immediately after words, "Silas wants 2 meet u with CPow and DRum at VP."

"When?" Cyrus replied.

"Thy'll fnd u." was the answer.

Several weeks after the Games, Simon called Cyrus on a new phone. The caller ID flashed a Ukrainian number.

"I'm back to Istanbul, Cyrus," he stated, his voice quick. "Can't say I have a good feeling about this one for some reason."

"You had better be careful. There'll be an awful lot of eyes watching you at the drop on the bridge," Cyrus said.

"Yeah, I'll call you when it's done," and with that, the line disconnected.

Turkish police were at the bridge. Eighteen elite units were stationed on either side of the footbridge over the Bosporus. At 11:15am, Simon walked towards the Ataturk bridge linkage from the northern side leaving the café just below the Galata Tower where the Whirling Dervishes rehearsed the night before. As Amal and Hafez walked out to meet him a voice rang out. Simon felt an object slam into his back knocking the wind out of his lungs. A second blow came as gunfire erupted around him. With searing pain shooting through his back and leg, he collapsed in a heap losing consciousness before he hit the ground. Did he drop the cases or had someone grabbed them as he fell? Amal's blood pooled beside him on the pavement creating the appearance that he had been the one who had been hit. To the casual observer, he appeared dead. The medics would pick up his body and that of Amal's, zip them both into body bags, and rush them to the hospital. Anyone watching would report that a Greek tourist had been caught up in a shootout. Simon could come back a new man, literally.

Driving into D.C. that night, NPR announced that the Kennedy Center was hosting the Dervishes for a special celebration of U.S. and Turkish relations. The costumes and staging would arrive in huge containers – large enough to fill with explosives which, at a minimum would severely damage or destroy the theater. If timed right, the trucks carrying the equipment would be able to detonate closer to the White House hopefully taking out the front of the Old Executive Office building. Cyrus called Carey.

"I bet you should have the Bureau take a close look at the cargo accompanying the Whirling Dervish exhibition performing at the Kennedy Center tonight," Cyrus began.

"What do you know?" Carey's voice quickened.

"Well, let's just say that some upset customers may not have received their second installment of funds if the Turkish police reports are accurate."

There was a long pause.

"We'll get on that right away. Cyrus, thanks for this," Carey said genuinely.

⊠

Steve called Ayman who was in New York for a few days having just flown in from Dubai.

"My friend," he started in a measured tone, "it appears that we need to assist the Naval Observatory with an asset transfer. Two sixty million dollar transfers to be precise. And, we'll need them run through the National Bank of Pakistan drawn from an account at Goldman Sachs. ISI is blinking for us so that no one detects the transfers."

"Whose money are we moving?" Ayman inquired.

"Yours, my good man," Steve replied. "Turns out that Jonas has been setting up some proprietary trades and is doing quite well. We've close to doubled our book and that is after we've returned the Ambassador's investment in its entirety."

"And for the trouble?" Ayman asked, half expecting no answer.

"Why don't you take a management fee on our treasury for the coming year. We'd like to have you intermediate some credit default swaps for us as these appear to hold promise for future undetected transfers and we'll give you 50 basis points on every trade," Steve was more than generous.

"Seventy-five bips is my fee when I have to run interference," Ayman replied.

"Done," Steve came back. He had no time for negotiations and, with as much cash as he was sitting on, the more diversified the portfolio, the better.

# CHAPTER 7 - THE HALL

Greydowns was a sweeping estate about 30 kilometers out of London down the A3 motorway. Lord Haverford had maintained the place with impeccable precision. The gardens were manicured to perfection save a stand of crepe myrtle which stood fully 8 meters high, branches sweeping to form a canopy that resembled the gothic interiors of England's finest cathedrals. When in bloom, the light filtered through the pinks, whites, and lavenders creating a sky-light of stained glass appearance. To the right as you walked towards the lower lawns and hedgerow, a small brook tripped out of the hill rising behind the house. His family had been granted this title in part due to their loyalty to James I and his court. The two story house had a crushed stone drive that meandered for close to a kilometer from the road, just beyond the White Thistle, a pub that had been in operation for close to four centuries built out of the grey stone quarried from the hills on the estate. During the Second World War, German bombers eager to dump their payloads would empty their bomb bays over the hills around the place and, as a result, the grounds and hilltop were littered with small ponds, each about two meters deep and about ten across. Lady Haverford had seen to it that these relics of conflict were integrated into the garden plan and each crater was filled with copious flowering water plants which bloomed in abundance during the Spring of 2005.

Approaching the house, a high gate stood across the drive with a rather tasteful, yet foreboding security perimeter clearly visible stretching in both directions. A keypad stood about 15 meters in front of the gate and Cyrus watched as the driver keyed in what appeared to be eight digits. The first one was 0 followed by quick movements and ending in '1', '8', '1', '5'. Closer to the house, a second keypad with another number series ending in '1', '8', '1', '5'. Cyrus let his mind race. What could be the obsession with 1815? Lord Haverford met him at the front door of the castle dressed in English stable fare. He wore boots which rose to mid-calf. His wide whale corduroy trousers fit loosely around his legs and he had an oversized tweed shooting jacket on over a pressed Oxford shirt.

Walking towards Cyrus, he extended his hand in a cordial welcome.

"Welcome to Greydowns, my good man," he said, his voice rich with refinement and courtesy. "Do come in won't you as it appears you brought a bit of rain from the City."

"Thank you, Sir," Cyrus obliged and entered the house through the informal entrance on the right hand side of the drive.

A tall dog, a hound of some sort, came loping across the wet grass and stopped briefly for an approving pat from his master before he glided into the house. Cyrus had seen no vehicles – not even evidence of a garage – so he had no clue as to the number of guests who may be staying at the castle for the next few days. The pretext for his invitation had been a discussion on asset management strategy in the wake of a growing sense of unease at the mounting deficits in the U.S., the increasing use of synthetic investment products by pensions and treasury managers, and an all too memorable exposure that the U.K. had to similar risks during the horror of the Lloyds credit insurance debacle. Lord Haverford had mentioned that he may be inviting a few of his continental colleagues but had not identified anyone save the Chairman of a 'major global consulting concern'.

Inside the dark wooden hallway a series of doors led off to the right and left. As they made their way down the lightless hall, Cyrus looked through the open door on his left to see a brightly lit, floor to ceiling windowed hall with a black and white marble checkerboard pattern across the entire room. In the room in front of what appeared to be the formal entrance into the ballroom, two plate armor statues stood vigilance. They continued down the hall and entered a room at the back of the house. The ceilings were at least 6 meters high, rich walnut panels trimmed with elegance Cyrus had only seen in cathedrals and palaces. On every wall, pale Victorian images on expanses of canvas glowered down onto the occupants of the room.

"We don't have much of an interior decorating budget, I'm afraid," Lord Haverford apologized as they entered the room watching Cyrus gaze at the imposing gallery.

He heard voices coming from a room opposite the entry through which he had just passed. As they neared the room, he thought he recognized a few of them and, as they appeared in the doorway, the mystery of his invitation unraveled with each entrant. He had seen Henri Giroud at the meeting back in '99. Gabriela hadn't aged a bit nor had her tanned skin faded. Steve and Jonas came in together accompanied by Robert Chapman – his tall physique and silvering hair still every bit as commanding as the first day they'd met. While he had not been formally introduced to the Southerner at their first meeting, no one with a television would be incapable of picking Jerry out of a line up. His face was a fixture anytime you saw the Vice President at any function. He was on the news and, of course, his Sunday broadcast. The last in the door was Chan Siew looking a bit more pale and obese than he had six years earlier.

Once drinks were served, they walked through the casement doors onto the stone veranda where afternoon cakes were generously laid out on each table. It was abundantly clear to Cyrus that the import of the meeting was not going to be surfaced at this early reception. An observer would have looked onto the assembly and gathered that a rather eclectic group of aging executives had traveled to the countryside for a weekend outing. Nothing was particularly noteworthy *save the absence of any vehicles*, thought Cyrus.

For the better part of two hours, tea and scotch were kept flowing by three house staff adorned in afternoon formal dress and spotless white gloves. Each of the seven guests made a point to chat with Cyrus who thrived on stimulating conversations ranging from geopolitics to economics. Save the twinge of misgiving surrounding his invitation to this place which had been quite hurried – he'd only heard of the trip five days prior to his arrival – his capacity to engross himself in idle conversation on an expansive array of topics was maddening to many and charming to a few. And it was clear that his guests had been briefed on his affairs of the last few years. They had all seen videos of his speeches on the economy, his testimony in Congress, and his talk at TED where he'd been audacious enough to suggest that the next breakthrough in technology would likely be seen arising from Vietnam or China – countries capable of inspiring feats of intellect rivaling the lunar missions in the U.S. decades earlier. Whether it was organic solar energy, electroconductive carbon nanoparticles, rapid genomic sequencing, fuel cells, or next generation multiplexing, these countries had both the brain power and resolve, he argued, to rival anything the U.S. could muster.

"You don't seem to concern yourself with making friends, Cyrus," Chan Siew had said looking over his third single malt scotch.

"If by that you mean that I'm tired of seeing people fall for the constant supply of experts from U.S. business schools who, when they see their futures wane in the States, choose to peddle their nonsense to WTO members in the Gulf, Southeast Asia, Eastern Europe and South America, then yes, I can't say I'm looking for those types to be friends and I'm not on any of their greeting card lists," Cyrus said. "I don't make the news, I just find the signal in the noise," he continued.

"Henri's firm is most upset. It seems that you've been making statements which would suggest that his partners don't have a clue about what's happening in technology or the economy," Chan Siew continued. "In my business, I've come to appreciate the advanced warnings I glean from your speeches, I hear you're becoming quite a threat to the professional class."

"I'll take that as a compliment," Cyrus replied, his response dripping with condescension. "If a few less charlatans fill their rice bowls with the excesses of Dubai, Riyadh, and Kuwait, so be it."

Dinner was a capital affair. Guests were given a few hours to freshen up and arrive in formal attire. While everyone came in suitably fashionable should one be using the money spent on clothes as the metric, it would have been the appearance Lord and Lady Haverford had desired. It was tragic, they thought, that civilization had advanced to the point where people no longer knew what 'formal' meant. Gabriella certainly had not forgotten. Her emerald evening gown was easy on the eyes, her tanned skin bursting through a plunging neckline accented with an exquisite necklace, simple and understated yet exuding good taste. The gentlemen had it a bit easier given the advice that had been included in the invitation. 'Black tie' was the simple instruction. Most seemed to know what that meant. Most, except for their own son, Nate and his latest fling. He came to dinner in a black jacket, pink shirt unbuttoned down from the collar, and jeans he'd picked up in his afternoon run to

Jermyn Street. Elana, if that really was her name, wore a silk blouse a bit too small for her voluptuous chest perched aloft an otherwise emaciated frame and a skirt that looked like it had been issued to a prep school girl half her age. Lady Haverford found Nate and his girlfriends most distasteful and whispered to Lord Haverford as they entered, "Can't we ask him to leave?"

"No," was the curt, nearly silent reply. "I would be most obliged to have him see the quality of our guests in hopes that some semblance of propriety rubs off on him."

The dinner service was formal and the food announced to be organic through and through. Courses were paced with a choreography befitting a head-of-state. The crowning achievement had been the venison which had been prepared to perfection in a Chardonnay reduction touched with cumin and cinnamon. No hint of game, the meat melted on the palate and drew the approval from every guest. And, dessert was a decadent chocolate mousse cake garnished with cream and blood orange. The dinner conversations were intimate with no more than two guests participating in each until, mustering all the courage he had, Lord Haverford elected to give Nate an opportunity to impress the guests with his latest enterprise.

"Well, you know that my da' has been a pioneer in on-line gaming which has been a modest financial success," Nate continued following his bumbling attempt to introduce the importance of his inherited speculation fund of 100 million pounds. "Couldn't have done it without some of the blokes who diligence deals for the Flemings and Rothschilds. However, we've sorted a tax-advantaged strategy which will more than double our yields and we've got a team in Bangalore that's making sure that we profile users to increase their playing time. I've had to visit all the casinos of any repute around the world – Macau, Vegas, Monaco, and Australia – for our gaming diligence. Picked up a fair piece of knowledge on how Aristocrat and Green Acres keep people addicted. Trips were most taxing on the old frame but," he squeezed Elana's hand, "there were certain, shall we say, side benefits I picked up along the way."

The dinner guests were not impressed. That is until he got to the part about aggregating credit information and the multiple users of their data including a number of governments who, while protesting the immorality of gaming in many instances, were using the data they were collecting for financial behavior analysis. The degree of intrusion into what most consumers would find to be privacy invasions was brilliant and the more behavior could be linked to inducement into ever greater amounts of indebtedness, the better. The average user, among their over 35 million profiles, had actually dipped into home equity loans to support their on-line obsessions. Jerry had injected that, in his experience with 'on-line entertainment', the more you made impulsive credit available, the more lucrative the usury side of the business. While he kept the conversation PG, everyone knew that his adult business was bursting out at the seams with the massive improvements to streaming video. He was now making more than double the 'lord's work' on every form of deviant sex fetish he could peddle. This year, he'd gross over $400 million across his adult empire. He proposed a private, cross marketing conversation to Nate who was more than happy to suggest that they retire to the upstairs gentlemen's lounge for a drink after dinner.

Cyrus was deeply aware of the link between on-line content and the deepening indebtedness of the American and European consumer. Horus Global, the firm he'd founded in 1995 had been monitoring the growth of real estate inflation driven not by asset appreciation but, rather, by tax and credit incentives promulgated by governments seeking to spend their way out of their own excessive, debt consumption orgies. They had seen that the more extensive the use of no-documentation loans, interest only loans and the like, the more you could predict excessive experience consumption. In short, people who were predisposed to extravagant and unsustainable indebtedness on palatial homes and cars were spending more on entertainment, leisure and media than those who maintained historically conventional credit. Listening to Nate and Jerry rave about the inducements that they were using to prey on compulsive addictions was not any surprise, just unsettling to see the frenzied passion they seemed to share.

"Too much effort for my tastes," Jonas chimed in. "We've taken real estate as close to every exchange as we can get for our automated trading desks. We can get in and out of stocks before most people ever know that an inflection is coming. Funny thing, you all have to build elaborate interfaces and businesses to induce people to game –

I just take their money going and coming every day. With every day trader, pension manager, and institutional investor, we've got their holdings and the behaviors perfectly modeled so we know what's going to rise and fall before they actually execute a trade. We don't make much on every transaction – we just make a lot of transactions."

"I've never understood precisely how what you do is legal," Robert Chapman broke his silence.

"Well my friend, when the law hasn't even contemplated what you're doing, that is a binary condition we don't concern ourselves with," Jonas stated dismissively. "We're living in a world where regulators have bigger fish to fry and they've got no clue about the products they think they understand. I'll be long dead before they even see how much money we've taken off the table and, by then...,"

"We'll have the White House," Steve exclaimed. "With Phase II, there's no chance that we'll ever have a political environment that dares to touch our business model once we've got our Enterprise fully operational. The Baron could take the Bank of England on emotional behavior nearly two centuries ago and, to mark the bicentennial, we'll have an even bigger haul. To Waterloo," he stood, raising a glass and toasting the table.

"I'll drink to that," Lord Haverford stood, glass raised. "And, now my dears, I would like to propose a bit of rest as I've arranged an event tonight. I would like you all to join me in the foyer precisely at midnight."

The guests milled about the expansive house in twos and threes. Cyrus, looking at his watch, stepped out onto the balcony of his room and called Emilie.

"What's going on over there?" she inquired.

"I don't suspect that I can tell you much over the phone, my Lady," he replied, "but I can tell you that you'd love to see this place. It's quite an experience and I'm staying in a room that has reportedly been the chambers of one or two queens."

"Well, it's a shame I'm not there to make you feel like a king," she teased.

"Doubt you'd like the company too much," he continued. "This is a reunion of the '99 meeting that John Michael set up. Do you remember that?"

"You mean the one at the Gramercy?" she was pleased that she'd deciphered his clues, something that she seldom seemed to get intuitively these days.

"We've got him on the balcony – talking to his wife," Emma said as she turned to Sun who was running the video observation.

"I've got him on circuit 4," Sun said, "do you have audio?"

"I'm connecting now," Emma said exasperated by Cyrus' irritating habit of switching off his mobile prior to his movements.

"How are the kids?" Cyrus inquired.

"Damn," Emma exclaimed, "we missed the first part of their conversation and now she's going to go on about school, games and he's not going to give us anything."

Emma got up from her desk and walked over to the bank of monitors where Sun and Carey were hovering. There was no doubt that, in the seven years that they'd followed him around the globe, the fact that he never broke cover was the source of both admiration and frustration. This night would be no different. At least not until the proposition. Then there was an outside chance that he'd finally come across to the Enterprise and they'd get to put an end to this level of intrusion.

"Will you call me tonight?" Emilie's voice did nothing to mask her attempt to solicit a romantic guarantee.

"Don't know when I'll be done this evening, babe. I'll call you if I can. Otherwise, I'll get you in your morning," he concluded.

"I love you," she lowered her voice. She knew that he wouldn't call.

At midnight, Lord Haverford and Robert were the only two in the foyer when Cyrus walked in. Emma and Sun had succeeded in getting the cameras to sequence correctly this time so they could follow his every move through the sprawling house.

"Where is everybody?" he inquired walking past the coat-of-arms to his left as he entered the room.

"I thought I'd take you on a little private tour before we meet up with the rest," Lord Haverford volunteered. "Robert and Steve have informed me of some of your interest in history and I thought you'd like to see a bit of it."

"Wonderful," Cyrus cheerily replied, "I'm sure there are plenty of places to hide secrets in this place."

Lord Haverford opened what appeared to be a panel in the left corner of the room which gave evidence to a staircase heading down from the ground floor level. The stairs were sparsely lit with footlights so the first few seconds required a bit of adjustment to the low light. The stairs gave way to a long hall which was, in its day, the armory for the estate. More medieval weapons, chain mail, coats of arms and the like. Cyrus was absorbed in the history that went unspoken save the visual feast. They proceeded diagonally across

173

the room, the only path one could take without running the risk of being impaled on one or more of the weapons which festooned the place.

"Glad the lights work down here," Cyrus quipped.

"Yes indeed," Lord Haverford responded, "you'd be out of luck if it was dark or you were too pissed," he added.

A low arched doorway was in the corner and next to it was another keypad. As Cyrus glanced at the code, he recognized it as the date of Napoleon's exile. There it was. All the security codes in the place were a progression of notable dates in the Napoleonic Wars and their aftermath. They stooped to enter what appeared to be a cellar of some sort. However, it was evident upon entry that this subterranean space was a labyrinth of chambers and no expense had been spared on the security or climate control. Skins and parchments were carefully preserved behind glass in elegant cabinets. Leather bound volumes were precisely placed on row after row of three-shelf book cases.

"I'm told that you have a certain fondness for the Magna Carta and the Charter of the Forests," Lord Haverford began, beaming with the satisfaction clearly evidenced on Cyrus' face.

"Indeed," was the simple reply.

"Well, my dear fellow, there's the story that you've been told and then there's what we have here," he said as he pulled the vellum from a drawer on the right hand wall about halfway through the second room.

"I thought that this was in the museum...," Cyrus began.

"Most people make the same assumption," Lord Haverford began. "The last of the originals of this and countless other pieces that our family had placed on loan back in the last century are now all home here. Safely out of reach of opportunistic thieves and thankfully, a bit too deep for any bombing run to so much as dust."

Cyrus poured over maps, letters to and from nobility going back over centuries of history. Cromwell's letters were bound in three informal volumes. The official transcript of the trial of, and judgment determination for, Guy Fawkes. He could have stayed here all night and well into the rest of his stay at Greydowns.

"A fair few scholars would give their right arm to spend time here," Lord Haverford commented. "But few would appreciate the experience as much as you, Cyrus. You know that few people accomplish the sweep of consequence you've done in your short life and, save your relentless obsession with all matters to which you can place your thoughts and inquiries, one would wonder if you're not some anomaly of nature."

"I have been fortunate to have some pretty amazing opportunities," Cyrus responded still absorbed in the history that lay around him. "I figure that there is a certain duty that comes with this experience."

"Indeed, indeed," Lord Haverford stated in a more somber tone. "Which leads us to the real purpose of this evening. Robert," he prodded their silent companion.

"Cyrus, you undoubtedly know that several of us have had time to reflect on our meeting in New York a few years ago. And, you may know that times have changed quite significantly since then. Now, we're quite satisfied that our Enterprise is coming along neatly – no major gaffes or challenges. However, as you've seen this evening, we are realizing that many of us are, well, a bit aging. Now, nobody's dancing on the grave, mind you. But, we did have a death in the 'family' and it put us to thinking that we don't have a high degree of confidence in the next generation."

He paused long enough to try to take the measure of how Cyrus was responding so far.

Nothing.

"We'd like you to come up to the chapel with us where we'd like to make a proposition to you. All we ask is that you hear us out. Would you do that?"

"Sure," Cyrus responded, his voice dropping into a flat affect that, for those who truly knew him signified that what was to follow was already certain.

They exited the catacombs and reentered the armory but this time proceeded to a door that had missed his glance when Cyrus came through the first time. A spiral stone staircase ascended the broad circular tower into which the three men entered. They proceed what felt to be the equivalent of two or three floors without the aid of any light. At the top of the staircase, a door on the left opened into a darkened room with one red votive candle lit in the front. As they entered, Cyrus was immediately aware of the presence of several people though he couldn't immediately count them all. They made their way up what felt to be a center aisle in a chapel, the latter being discerned with the spacing of what felt to be pews on either side of their path. As his eyes adjusted to the darkness, he could now make out the shadows of eleven people sitting in the first three rows of pews – all of them facing forward and all appearing to be hooded. Lord Haverford led Cyrus to the front of the room where two large chairs faced the assembly.

"Have a seat, won't you," he offered.

Cyrus sat in the seat on the right. Lord Haverford sat next to him and Robert turned and left the room as if instructed that he'd gone as far as he could go.

"Damn night vision," Sun exclaimed as he pointed to the thirteen glowing bodies illumined in a bright green. "You can certainly see who's got just their robe on with nothing underneath," he said as he panned the camera inappropriately picking up some of the more brilliant features quite visible in infrared.

"You're a creeper," Elizabeth and Emma said in unison, evidencing their disgust for the immaturity of their geeky colleague.

"You think he's going to go for it this time?" Keith inquired of his fellow voyeurs.

"Doubtful," Emma began, "but, who knows. We've been putting some pressure on Horus – got a couple of key accounts to cancel – so he could use the money unless…"

"Unless he's getting paid by somebody we can't track," Keith interrupted.

"Keith, you need to face the facts that we haven't been able to find anything – no bank account, no spending, nothing – that would indicate that he's getting paid," Elizabeth retorted. "If he's getting paid, you'd think that we'd find something somewhere that would have his name on it."

"Nobody would do what he does without being highly trained by somebody and that somebody has got to be compensating him somehow," Keith was relentless.

"Shut up, Lord Haverford is speaking," Emma halted the conversation.

"Cyrus, we know that you elected to pursue other paths in 1999 and, to be perfectly honest, it appears that you chose wisely then. You've gained access to powerful people around the world and you've been involved in some consequential events. Let us be clear, we are all great admirers of what you've accomplished. Regrettably one of our number passed away a few years back – terrible bloody unfortunate situation – but, it put us to thinking. We'd like you to take his share and, you'll need not put up any money to join – just your commitment to help us in Phase II. You see, none of us have children we can trust and, God forbid, something should happen during the next few years, we need to know that our endeavor will not falter. We're unanimous in our decision to offer this twelfth seat to you."

The room was silent. Cyrus was studying the darkness around him willing for the candle to burn just a bit brighter so that he could get a good look at the faces upturned awaiting his response. If only there was a full moon or some other light to offer succor to the flickering light but, that was not to be.

In the years that had past, his impulsiveness had tempered slightly. His ability to control his spontaneity and tact had refined immensely.

"I'm honored with the hospitality and effort you've afforded me," he started. "There's no question that, in the wake of this past election, the notion of buying the Presidency can no longer be considered novel so my moral revulsion notwithstanding, it is clear that the Presidency of the United States has nothing to do with qualifications or merits as a leader. Any country that will follow an illiterate, being controlled by one of the coldest, most calculating and corrupt to ever occupy the Observatory residence has evidenced that what I thought madness in 99 is now de rigueur."

The occupants of the room began to relax. In contrast to his surgical rejection at the first encounter, it sounded like expediency and inevitability were beginning to take hold.

"However," he continued, "I find that the vector of your enterprise violates, at its core, a principle that I find growing more attractive with every passing day. If you could find a path to be transparent in your identities and efforts, I could actually find myself aligned with your conclusion that the useless illusion of the nation-state as the preeminent organizing structure has run its course and that it may well be replaced with transparent corporate interests. Your impulse to change the model makes sense given the hopeless condition of nations at present. I just find the opacity an affront to values I hold dearly."

"Cyrus, do have any idea how rare is the opportunity we're affording you?" Lord Haverford implored.

"Yes I do," Cyrus replied. "And I am deeply honored. But, while we will share our commitment to alter intolerable conditions passing as public service, I must, once again, with deepest regard for the impulse leading to this offer, respectfully decline."

"Pay up, Dan," Emma held out her hand. "I told you that no one can find a way to turn him."

"Well, Emma," Dan said with his voice lowering into that thick Israeli accent, "we've used the soft touch until now. Now it's war. We'll find out what he's up to. You watch. If we've got the cockroaches in Guantanamo singing, I can assure you that we can get him to crack. Just a matter of time and some well positioned friends I've rounded up for occasions that call for aggressive techniques."

In the morning, all of the night's guests were gone. Cyrus awoke with the sunrise, slipped on some running shoes, shorts and a sweatshirt and went out for a run across the expansive lush ground of Greydowns. Emilie would be sleeping for another several hours and, while he had thought about calling her when he retired to his room at 2:30 am, he had been too exhausted. A good run and a hearty breakfast would recharge his batteries. When he returned to the house 50 minutes later, he entered the field entrance and was greeted by a charming Lady Haverford.

"I'm terribly sorry, Cyrus, but you just missed my husband. He's been called away but has arranged for a car to take you back to London this morning."

"Well, I'm the one who should be sorry. I just felt like a bit of exercise this morning would be in order and I didn't hear the house stirring when I got up," Cyrus replied.

"Oh no, not at all," she continued, "Lord Haverford was most apologetic for his sudden absence. It seems that a situation has come up requiring his urgent attention."

Cyrus showered, dressed and went to the entrance. Within a minute or two, a black Range Rover pulled up and the driver immediately spirited Cyrus' luggage into the back and opened the rear passenger door.

"Le Meridian at Piccadilly, Sir?" he inquired.

Cyrus had not made any arrangements but was in no mood to protest what was certainly hospitality that had been arranged in the contingency of his refusal the night before.

"Certainly," Cyrus replied.

He decided to take some extra time in the gym – his favorite in London. After an amazing workout he sent a text to the bankers he was going to meet over in Jewry Street. He'd shoot to arrive a little later, closer to 10 instead of their previous plan to meet up at 9 at Pret a Manger. He stepped out of the steam room and saw everyone crowding around the television screens in the aerobics area. There had been an explosion on the Tube. While he couldn't see the details without his glasses on, he could make out the intersection. The unmistakable façade of the Aldgate Station was intermittently shrouded in billowing smoke. Several of his colleagues were usually arriving to their offices in the blocks surrounding Aldgate at that time. He ran up to the room to call them. No service – all the circuits were overloaded.

A bombing in London the day after the Shareholders had all left. Was this another Distraction or was it just a bunch of random acts of violence? The thoughts swirled in Cyrus' mind as he stepped into the shower. He had missed his scheduled meeting on September 11 because the executive team from Boston had canceled their trip on Sunday before the Towers. Working out in the Le Meridian gym too long – a good hard sweat – had preempted his date with destiny today. London was eerily quiet which gave Cyrus time to think. *There's got to be a connection,* he thought. *Too many coincidences.*

"I've been told that my relationship with you has become compromised," Carey said when they met at the airport upon his return from Heathrow. "They say that field officers are supposed to report on requirements and foreign intelligence, not wade into analysis and certainly not advocate for ideology."

"What are you talking about?" Cyrus said incredulously. "You're not advocating for anything nor am I. I'm just providing a perspective that your door-kickers can't get. You know that your employer's sources and methods are precisely why we're operating in the dark all over the world. If you actually walked through the front door rather than breaking in through the guarded windows, you'd find a world that is quite accessible."

"I may want to agree with you but, unfortunately, it's come down to me either cutting off all contact with you, being relocated, or quitting," Carey said. "I can't say that I'm thrilled with any of those options but, this country's not ready for the likes of you and I can't jeopardize what I've worked to create for myself and my kids."

"If you ever want a change of scenery, my friend, I would be happy to find a place for your skills at Horus," Cyrus said, his voice filled with genuine compassion for the impossibility of Carey's conundrum.

"From the sounds of things," Carey replied, "I think it's best if we stop communicating."

"From the sounds of things? What sounds of what things?" Cyrus inquired.

"You've pissed off some pretty powerful people, Cyrus. I sure wish you'd just lay low and focus on your business."

"I don't know what you're trying to warn me of but I can't say that it'll do much good," Cyrus replied. "Once you have chosen a path and your light scatters the rodents, you're likely to keep pressing on if you're me."

"You may regret that position, Cyrus," Carey said directly. "I'd think about Emilie and the kids before I'd make another move. Oh, and by the way, that thing you said a while back about how people were moving assets in zeolite – turns out that we've tracked at least two bombings to platinum and other precious metals shipped that way. Good call."

"Thanks. We've been watching some of Bart's recent moves in China and Mongolia. Seems that Asia is good for him and the outlook is bright given the fact that the Chinese are going to have to move away from their Treasury addiction and start getting real assets into their strategy. Nothing like the world's luckiest prospector to make that a reality."

"He's more dangerous than the lad's you lunched with in London, Cyrus," Carey cautioned.

"No question about it," Cyrus agreed, "and he's got Goldman wrapped around his finger. Given the fees they get for financing his deals, the fact that he's leading countries into economic and political ruin is beside the point. And best of all, Resilience Global is papering every financial institution with white papers extolling the virtues of his projects."

Lord Haverford received the phone call at his hotel room at Aggie Grey's next to the airport in Apia.

"We don't have the toxicology report back but the security tape shows Nate entering the armory at 1:30 am with two girls. It looks like he was either drunk, drugged or both. One of the girls started taking off her skirt when she fell back into one of the plate armor mounts. A battle axe came down square on Nate's head. I'm so sorry."

"Do you know who the girls were – was it Elana?" Lord Haverford's voice trembled slightly.

"No, she wasn't there. They were two girls he picked up down at the West End tonight. Neither of them had any ID but Keith thinks they're Serbs."

"When are you getting the lab results back?" Lord Haverford dropped into a calculating tone.

"Should be within the hour."

"And my good wife, where is she?"

"She's resting at the flat in Kensington. Doesn't want to be anywhere near the house. I've made arrangements for you to take the Air New Zealand flight tonight and you'll be home in 20 hours."

He looked out the window across the close cut grass lawn spreading downward towards the South Pacific Ocean. The sun was orange in the east and was casting golden and orange hues on the palms that were outside his window. He interrupted his thoughts which he recognized were terribly out of sorts considering the news he'd just received. If only he had had a son who could step into the gravity of his role in the world. Instead, he had an insatiable, weak playboy who cut his life short with two hookers he'd partied with the night before. "If only I had a son like Cyrus," he thought, "I could've reclaimed my destiny."

# CHAPTER 8 – ALL THE PRESIDENT'S MEN

In the second term of any President, most of the fawning sycophants who would do anything for White House credentials at the inauguration and during the first term realize that the luster of being next to an ineffectual decoy can actually be bad for a career. Defections in the second term are made worse by the recognition that the trajectory of the economy did not bode well for an incumbent party victory. Not a prayer that the country would vote for Satan's minion and the Republican field, if one were to go as far as to suggest that there was a credible candidate, was anemic. So, by 2006, the hangers on were ideologues whose sole purpose in life seemed to be to last long enough to land gigs with AFN, conservative talk radio, or K-Street addresses to turn their focus to Congressional influence peddling. Whether the Democrats could pick up midterm seats or not, one thing that was certain was that the Administration was doing nothing to help the economy. The War on Terror was starting to get tiresome with the monotonous drumbeat of casualties and there was the constant reminder that, with the entire intelligence and military apparatus of the United States, we couldn't track a medically incapacitated, master-mind of evil.

And there was the gnawing reality that Iraq oil concessions were being negotiated with China, Iran's oil, natural gas and nuclear infrastructure was being financed with U.S. Treasuries, and the morality of the conservative right's war was being marred by pesky pictorial essays released by an ever expanding network of inquiring minds. For the first time in American history, save the cooperation from phone companies and banks which insured ready surveillance on every American dissident in the name of national security to limit organization of true inquiry, there was a possibility that the revelations of significant abuses could lead to war crimes against a U.S. President or Vice President. The specter of this threat was so great that the Administration had to be the first in U.S. history to officially silence the 'human rights' rhetoric against places like China and Myanmar for a more diffuse proclamation of 'freedom'. The ineffectual puppets in Iraq, Afghanistan and the attempts to manipulate events in Pakistan had clearly shown that no lever of control seemed to be working.

And so, against this backdrop, the Enterprise could do nothing but celebrate. Distraction had been brilliant. The fact that the Ambassador didn't live to see the consummation of his work was regrettable. Jerry had succeeded in making diatribes on 'marriage' and 'family values' the constant anesthetic to the masses – a strategy that had conveniently crescendoed at the slightest hint that investigations into any part of the War on Terror and its aftermath might gain traction. While a few thousand men and women were dying in remote deserts and thousands more were being pressed into extended tours, the stage was as close to perfect as they could have imagined in 1999. Save a few loose ends – those puzzle pieces that constantly gnaw at the back of the mind like a few termites in a load-bearing timber – and the biggest loose end was having increasing success around the globe as the Enterprise seemed to lose control of his movements at home.

Cyrus and his colleague Edward were sitting outside the Montana Grill in Union Station after spending the morning on Capitol Hill with some Senate Finance Committee members and their staff. They had just finished a late lunch when a tall African American gentleman in a handsome grey pinstriped suit approached from the direction of the coffee shop in the center of the reception hall.

"Dr. Alexander," the man said as he approached the table.

Cyrus looked up into the face of someone he had never met.

"Yes," Cyrus replied.

The gentleman had an envelop containing a hand-written note from a former Senator who had been quietly asked to inquire into domestic and foreign intelligence capabilities and vulnerabilities which may have contributed to failures prior to the actions in the Middle East.

"Do you see that bank of phones over by the Amtrak kiosk?" he asked.

"Yes," Cyrus responded looking to the far opposite corner of the expansive building.

"If you would be so kind as to answer the third phone when it rings, we would be most appreciative," the man continued and then disappeared into a crowd of commuters rushing for their 2:30 departure.

"Sounds like some sort of espionage thriller," Edward said looking at Cyrus after the man departed. "Kind of cliché, don't you think... 'a phone will ring and you will follow instructions'..."

"Given the creativity of this government, nothing seems cliché any more," Cyrus said evidencing his frustration. "Of course, we get the country we deserve, and from the way we're behaving, we shouldn't be surprised that we have a President swearing to defend a Constitution he's never read."

"Go find out what the phone call's about," Edward changed the subject.

Cyrus crossed the station hall and, within a few seconds, the third phone in the bank rang.

"This is Cecil," the voice began. "You are to take the black Town Car in front of the station – the Senator has asked that you come alone."

The voice was heavily masked to defy anyone knowing the speaker's age or gender.

"I wouldn't go if I were you," Edward said as Cyrus walked back to the table.

"Listen, call Emilie and let her know what I'm doing. I'll leave my phone on so if anything happens, I'll text our code and you'll know that I'm in trouble. I'll catch up with you back at the office in Arlington."

"O.K. compadre – have fun," Edward called to Cyrus as he hurried towards the entrance.

A black Town Car was waiting at the curb. As he walked over, the back door opened and he saw the gentleman who had carried the note inside.

"Thank you, Dr. Alexander," the man said as Cyrus entered the car. "I'm Alan Jefferson, you may have heard my name from Senator Simpson."

"I'm afraid not," Cyrus replied.

"The Senator has been advised that you have some information about the adequacy of our intelligence apparatus and he's asked for a few of his retired friends and colleagues to launch an informal inquiry to see what we knew and when we knew it. If your past performance is any indication – Hill testimony and public statements – you must have an opinion on this matter."

"I haven't been often accused of being devoid of opinions, Alan," Cyrus replied with a smile.

They arrived a few minutes later at the Four Seasons in Georgetown. Walking past the reception desk, they went to a suite on the second floor filled with chairs occupied by a group of people Cyrus didn't recognize save the retired Senator.

"Thanks for coming, Dr. Alexander," the Senator began. "My former colleague, Senator Simpson, says that you provided some unique and valuable information to his office back in 2001 and he suggested that you may have some insights as to the predicament in which we find the country at the moment."

"What insights are you looking for?" Cyrus replied.

"Well, it seems that you've had a number of opportunities to supply vital information to law enforcement and intelligence over the past few years – some of which has been appreciated and some of which – well, shall we say – has been viewed as contentious."

They fell into a long conversation about a variety of topics. The irony of tracking financial events and actors like the insurance and pharmaceutical transactions in 2001; the financing of bombings in

Jakarta and Bali; the movement of assets through Russian and Ukrainian institutions; the shipment of armor-piercing munitions to Hezbollah and the list went on. At the end of 3 hours, Cyrus looked at his watch.

"Ladies and gentlemen," he said, "I need to get back to the office to wrap a few things up before I head home. If you would like any more information, you know where to find me."

"Many thanks, Cyrus," the Senator responded. "We'll certainly follow up with you shortly."

⌨

He hailed a cab and was shortly crossing the Potomac into Virginia. His D.C. office was up near the Courthouse Metro station and traffic on 66 leaving downtown was already at a near standstill. The last mile or so took close to twenty minutes and he kept resisting the impulse to get out and walk. He was so distracted by the day's events that he paid no attention to the two cars that had followed him from the hotel. One had turned east towards Fort Meyer Drive while the other stayed one behind the cab separated at all times by a single car.

He paid the driver and gave him a $10 tip for the inconvenience of having to cross out of the District at rush hour. As he approached the door to his office, two men in suits approached him from behind.

"Dr. Alexander," one of the men said as he got close to Cyrus.

Cyrus turned to see who was speaking. Before he could respond, one of the men placed his hand on his shoulder.

"Emilie knows not to expect you home. Edward received word that you were needed for a meeting in New York and you've already left her a voice message on your home machine telling her that you'll be away for a day."

"I left no such message," Cyrus protested.

"Actually, in a manner of speaking you did," the man continued. "You see we've got hundreds of hours of your speaking on file and we can have you say anything we want."

"Yes, but she'll know that this is unusual and she's not likely to just sit around if I don't come home," Cyrus persisted.

"We'll take care of that," the man said and, grabbing him firmly by the arm, escorted him to the car.

⊟

At times of considerable physical stress, the mind does some rather unusual things. He could recall a building with a dark gray interior. There was an older looking chair, light yellow upholstery on it with wooden arm rests to which his arms had been strapped. There were electrode leads on his hands, forearms, neck and chest. He couldn't remember if the straps at his ankles were fitted with electrodes or just immobilizing him. There was a woman in her late forties or early fifties who had connected the various leads to a variety of boxes, backs all facing him. Time seemed to slow to a near stop. The woman had left after 'testing' the equipment – testing for evoked potential she had explained.

"Have you had any contact with any foreign intelligence officer in your travels?" the young man dressed in a military uniform yelled louder after Cyrus had already replied.

"Of course I have," he replied. "You can't travel in and out of the countries I visit without having many contacts – both formal and informal."

"So you're admitting that you have contacts with foreign intelligence officers," the young man said, his voice dripping with disgust.

"Ever since Moscow and Nicaragua, and up until the present, I am sure that many of the people I've met in government functions are connected in some way to foreign intelligence. In fact, I know that our government has sought to exploit several of those relationships," Cyrus went on.

"In your present condition, mister, I wouldn't be so careless about admitting to contacts like this," the interrogator started.

"You asked the question, Sir and, given my present condition, I figured that you'd like a straightforward answer," Cyrus said.

"You think that you can continue to do what you're doing, jeopardizing this country's security and just get away with it?" the interrogator resumed his hostility.

"Far from it. I know that I'll continue to do what I've been doing for years because what's happening in our government is actually destroying our security at home and abroad," Cyrus said coolly.

From the surge of current that flowed through his body, he knew that this was the 'wrong' answer. A ranking military officer came in the room after a series of loud questions. He spoke in a very contemplative tone.

"Do you really think that your actions are worth dying for?" he asked. "Do you think this country is worth dying for?"

"I can't say this country is worth dying for, Sir, but I can say that it is worth dying for a country that would be worth dying for."

The next memory from interrogation was being dropped off in front of the Trinity Building across from Wall Street. How he got there and from where he didn't know. What he did know was that while he was standing on the curb looking south to the Trinity Church graveyard, the front door opened and out stepped Marvin Goldblatt. Marvin was an icon of the New York Stock Exchange and served on countless boards. He was connected to everyone who moved in the capital markets.

"Cyrus," he said standing at the top of the stairs, "come on up. Everybody's in the office waiting for you."

His head was still a bit hazy but he found his feet and followed Marvin up to the sixth floor. The narrow hallways were papered with stock certificates from notorious deals – both winners and losers – including one giant framed certificate for their shares in Enron with a brass plaque engraved with the words "Never Again".

"We've received word from our sources that Horus International is for sale," Marvin began. "We want you to know that we'd be interested in it… and you," he hastened to add.

"For sale?" Cyrus said still wondering if he was in a bizarre dream.

"Yes, some of our friends in D.C. told us that you had run out of funds and were putting the company up for sale. With the data you guys have and the technologies you've developed, we have interest in the firm for our own purposes and we've got friends both here and in Israel who would like to find more profitable ways to exploit your technology for, shall we say, other purposes."

"Marvin, you know that we've talked about doing a partnership with Goldblatt and Winer for years, but 'for sale'… I don't think so," Cyrus clarified.

"Cyrus, I invited one of my old colleagues here to meet you today. Let's change the subject for a moment. Would you please take a moment to describe your business to Lou Rosen?"

Lou was a white haired man, well into his 80s. He had a colorful life working with the Israeli intelligence service for years before coming to New York to work in the advertising business. While his appearance was unkempt to the point that you'd walk past him on the street and wonder if he was homeless, his mind was as sharp a mind as Cyrus had ever encountered.

"This sounds like some work we were doing after the war," he said adjusting his hearing aid with an excruciating loud squeal. "Never thought I'd live to see the day when machines could out-think humans, eh Marvin? Oh, I knew it would come along – things like that always do – but think about the potential of what you could do with what this young man is saying."

"I know Lou," Marvin replied raising his voice to insure that his guest could hear. "Why do you think I wanted you to meet Dr. Alexander?"

"You know, young man," Lou turned to Cyrus, "if you play your cards right, you just may be able to take over the world."

"Thank you, but I'm afraid there are too many people already vying for that job," Cyrus said, glad to see his wit returning after the recent events.

⊠

"In case of a water landing, your seat cushion serves as an approved flotation device. Simply place your arms through the straps, hold the cushion to your chest and exit the aircraft. In the event of a loss of cabin pressure..." the US Airways Shuttle flight attendant droned on.

Cyrus was preoccupied with his trip home. He hadn't talked to Emilie when he had left the house yesterday morning – at least he thought it was yesterday. They had another argument and had gone to sleep in that horrible state of knowing that both wanted something that neither was willing to give. It had been weeks since he had felt any connection with her and, for that matter, the intervals between moments of passion had stretched so far that he was not entirely sure what had gone wrong. What he knew was that the events of the last 48 hours would not be easily forgotten and he was not motivated to talk about them now.

Emilie met him at Reagan National waiting by the curb. He was wearing clothes that were purchased for him by someone somewhere

– no luggage, no briefcase, just the shell of the man she saw last in anger a few days earlier.

"Hello honey," she had her arms outstretched waiting for an embrace.

"Just let me go home," he said.

The drive home was painful. Neither of them spoke. In their silence, the mists of every doubt either one had ever had settled in like the dense blanket that covers a warm river on the morning of a first frost. Ironic, isn't it how when one is warm and one is cold, the result is fog? The kids were already in bed when they got into the house.

"Are you going to tell me what happened?" Emilie softly prodded.

"Not tonight – I'm going to bed."

✉

"Says here that during the whole interrogation, he never mentioned us once," Keith said looking up from the official briefing he received from Silas.

"Sure would love to have him teach his technique to our teams at the Farm," Carey said. "With what they put him through, I've never seen anyone's vitals stabilize so well."

"Yeah, what's the deal with that? Where did he get his training? He spent time in Moscow in the early 90s long before we were following him. Details of that time are sketchy and the people he worked with have all drunk themselves to death. A cardiologist who steadied his nerves with 7 or 8 shots before entering the theater wound up killing himself with alcohol poisoning after his wife left him for an oil tycoon. A young materials science researcher who disappeared – no trace of him. And a reclusive doctor who moved to New Jersey only to be hit by a bus in 96. I suppose the other option may be something that he learned in Central America. You know he penetrated into Sandinista territory on more than one occasion – met a bunch of ours and theirs. All of these seem to be dead-ends but we've watched him long enough that I have to wonder if he was trained a long time ago," Keith paused trying to put together the mystery.

"You know that he was in one of the government's 'gifted' programs back in the early 70s. When Hal and Ingo were running their experiments at Stanford, several projects in California and Arizona tried to find young people with identified anomalies and studied them – God knows what that means. We found some records from one school suggesting that Cyrus may have been part of the project that kicked off when the CIA officially announced the de-funding of their remote viewing experiments. You know the Agency. When they announce that they're not doing something, you know that's when it gets serious," Allen observed.

"Do you mean to tell me that a kid could be trained to resist interrogation before the age of 9 years old and keep those skills into adulthood?" Emma asked, her voice incredulous.

"We have demonstrated this with a number of operatives," Fengming contributed on the conference line. "All of our observations here in Beijing indicate that he can detect observation – both physical and remote surveillance with an uncanny efficiency. He wears hats with a precision that defies easy facial recognition, conducts near robotic precision routines when he's in a hotel room any place on the planet. Whoever trained him did an amazing job."

"O.K. team. Back to the point. Why would he protect our identity when he's put under the screws?" Keith tried to end the speculation. "What is he waiting for? When is he going to 'out' the Enterprise?"

"Well, our best guess is that he'll start making noise as the Presidential election starts heating up in the summer of '07. After all, if he wants to sabotage the Enterprise, he would need to get the leaks springing no later than the conventions," Dan contributed.

"In that case, why don't we infiltrate Horus? Let's get people on the inside and have them see if they can figure out what he's up to," Jonas said, breaking an uncharacteristic silence. "I've got a cousin who works with a number of black ops and security types. A few of them have just enough eccentricity that it may appeal to Cyrus –

maybe enough to actually hire them and bring them into his circle of trust."

"I don't want to pour the cold water of reality on your plan," Emma began, "but I don't believe that you'll ever get Cyrus to trust anyone. After all he's been through, that guy will never let someone all the way in. Like the briefing said when we first picked him up, no one can figure out what moves him and nothing and no one ever seems to get his full trust."

Omega Resilience was a federated team of advisors assembled from a number of continental and U.S. consulting and government services firms. They had assembled their bona fides in the assessment and planning for government continuity and mission critical systems during the run up to Y2K and then were pulled back into overt and covert services in the wake of the Distraction. The team included ties to Israeli, Italian, Greek, Australian, and U.S. intelligence services. They had worked together on a couple of financial investigations – not as leads but with enough proficiency to be of potential utility to Horus.

In August 2006, an invitation-only gathering was hosted by the Global Foresight Institute for which Cyrus was to deliver an economic assessment of U.S. and European markets in light of the growing competiveness emerging in the Brazilian, Indian, Russian and Chinese economies. The room at the University Club was large enough to comfortably host 40 people. The event would be videotaped and posted on the GFI website. Omega's founder and Managing Director, Hank Peterson would attend. Three days before the event, Hank contacted GFI and succeeded in pleading for one more seat for one of his deputies, John Roberts.

After an hour presentation and an hour question and answer session, Cyrus was surrounded by a number of the audience asking questions ranging from investment strategies to sources for more information on the themes he had covered. Hank and John approached him as the crowd was thinning.

"How about joining us for dinner tonight?" they offered. "We'd like to take you to McCormick and Schmick's on K-Street."

"That would be lovely," Cyrus responded.

On their way to the restaurant, they called Steve. "Looks like we've got some alone time at the location."

"Excellent, we have great sound from your wires. By the way, how the hell does he keep all that data in his head?" Steve inquired.

"Yeah, he covered more material in an hour than I thought was possible," Hank said. "Do you want us to shoot for an advisory position or shall we try to go all the way in?"

"Let's shoot for a full penetration. At least one of you should be available to work on the inside – he hates consultants and, for good reason," Steve added.

"Roger that," Hank said, "we'll make John unemployed."

"We've got a guy to throw in the mix too," Fengming added. "He's loosely connected to some of our people in Hong Kong and he can offer some Asia bench depth for Cyrus since they're looking to expand their activities out of Singapore into the rest of the region. Make sure you mention Richard Hoffberg when you meet tonight."

"Will do. We're here. Out," and Hank hung up.

"Are you dining with us this evening?" the valet attendant asked as he opened Hank's door.

"Yes, dinner reservations for Peterson – they'll be three of us."

"Very well, Mr. Peterson, just leave your keys in the car and I'll have someone park it for you."

They entered the restaurant and sat at the bar until Cyrus arrived 10 minutes later. Stacey, the young lady at the hostess desk showed them to their table, a small round table towards the back.

"I believe you like sitting with your back to the wall," Hank pointed to the seat facing the restaurant.

"Why, yes I do," Cyrus said, "thank you."

They sat down. Falling into conversations about geopolitics, economics, history, and religion they interrupted conversations long enough to choke down a few bites of tuna, steak and pork chops ordered for the table. The food was forgettable – no wine tonight. But the depth of inquiry and the breadth of topics was an elixir for Cyrus.

"We'd love to learn more about your operation," John volunteered over coffee at the end of the meal. "Is there any chance we could come to your offices and meet your team? I get a sense that there's a lot we could do together."

"Sure, are you guys local?" Cyrus replied.

"Yes, we both live out near Manassas so we can stop in whenever it's convenient," Hank said.

After a long afternoon meeting the following Wednesday, Cyrus invited Hank and John to the house for dinner. Emilie was used to this drop in hospitality that was inextricable to Cyrus' style. It was common for Cyrus to get his family's instincts about people as part of his due diligence. Anna's perception of people was razor sharp as a young girl and, while blunted and jaded over her broadening life experiences, she still had great insights. Sorin would either warm to people or not. And if he didn't Cyrus always made a note of his response, particularly his comments after people left the house. And then there as Admiral Wellington – a rescue that thought himself more human than dog. Admiral Wellington was abused as a puppy and was one of the best barometers of human character. People who were genuinely good would evoke a long-lost-friend effervescence when they'd walk in the door. People of unremarkable character usually got a sniff and then benign indifference. But when Admiral Wellington was hostile, you knew that he found something in a person that was worth remarkable caution. Cyrus and Emilie came to trust Admiral Wellington implicitly and the more they trusted the beast, the better he performed.

Admiral Wellington ignored John as he entered the foyer next to the study. However, as Hank neared the doorway, he barked, bared his teeth and growled. When Cyrus reached out to shake Hank's hand, Admiral Wellington ran into the living room as if to defend the house from whatever was entering his domain. Cyrus and Emilie looked at each other with a knowing glance. After dinner, the conversation turned to the family life and experiences. Hank was unmarried but recently met a blonde who had clearly claimed his heart and other parts as well. John had a young family and was one of the casualties of adjustable rate mortgage stress arising from their purchase of a house at the peak of the real estate bubble a few months back. Business was unpredictable for Omega Resilience and so there was a lot of strain on the family. If there was any way that he could be of assistance on any client relationships for Horus, he'd be delighted to get the experience and the financial comfort of a more reliable paycheck.

⊠

"We're in," Hank reported to Steve three weeks later. "It looks like John will be embedded and he's talked Cyrus into a very generous package. Kind of strange, he tells me that Horus is quite the environment. On the one hand he gets phenomenal access to clients and relationships – far more expansive than we ever thought. But when it comes to the guts of their data and how they do their analysis, it appears that Cyrus has engineered it so even his systems engineers don't know the full scope of what the entire capacity is or how it all fits together."

"No surprise there," Steve responded. "We're dangerously close to believing that he's just got a 'gift' since Sun has been incapable of breaking into anything that could explain what he does and how he does it. We have found what appears to be a spider that scours the world for data – but we can't figure out what they do with it once they bring it in."

"Well, John is worthless when it comes to anything to do with computers. He's a Mac guy and wouldn't be able to make heads or tails out of anything resembling code," Hank confided. "See if you can get him to arrange a client which would demand system access as part of their due diligence."

"Already tried," Hank responded. "Brought in L3 with a lucrative proposition. He sat with their engineering team for 45 minutes and they all came out shaking their heads. They couldn't even grasp what their systems were engineered to do… and the code, forget about it. They couldn't get a grasp of any piece, much less the whole enchilada."

"Well, keep trying," Steve said. "See if you can get a big bogey. Hell, we may actually offer up some of the Shareholders to see if they could make a proposition that he'd bite on."

✄

Cyrus and Edward were asked to come to D.C. The incursion into Lebanon by Israelis had been met with RPGs which, much to the world's surprise, stopped Israeli tanks just across the border. The only people, it seemed, that weren't surprised were Cyrus and Edward as they had briefed the FBI a few months earlier about the procurement of the weapons. The shipment, masked as telephonic equipment had been shipped by a Moldovan arms dealer through Lithuania and then onto Norway before being transported to Lebanon for a World Bank financed project to build out the wireless networks around Beirut. By the time the crates were in Norway, they were indistinguishable from their Nokia decoys and no one bothered to inspect them at the three transshipment stops en route through the

Mediterranean. An inspector in Cyprus got suspicious when the manifest and the crate count didn't match but, a timely payment turned inquiry into expediency and the shipments got through. Horus International had been monitoring the known recipients of Olympic security funds and this shipment was the only known diversion that had not supplied material for IEDs in Iraq, Afghanistan and Pakistan. The Bureau was briefed in May, well before the incursion. They had paid no attention because they couldn't independently corroborate the information. John asked if he and Hank could come along.

"You are not cleared into this conversation," Edward explained. "There are details about what we know and when we knew it that we agreed to keep confidential – they've since been classified by a number of agencies."

"We've both had clearances – they're just not active at present because we haven't found a place to park them," John protested.

"John, the sooner you learn to only go where you're invited, the easier your life will be," Edward rebuked his eager colleague. "This is not a matter for casual observation. If Cyrus wants you to be part of this segment of the business, he'll tell me and I will tell you. Until then, focus on your training and your business development activities."

Edward had very little use for John and had raw disdain for Hank. His aversion to the two of them grew out of his two decades of experience with White House and Congressional advisor wannabes. Add to that the fact that he thought Hank was a mole for someone or something and he relished any time he could deflate their air of self-importance.

Dan was livid when Silas met them in the New York control center.

"You mean to tell me that we had three months warning before the incursion and my brothers died an avoidable death," his voice cracking with rage.

"We're running into a dry well with public support for Iraq and Afghanistan – no WMDs, no Osama – and we need to have fresh meat in the 'enemy' camp. We figure that everyone will blame Iran for the arming of the Lebanese. And that'll help us keep the Homeland Defense engine running into '08 right up through the elections," Silas said in his vintage, calculating tone.

"This memo says that Horus briefed the Bureau on this topic in May," he persisted, his voice growing more agitated. "And it says that their intel came from our Olympic investment!"

"It's a messy business, Danny boy. Back when you were in the Army, it was so easy to bulldoze houses and shoot protestors. Now that you are old enough to see that this is just business, you're starting to have regrets. Listen here you little Hebrew shit. We created your sandbox because we knew that you'd never get along with your neighbors. The Jewish State could have been planted anywhere. By insuring that your people are right under the nose of the people who hate you the most, everyone got what they wanted. We've got an ally that the freaks in Jerry's world can fund in an apocalyptic frenzy. We're baiting the Persians. And we can count on your persistent state of war to insure that our defense contractors have plenty of business. If you think any of us give a shit about your religion, ideology or entitlements justified in fairy tales, you best think again. It's good business and a couple tank drivers are a tiny price to pay for the benefit their deaths will bring us."

Dan knew that Silas was right. He also knew that the experiment of the Israeli State was only as good as the U.S. financial support propping it up. If ever there was a waning of support – either out of boredom or, worse yet, economic weakness in the U.S. – the statehood concession publicly justified by acts of horror doled out on Jews, Gypsies, and others, in the 30s and 40s would evaporate like water on a roof-top in Tel Aviv in the middle of summer. And he knew that, in the end, it was looking more and more like China, the great pragmatic behemoth, may very well be assuming the hegemonic role occupied by the U.S. and they didn't have any use for the fairy tales.

"He's where?" exclaimed Prime Minister Benazir Bhutto when she first received word that Osama bin Laden's health had required location to a more secure compound in Abbotabad. "I thought ISI said that they'd insure that he stayed in Waziristan."

Pakistani Army Chief Ashfaq Kayani was not thrilled with the plan in the least. "Why don't we just let the rodent die? Without him the world would be so much a better place," he said shaking his head in that confusing wag that Westerners confuse to indicate dissent.

"I will not stand for this for one moment," Prime Minister Bhutto objected. "We're establishing a new Pakistan. One in which law and order are the rule. Overtly harboring this cockroach in my country is something that my people would never forgive. I will not stand by and let this affront to our sovereignty go on. Absolutely not!"

"I think, Madam Prime Minister, that I have not made myself entirely clear," continued General Gutierrez. "We're not really interested in your permission. We'll keep him under wraps – hell, ma'am, nobody will know he's behind the walls. It's just a simple fact that we can't have him die on us and we can't keep him alive in the hills. If we don't have an enemy ma'am, we cannot continue to justify our generous support for your military and, without the loyalty of your military..., well ma'am, I think you know what kind of situation that would create for you."

"Do we need him alive through the elections?" the General said when he called Steve on a secure line from his residence in Islamabad.

"No question, General, we can have a little progress on the war but, come November, we need to still have action – after all, we can't get the Left to vote for our guy if he can't pluck the heartstrings of every goddamn peacenik by promising to end something that he'll never alter," Steve replied.

"If that's the case, you should know that the Prime Minister, in my assessment, is a liability," the General replied.

"Can you contain her?" Steve probed.

"Sir, if you want your man alive, you're going to have to silence the Prime Minister. She's going to be campaigning in Rawalpindi – damn maze of a town where anything could happen," the General offered. "I'm not going to have any of our assets on this one. If it's a commercial op, you're going to have to run it."

"We've got plenty of assets in the area," Steve replied. "I'll send Carey since he's been on the ground there so many times."

"We've got it from pretty reliable sources she'll be there around December 26 or 27 – not a bad time to remind Americans that our allies are still under the constant threat of terrorists don't you think?"

the General was glad that he'd be free from any implication. It was hard enough for him to navigate the locals – killing the Prime Minister would be a bit much.

## *CHAPTER 9 – ACT II*

The Enterprise had turned out to be a brilliant investment. Darius was quite pleased by the fact that his contribution to the Distraction had remained the focus of only a handful of Postal Inspectors while al-Qaeda had gotten all the credit for September 2001. Funny how terror that could reach every mailbox was more acceptable than planes hitting buildings. His vaccine research had expanded well beyond anthrax – though that was still quite profitable. His foray into H1N1 had paid off nicely. And he never expected to get such a boost from the virginity-promoting campaign surrounding HPV. It's amazing what happens when you get a bunch of conservative Christians to promote chastity at the end of a needle. While his lab didn't get in on the science side of the deal, his investments were performing beyond his wildest dreams. He'd tipped Jerry off in time on this one. Jerry was picking the pockets of saints and sinners alike with his uptick in safe sex girl-on-girl porn, his investments in vaccine producers, and his stratospheric ratings buoyed by his vitriolic promotion of sex after marriage.

Gabriella was so pleased with the sale of 'Black Ops' and 'Ground Zero II" that she found herself forgetting about the Enterprise on all but the rarest of occasions. Henri couldn't hire enough people to keep up with the constant demand for business continuity plans. He'd partnered with Chris Cohen at Titan Capital on some amazing trading strategies. Henri hosted 'strategy' conversations with Chris' traders prior to and following client engagements. The SEC was so distracted with structured finance products and Ponzi schemes that the Privateers – as they had code-named their trading scheme – knew that their insider racket would never be detected. After all, timed trading without knowledge of counter-parties was tough to find if you knew what you were looking for. And the SEC had no clue to look, much less, what to look for. Ayman was trading so many swaps that he was clearing his principal investment once every six months and, since the quant model trades took over the market by total global equities trading volume in the Fall of 2007, Jonas was minting money.

Chan Siew's rubber and palm oil businesses were embracing the rise of the Chinese consumer and Patrick Cheong's RFTrax had found its way into everything from military hardware to tool tracking in every aircraft service bay in the world.

It was, however, a long wait for a few of them. Kate O'Connor seemed to be nearly invisible. Every now and then, she'd show up with an announcement about some major charity initiative. She was frequently photographed in the company of Hollywood stars at events to raise money for refugees in Darfur, tsunami victims and she co-hosted a fund-raiser in May with Connie for the victims of the Sichuan quake. Most of the Shareholders extrapolated that she was probably receiving handsome management fees for the billions of dollars of philanthropy that was passing through her various charities but no one knew. And worse than that, try as they might, they just couldn't figure out what motivated her involvement.

Lord Haverford, everyone knew, was in line for the big wins come 2011 in Phase III so, while the 10-year lock-up seemed ill-suited for typical greed, in true civilized fashion, he knew that his payday was going to be so considerable that a little patience wouldn't hurt. And Connie was more than happy knowing that, with Haverford, her winnings in Phase III were staggering in light of the cost of delayed gratification.

The Operators had laughed themselves silly when John McCain had announced that a nameless, ineffectual Governor from Alaska had been selected to be his 'choice' of a running mate. If listening to Bush stumble through a simple sentence unsuccessfully was charming, listening to Sarah exude raw stupidity was, well, you had to laugh. Foreign policy through your kitchen window because you can 'see Russia' from Alaska? Would Americans really be that naïve?

"Don't we have to make it look like a fair fight?" Dan had inquired of Steve when they returned from Anchorage.

"You'd be surprised how many Americans are going to fall for her. Chicks with guns are the fantasy of a solid 25 percent of the electorate. I can guarantee you that, up against Obama, they'll be as many guys who'd love to have a poster of her with a bikini and a Glock as there'll be bleeding heart liberals who believe in hope and change," Steve replied. "And McCain is just credible enough that we need to give him the albatross so that he doesn't go off and spoil our plans."

"And if that doesn't play out?" Dan continued.

"Trust me," Jonas said, "the Republicans don't stand a chance. We've got some economic news that's going to make it impossible for them to win. Remember the 'It's the economy, stupid'. Well, we're going to pull the house down so completely that no incumbent or his party stands a chance."

"Can someone explain to me how we're so damn sure that we're going to time a banking crisis to the election?" Emma asked what she found to be an obvious question.

"Well, it's actually quite simple," Jonas began. "To get out of the slump in 2002, the only plan anybody had was to get consumers to spend. Trouble was, no one in the Bush Administration had the foggiest notion about how to do it with two big exceptions. Beat the drums of war and terror and you can easily pump 25% of the GDP into direct and indirect military spend. And then, with Alan doing his patronizing best and with the Treasury in tow, the second leg of the stool was to use that delightful contrivance of 'The American Dream' – namely, home ownership – to get cash in the hands of consumers. With a tiny dash of tax incentives, Americans would use 'cheap credit' to take equity out of their American Dreams and leverage themselves to death. And, as long as easy credit was subsidized by 5-year Treasuries bought by the Chinese capitalists within the foreign reserve office and Gulf egomaniacs, we'd have a half decade of spending. Irrational exuberance would induce Americans into living well beyond their means and, hell, we have our recipe for a melt-down perfectly timed for..." his voice drifted off.

"You son-of-a-bitch," Dan interrupted. "You are so ugly when you're gloating."

"You know, Danny-boy," Jonas retorted, "just because my plan has gone to perfection doesn't mean you have to get all high and mighty."

Sun squirmed in his seat. The only time you could visibly see anything get under his skin was when he was reminded about the event years ago on the African coast. While conventional wisdom was that time heals all wounds, his image of the Ambassador going into the drink with his family haunted him and, when he heard Jonas talk about his 'perfect record', he knew that somewhere, he was being reprimanded for what, apart from his colossal fuck up, had been a decade of near perfect execution.

"So what happens in summer and fall of 2008?" Emma tried to get the conversation back on track.

"Well," Jonas dropped into his professorial tone, "when the debt comes due, we'll go to the cupboard and it will be empty. You see, to make the racket work, the financial markets have realized that they only make money by pumping debt into the market, not from actually servicing debt. So after they originate loans and second mortgages, they dump them as fast as possible. Hell, they make more money from fees than they do from actually being a bank. And the more the government needs the illusion of consumption, the more they're incentivized to print deals. What we've done is picked a couple banks who have been – well, shall we say, less than cooperative and we're going to take them down."

"If the banks collapse, wouldn't that be a disaster?" Emma insisted.

"Well, that depends where your check comes from," Jonas laughed. "You damn well better thank your lucky stars you're working for us because if you were working for the assholes employing all your friends, you'd be getting ready to pack your things and move into a trailer park in New Jersey."

"But aren't insurance companies and pension funds exposed to these real-estate assets?" Dan added seeking to demonstrate his awareness of the financial markets. "I mean, wouldn't a company like AIG get hammered if something like this went down?"

"Funny you should mention AIG," Jonas said. "There are a bunch of people who have a hard on to take out some of AIG's executives –

people who think the Greenberg's have gotten too powerful and, yes, THAT AIG is going down. But, AIG is fine. They've provided so much utility to so many of our friends that, while they'll appear to be punished for getting too cavalier, the firm will simply fall into the loving, opaque arms of the government and they'll be fine. After all, AIG is going to be the way we pass much needed liquidity to some of our friends. And since nobody knows what swap products really are, we'll be able to move money without anyone really knowing how to follow it."

Sun finally snapped out of his funk. "So what you're saying is that the Enterprise is going to actually move ALL the financial assets of the country into the pockets of..."

"No, my dear friend," Jonas responded. "Not going to. We already have."

"Does Steve know how all this is happening?" Sun probed.

"Steve knows enough," was the reply, "but, given the fact that he has been holding our money for a long time – and don't get me wrong, we trust him and all – we have needed to know we would win whether we got the White House or not. Turns out that we'll get the White House and, in a word, the entire Treasury of the U.S. in one fell swoop. And best of all, Americans will have voted themselves into oblivion."

"We have a problem," came the masked voice when Dr. Robertson picked up the phone.

"Cecil?" he blurted.

"Yes," was the response.

"What's the problem?" Dr. Robertson inquired, his Southern accent dripping from his voice.

"It appears that Cyrus has put together a few too many pieces of the puzzle and he could blow the whole operation. So we need you to see if you can do something to pull him off his game."

"What, precisely, do you have in mind?"

"That's up to you," Cecil replied. "Why don't you see if you can distract him?"

"Given what I've heard from Emma and Karen, that's no small task," Dr. Robertson replied.

His next call was to Hank and John. He wanted to know more about the threat that had warranted Cecil's call. He hadn't had a phone call like this, save a few invitations to gatherings here and there, for years so he figured that this was something of considerable import. Hank and John were not very helpful.

"You've had a year inside Horus," Jerry was clearly exasperated, "and you still don't have access to the black box?"

"Listen, Jerry," Hank replied, "last time I checked you guys have had the Agency, China's MII, and all Steve's team try to crack the code but, somehow he keeps showing up with information that no one can trace so, the fact that we haven't gotten in shouldn't be a surprise."

"But I thought you said that he trusted you – well at least John," Jerry protested.

"You know Jerry," John quipped, "I don't think Cyrus trusts anybody. He's an open book if, by that you mean you can turn the cover, but get on the inside, that's another story. Every page you think you find looks blank. But there's a bigger problem. He works all the time and we haven't found a way to hang with him. We may spend 10 to 12 hours a day with him but he'll show up the next morning having done 5 or 10 things that no one saw him do. At first we thought it was just bullshit but, the damn thing is that everything checks out. We've got no clue how to stay on top of it. If I didn't know better, I'd start believing that this guy actually has figured out parallel universes since he seems to be in more than one place at one time and he definitely gets more done in our 24 hours than you could do in a week."

"That's crazy talk," Jerry said. "He's a mere mortal like the rest of us."

"Good luck with that," Hank replied. "From the outside, that's what everyone says but if you spend anytime with him, you'll conclude differently."

"Well," Jerry continued, "how can we take him down? I've got orders that he cannot be at liberty to disrupt the elections – no speeches where he outs us, no op-eds, nothing – he has to be silenced."

Hank and John laughed. "Silenced! You've got to be joking. He'll never shut up."

"If you can't shut him up, can you at least make his life a living hell so he's distracted?" he was getting desperate. "Can we get to him through Emilie or the kids?"

"You know, lately home life's been a little rocky but, that's a dry well. He may never be happy but, since last Thanksgiving it seems that he doesn't even care about that anymore. Bottom line – the only way we could get to him is sabotage. He values his reputation and we could create some trouble there. However, you know we'll have to make shit up and, knowing him, he'll actually out us in the end so it won't be a solution – just a temporary set back," Hank said.

"Invite him up to New York in August. Kate is hosting a gathering of NGOs and let's see if we can appeal to his humanitarian weaknesses. I'll make sure that I have some great operators in the room and we'll get him distracted – you guys do your job," Jerry suggested.

"If we do this, Jerry," John said, "we need to know that you'll cover us when he finds out what we've done. He doesn't fire people but he'll cut us off when he knows that we were responsible for pulling the house down."

"You know, John, in my business, whores actually do a service first and then demand payment. You've got a lot to learn that your seminary didn't teach you. You deliver first and demand payment later. Hell, that's why we take the offering AFTER we tell people they're going to hell, Son. Guarantees that we'll get a 10% kick. The more hell fire I lob across the pulpit, the better the take. You high church folk could learn a lot from us Baptists. That said, we'll make sure that you don't go homeless," Jerry said.

⌧

"Bart Ivanhoe has taken his business model from Mongolia and decided that it's better suited for mineral and energy projects in Burma," Avi continued as he railed against the extractive industry abuses across the globe. "Whether he'll ever see his billions from the Gobi Desert or not is really not his primary concern. With water and infrastructure in such short supply, his business model is really the capital markets play and with Goldman in his pocket, it's working out quite well. Announce a major reserve, dupe a government into believing that they're a partner to get enough press releases to pump the stock and bail before any accountability darkens the doorstep."

"You know," Cyrus replied when they were speaking afterward, "we've seen this same story played out in Sierra Leone, Peru, Indonesia, hell, everywhere, and unfortunately, crooks like Grayson from the World Bank keep running around promoting the merits of these projects only to have the UN Millennium charities come along years later to mop up the blood after the Bank funded carnage."

"Any chance you'd like to join me on a trip this fall to Chile?" Avi asked Cyrus. "I'm sure Horus could provide some much needed financing and strategy to the government and a bunch of our friends down there. We could also explore some of our other community operations in Peru, Colombia and Venezuela around the same time."

"Sure," Cyrus replied, "I'd love it."

"Any chance you could get Emilie to join you on a trip down south?" Avi inquired.

"You know," Cyrus replied, "it just may be the change of scenery that would get her excited about life again."

"We're shooting to head down in October or November," Avi continued. "You'd be out of the country for the elections in all likelihood."

"That's not a problem," Cyrus was quick with his response – maybe too quick, "I already know who's going to win."

🗗

Carey was breathless when he returned to Control. The whole gang was there plus one new face. Anything or anyone new or different jumps out at you when you've spent a decade working with the same people all the time. With her arm draped over the new arrival's shoulder, Elizabeth was doing her level best to make it clear that she already had a relationship. The young man had rich brown skin, carbon black hair, and was dressed in clothes that suggested a recent splurge on Madison Ave. He couldn't have been more than 23 or 24 however, when it came to people of central Asian descent, guessing ages is a fool's errand. While Carey immediately focused on the young man, he couldn't help being distracted by the look on Elizabeth's face. Having spent 15 years of her life as a decoy to seduce countless men into whatever compromising act would inure to the benefit of her employers which left her with a persistent hard edge, she seemed rather softened with this young man and clearly was enjoying what looked to anyone in the room like flirting.

"I see you found someone new," Carey said, his voice tinged with a bit of sarcasm and jealousy. He, after all, would have given anything to have been one of her targets even if he had known that the whole thing was a façade. She was that hot. But, alas, they were colleagues and from his earliest days at the Farm, he knew that dropping anchors in local ports was taboo. He had numerous, hollow relationships with vacuous women he had lured into a moment of intrigue but, his elusive behaviors had killed any romance before it had a chance to bloom. So thankfully, he had cultivated a wonderful relationship with a sympathetic madam who had, among her clients Congressmen, aides to governors and mayors, U.S. Attorneys and countless other men who required discretion. She was old enough to be Carey's mom but, for reasons he didn't understand, she just wanted to be his caretaker. And so, in the last few years, she would arrange a social life for Carey that, while episodic, was anything but monotonous. But what he would have given if he could have ever lived even one of his fantasies with Elizabeth.

"Indeed I have," Elizabeth gloated. "This is Munkhbat. His father is a member of the Parliament in Mongolia and he's here doing an internship at Goldman Sachs. It seems that they needed to have someone with Mongolian expertise to pull off their recent debt instrument with the government and he made them millions so they're giving him a nice piece of the action."

"Looks like he's getting more than just a piece of Goldman's action," Carey sneered.

"Oh, you poor little boy," she said reaching over and pinching Carey's ass. "You don't actually think that I'd ever fall for a playboy like you, do you? After all, what would all those hookers think if you settled down? You'd break all of their hearts."

"Focus, please," Sun interrupted the tiff. "What did you find out at the gathering over at the O'Connor event?"

"Well," Carey started, composing himself, "it looks like we've got a two-pronged strategy to keep the lads at Horus distracted and to keep Cyrus from outing us. What we're doing is leaning on John and Hank who've agreed to start leading a bit of a palace coup at Horus. They've got several shareholders and few of the board to go along with an asset sale boondoggle where they'll start rumors that Horus' technologies are going to be sold to a few government agencies. And, it appears that Cyrus is going to be heading out of the country in late October for a few weeks so we'll have open access to the offices for a minimum of two weeks while he's off meeting the natives in South America. He'll be off the grid and we'll take as much apart as possible while he's gone. Hank and John don't think that they can get us into the heart of the data systems since they've never been cleared but we can at least lean on the staff at Horus to see if we can get somebody to cave."

"Hell, if you get me in the room with enough time, I'll tear through his hard drives and find out where he sources his data and where he stores the evidence," Sun gloated.

"Not so fast little fella," Jonas chimed in. "You may have Cyrus out of the office but I can guarantee that there's more to Edward than meets the eye and I wouldn't be so cock sure that you'll just waltz in there without having a bit of opposition."

"He doesn't know a goddamn thing about computers," Elizabeth interrupted.

"Yes, but he defends Cyrus to the end and he's just the sort who I wouldn't want to underestimate. Hell, with his gun collection, I wouldn't put it past him to bring a Glock to school one day and take us out if we started looking suspicious," Jonas had a greater concern in his voice than was customary.

"Well, at a minimum, we know we can walk in the front door with John and Hank instead of trying to break into his little fortress," Sun reassured the group.

"And what am I doing here?" Munkhbat interrupted.

"You're with me, my little Khan," Elizabeth said. "You're just going to call your daddy and make sure that Steve's money is safe in his mining deals."

"Now that we've got Rio in the deal, his money is very safe. I've been assured of this by Dan and the rest of my friends at Goldman," Munkhbat replied.

"Friends at Goldman! Now that's an oxymoron if I've ever heard one," Emma sneered. "Once you're no longer useful, I can assure you that they won't give a damn about you, Mongolia, or any of the thousand empty promises they've made to you and your government. You're only purpose is to sell out your country and, from the looks of things, you're doing a great job. But when you're in our business, you learn very quickly that traitors don't have friends."

"Well, who woke up on the wrong side of the bed this morning?" Jonas snapped, sending a cold stare towards Emma.

"Listen, Jonas," Emma retorted uncharacteristically, "I've been working this gig for 10 years and I've seen us destroy thousands – no millions of lives, fortunes, even whole countries – and I know that if anyone ever knew that any of us had anything to do with one tenth of what we've done, we'd be strung up. And with what you're about to do – sending millions of people into unemployment, destroying retirees' lives – I hardly think there's a better word than treason for what we're doing"

"Oh, my naïve little Emma," Jonas cajoled. "You have to remember that it's the ignorance, stupidity, and greed of every citizen that led them into debt. It's their unwillingness to be informed that lured them to let their money be managed by incompetence. And, the only thing we're doing is harvesting the grapes of wrath that they left untended. If an obese person can't walk past Dunkin Donuts without realizing that another glaze-filled pastry is going to speed their heart attack, do we blame the doughnut? If a thoracic surgeon finishes a lung transplant and then goes outside to have a smoke to calm his nerves, do we blame a cigarette? We're not stealing, we're salvaging. And there's no victim. Just a bunch of lazy Americans and Europeans who have decided that letting others take their money to chase greedy returns was a good idea while they dug themselves into a cesspool of debt. We didn't make the hell – they did."

⊟

Jerry flew Hank and John out to the *Genesis 2:25* in San Diego for a small gathering of a few of the Shareholders. Henri and Patrick were there. For the life of him, Jerry couldn't figure out how he could follow through with Cecil's order that he coordinate the distraction of Cyrus and the Horus team. But what he did know is that no one could justify more waste, fraud, and abuse in government contracting than Henri and his band of ex-government and agency wonks at Resilience Global. Patrick had weaseled his way into enough Asia Pacific post-Avian flu working groups that between the two of them, they should be able to arrange a soft landing for the turncoats if Cyrus landed on his feet after being knocked off the horse. Gabriella would be on the boat but she had agreed to be

234

playing the role of 'hostess' for the gathering so the Shareholders could get a sense about the character of the two. Ever since Hank's wife had died, rumor had it that he had been starting to color outside the line with his lifestyle and, who better than an amazingly beautiful, mature Brazilian, to see if the rumors were true.

"When you were in seminary, John, did your professors teach you how to turn the pulpit into a yacht like this beauty?" Jerry asked, putting his arm around John as they came aboard.

"I'm afraid that we Anglicans are a few paces behind you when it comes to yachts," John laughed. "We're more the dinghy type," he added as he soaked in the opulence surrounding him. "Our Lord could walk on water but he wasn't big on party boats."

"Well, have I got a gospel for you my dear shepherd... Scotch anyone?" Jerry was tired of waiting for his drink.

A silver tray filled with glasses materialized around the aft cabin door borne on the twiggy arm of a young lady who appeared to have walked right out of a Sports Illustrated swimsuit model shoot.

"Where do you find them, Jer?" Patrick asked his eyes glued to the young lady serving drinks.

"Turns out that when some of our wayward ladies come to the Lord, a few of them need sanctuary in service to the mission," Jerry replied. "It is a mystery how they find us."

"I think I saw the website that unveils the mystery," Hank offered. "I've found it a great source of inspiration since Linda passed."

Dinner was a lavish affair but no one came for the meal. This meeting was serious business. Jerry had orders to make it impossible for Horus to have the capacity to disclose any of the Enterprise, its members or its plans. John and Hank were worthless on the technical front. They had tried, in vain, to pick one of the Horus team to turn but, as fate would have it, they picked a junior member of the IT side who did not know any of the advanced systems that Cyrus had built. Edward shut down every attempt to probe details out of the rest of the team.

"We're pretty sure that he's storing data overseas," John said as dessert was being served. "Over the past several months, he's been heading to a number of places where he's off the grid for 3 to 5 days at a time. There's no telling what he may be doing or with whom he may be meeting when he goes dark."

"There are a few places he's been going lately – some in South America, some in Southeast Asia and a few spots in China – and we think that he's probably taking back up files with him," Hank added.

"What kind of data can Horus track?" Henri inquired leaning forward from his chair.

"Well," John began, "what we know is that he talks about tracking all manner of transactions in the U.S. and Europe. During one of his trips to China, he was able to access a large batch of IP addresses in MII and, from time to time, he's implied that we still get signals on those wires."

"Damn it," Jerry blurted, "with all the geeks we've got on our payroll, why can't anyone actually find a way to break into every piece of equipment he touches and settle this once and for all?"

"That's the problem," Hank replied. "We think we have done it. We had several weekends when we had access to all the office hardware and we had some of our best pouring over every box and...," he paused, "we couldn't find a thing."

"You mean to tell me that Horus is just a decoy for whatever Cyrus is really up to?" Henri asked.

"That's what we'd all conclude except for..." John's voice abruptly stopped as he shot a glance towards the sunset just off the starboard bow.

"What in God's name is that?" Hank said as they all watched what appeared to be a rocket trail launch into the evening sky.

The trail of smoke rose into the darkening sky. No explosion. No noise at all. Just a brightly lit contrail emerging from the sea and stretching into the heavens.

Patrick watched without flinching. His lack of surprise would have been noticeable though no one was paying attention. He knew that one of the three Pakistani subs had passed through the Straits of Malacca just a few weeks ago – rendezvoused with a Korean flagged fishing vessel – and then dove into the Pacific. With their anti-cavitation propulsion systems designed by the French, they could run anywhere without easy detection. While he didn't know what the payload was, he knew who would know and he was going to pay her a visit in a few days.

"Gentlemen, a few fireworks can't distract us from our mission," Jerry tried to regain control of the evening.

"If Horus is a cover operation for whatever Cyrus is up to, let's choke it," Henri said.

"We can send all of Horus' client information and contract data to Resilience Consulting and at least cut off the supply of cashflow," John suggested. "After all, if he can't make payroll, it's going to be a hell of a lot easier to flush out where he's really getting his support."

"Yeah, and when we see who he runs to next, we'll at least have a better idea where to start looking for what he knows and who he's working for," Hank added.

"Have you contained the problem?" Cecil asked on the phone that rang on the bridge.

"How do you know that I'm on the *Genesis*?" Jerry asked in disbelief.

"Jerry," Cecil continued, "do you honestly think there's been a moment since we first met that I haven't watched every move you make?"

"Well," he began, his voice lowering, "we're going to kill Horus. Kind of like the old Egyptian myth.  You know, kill it, chop it up and make sure that the pieces can't ever get put back together."

"Jerry," Cecil was not amused, "you didn't read the end of the story did you?  Because in the story, the Eye of Horus becomes all seeing. We've got enough problems with Cyrus as it is.  The last thing we need is for him to see more."

"Bad analogy," Jerry responded.  "We're going live with our plan immediately.  John and Hank are going to kill off the oxygen to Horus and then take all its clients to Henri's operation."

"I will inform the team at Control and make sure that they monitor every move Cyrus makes," and then the line went dead.

As they were closing the bridge, Sam pulled Jerry aside.

"You know when that missile went up?" he began.

"How could I have missed it, Sam?  What the hell was that?" Jerry replied.

"Well, Sir, about 15 seconds after it went up, all the comm went dead," Sam continued.

"What do you mean, went dead?" Jerry asked, his voice holding an awkward urgency.

"Sir, I mean everything blacked out.  We were on battery for about five minutes to keep your party going but we couldn't communicate with any systems on the bridge – no radar, no radio, no phone, no GPS – nothing.  A complete black out."

"And did you get everything back up after that?" Jerry pressed.

"No Sir, all the computers onboard appear to be fried.  I brought the *Genesis* back on full mechanical, Jerry, not a goddamn system operating," Sam was clearly agitated.

"What do you think that was?" Jerry asked.

"Damned if I know, Sir," Sam composed himself.

"See to it that you send the hardware down to our friends at the lab so they can check it out," Jerry said as he turned to walk away to join the others.

"Yessir."

## CHAPTER 10 – GIPPETTO'S THEATER

Wolf Blitzer raced onto the stage at CNN's Election Night headquarters. He was out of breath.

"We can call it," he said to the twenty or so on and off camera staff and pundits assembled for the Presidential election.

"We are going to announce that Barack Hussein Obama has defeated John McCain – I can't believe it," his voice was filled with amazement.

The Operators had decided to spend the election night out of the country. It's kind of anticlimactic to pretend to be surprised by an event you orchestrated. And, this was no time for celebration. While Steve's grand vision had been accomplished – the Enterprise had, in fact, bought the White House – most plans are highly vulnerable when participants prematurely celebrate. So, together with Jonas and Connie, he had decided to up the ante. Yes, the Enterprise was firmly in control of the Presidency and, thanks to Jerry's media empire, controlled the mindshare of over 40% of the American electorate. And while Dan and Sun had failed to find any new evidence of what Horus knew or how Cyrus operated, Hank and John had, indeed succeeded in gutting the operation so, for the moment, the threat appeared contained. Everyone was in awe of how much money had been transferred into the Enterprise accounts in full view of a world who believed that a financial crisis had hit the real estate market. Who would have thought that a Republican lame duck president would actually convince the country to use its last gasp of credit to put the Treasury of the United States into the pockets of twelve private interests? And now with their puppet on his way to Pennsylvania Avenue, all the 'no more torture' and 'close Guantanamo' rhetoric would die off in the practicalities of solidifying the asset transfer.

The Operators all received confirmation of their promised bonus payments at an evening dinner on the third night of their offsite. The payments were a combination of gold, bonds from Australia, Canada, and Norway, and a small equity stake in the firms controlled by the Shareholders. All funds were placed into trusts domiciled in Lichtenstein. They were all sternly reminded that the money was theirs with a condition. If any of them ever spoke of The Enterprise or any activities undertaken thereby, all trusts would be confiscated. If they played their cards right, they'd all weather Phase III with more money than virtually any other person on the planet.

"Whatever you do," Jonas said, "do NOT put any of this money in U.S. dollars."

"I don't suppose it will do any good to ask why?" Carey said as his mind raced through the portfolio summary he'd been given.

"Nope," Jonas replied.

"How do we access our money?" Elizabeth asked.

"You'll each have a crypt-account and you'll speak to Cecil," Jonas replied.

"And if we can't get Cecil..." Sun began.

"You'll get Cecil and Cecil will find you," Jonas cut him off.

The Inka Terra resort receives the morning sun an hour after it's done the fog-burning magic on Machu Picchu. The Operators had been out in Aguas Calientes late into the night celebrating their decade of hard work. There was little chance that any of them were going to make the early bus up to the mountain opting instead for a lavish breakfast of quinoa pancakes, fresh fruit and enough coffee to take the edge off their hangovers. They had each received a note under their doors early in the morning that there was to be a gathering in the private dining room for dinner that evening – formal attire mandatory.

Elizabeth and Munkhbat didn't even make it out of their room. For a woman who had spent her life seducing men to extract information, she was intoxicated with her young lover and the furthest she'd go today is from the beautifully appointed king-sized bed to the toilet and back. The nearly fifteen years of age that stood between her and Munkhbat was the perfect spread. He was still in his over-eager physical insatiability and she was hitting her 40-something appetite for sensual sex. It was working for both of them.

Carey, Dan, and Emma boarded the bus at 10am to head up to Machu Picchu and agreed to join Keith for lunch between noon and one. With any luck, they'd cross the ruins and head over to Wayna Picchu, do the climb, take a few pictures, and get back in time for lunch. Climbing the last 100 feet up the closely cut stairs, they paused for a moment to catch their breath and take in the sight. To the west, the Sun Gate was now fully bathed in late morning light. Small bands of tourists were milling about down below. Up above, a few intrepid climbers were at the summit embracing one another. From their appearance, it was clear that these early risers were some of the more hearty tourists – the ones who do the five day trek on the Inca Trail to arrive into Machu Picchu. Most in the group were women. They were smiling and chatting. They lined up along the rocks, backs facing the ruins, and one of the group took a number of pictures on an impressive looking camera. By the time the three reached the summit, the early group was beginning its long descent.

"Isn't this magnificent?" Emma said, putting her hands on her hips as she surveyed the panorama. "The Shareholders really picked a winner for this little gathering."

Dan and Carey were a bit winded and just nodded in approval.

"Are you going to stay on?" Dan asked, sitting on a rock next to Carey.

"I don't know," Carey replied. "You know, I've always wanted to start my own restaurant – maybe own a doughnut franchise – who knows."

"Doughnuts!" Emma laughed. "Where the hell did that come from?"

"Seriously," Carey continued, "I'd like to hang up all this nonsense, start a family and do something that just makes people happy."

"The money they're offering for Phase III is tempting," Dan said, turning his attention to Emma.

"Yes, but there's something that I don't trust about Jonas," Emma responded. "I can't put my finger on it but it seems that he's running more of the show than Steve and I'll bet that there's going to be a blow-up at some point. Can't say I want to stick around to see what happens."

"I know that Fengming is staying around and Munkhbat's going to follow Elizabeth wherever she goes. Sun's already in," Carey offered.

"I'll see what they're offering tonight," Dan said. "I've got nowhere to go and I've got no clue what I'd do so, if the money's right, I'll stay."

The Operators had no idea what was in store for the evening. They all showed up more or less on time and were each greeted with Pisco Sours. Connie and Gabriela were both there when the Operators arrived – both wearing stunning Jimmy Choo shoes perfectly coordinated with their gowns. Lord Haverford arrived in the company of Steve and Jonas.

"A few of the Shareholders couldn't make it this evening and, as you all know, we can't all be together at one time anyhow," Steve quieted the room. "However, the Shareholders have agreed that we wanted to thank you all for your decade of service," and he raised a glass to toast his team.

"Here, here," Lord Haverford bellowed. "You have all done your duty with honor and we, the Shareholders are eternally grateful."

"Whoa," Keith blurted, "sounds like we're about to get fired or something."

"On the contrary," Steve continued. "Now that we've successfully taken the Presidency, we've decided to reach a bit further."

Over dinner they reminisced about the highs and lows of the Enterprise. Certain topics never came up. The conversation focused more on the gains – vaccines, media, security, consulting, finance. No one mentioned the Distraction. No one mentioned the Ambassador. In fact, no one mentioned anything that would have suggested the audacity of what this small group of people had accomplished. Best of all, Steve and Jonas seemed to be getting along fabulously.

Emma kicked Dan under the table.

"Would you look at that?" she whispered nodding her head down the table. "Looks like those two have kissed and made up."

"Appearances, my dear, are not to be trusted," Dan mouthed back.

"Cynic," Emma whispered.

"As you all know," Steve stood up from the table, "we're on course to move about $1.4 trillion into our Enterprise through our current activities in Washington. Conveniently, we've convinced the Fed and Treasury to hire Goldman, Black Rock and a few of our friends to pick up transaction fees for managing the government's bailout and we've been assured that our friends in Beijing are going to continue to buy short term debt to keep the funds flowing. One of the Shareholders has secured energy and metals deals for China in Iran, Iraq, Afghanistan and Pakistan in exchange for some additional

Treasury support. And, as long as our President – don't you love the sound of it – keeps distracting combatants in the name of national security, China's happy to help prop up the illusion of the dollar for a bit longer."

"So China buys U.S. Treasuries, uses them to pay for their global resource conquest, and gets a return how?" Elizabeth asked the question that several of them were thinking.

"Well," Jonas chimed in, "don't think of their investments as conventional foreign exchange. Think of them as the price they're willing to pay for us not to compete on their resource deals."

"Yes, but wouldn't they want to be repaid?" Dan inquired.

"Ah, you see that's where this Enterprise gets its big win," Jonas said, once again dropping into his signature gloat. "These Treasuries are never going to be repaid."

"Why? Is the U.S. going to default?" Elizabeth asked.

"No," Connie couldn't wait to get in on the act. "The Treasury is going to be erased."

"What the…" Sun blurted out, startled at what he had just heard.

"Yes, friends, we are going to erase all the tracks of the Enterprise," Jonas continued, his voice assuming a patronizing severity. "And to be clear, any of you who breathes a word of this will be erased immediately too."

He wasn't joking. They all knew it.

"It's going to start out fairly simply. We'll begin a series of low impact cyber intrusions – you know, hacking a few credit card accounts – and get the public used to knowing that cyber security is critical. We've got a group in Sweden who is going to anonymously target a few government agencies – the CIA, the DoD – just enough to make sure that people know that our Enterprise is a victim too," Jonas began. "Then, we'll amp it up a bit. Gabriela and Lord Haverford are going to have their gaming empires 'intruded' with identity theft. Nothing too serious but enough to get the buzz going a bit more. We've got cooperation in Malaysia, Singapore, Vietnam and the Emirates where we can launch the attacks and, with our mirrors, the interruptions and intrusions will be blamed on parties of expediency. Before long, the official response will be to consolidate records of Treasury, Fed, and pension data into a few clouds, and then…"

"I feel a storm coming on," Emma broke the seriousness of a moment and the room all laughed uncomfortably.

One floor below in a dark room overlooking the river, a quiet figure sat next to a stone around which the room's foundation had been poured. The acoustic properties of stone are fascinating and little understood. To most people, that is. Not to this man.

Few Americans take the time to read what goes on under their noses. Even fewer would recognize a genuine threat or vulnerability even if they saw it. Steve knew this. His years of work on the Hill as a staffer before he fell into the insurance and banking industries gave him ample opportunity to know that the best way to effectuate a plan is to get a government agency that no one understands to do your bidding. So, after the launch of the Enterprise, few could have recognized that a letter from Louise L. Roseman, Director of the Division of Reserve Bank Operations and Payment Systems for the Board of Governors of the Federal Reserve System would actually lay out the anatomy of the fatal blow that would take down the U.S. economy for good. Buried in a GAO report, the Federal Reserve Banks, The Department of the Treasury's Financial Management Service and the Bureau of Public Debt, 29 reported vulnerabilities were identified and, this apparent thoroughness would create the illusion of a comprehensive review. What was *not* included would be the Achilles heel. And, like every other national tragedy, no one would ever have the presence of mind to go back and look at the public record in the midst of the storm. Steve knew this. So did Cyrus. And, in the weeks leading up to the inauguration of President Obama, Cyrus knew where the final blow would be dealt.

He knew that the Enterprise would cover its tracks by destroying all digital records of financial transactions. And best of all, he now knew how.

Barack Obama was far more malleable than some of the Shareholders had expected. His ability to backtrack from campaign pledges was predictable. His willingness to leave President Bush's appointees – actually, the Enterprise's appointees – in their positions came without so much as a whimper. Far from scaling back conflict in the Middle East, he went along with the privatization of the conflicts in Iraq and Afghanistan. For every enlisted soldier brought home or redeployed, two private mercenary contractors at three times the pay would be hired. More blood, more revenue, no national guilt. Any attempt to investigate treasonous acts from the previous administration was quashed before it could build up any steam. The Enterprise was not only fully in control but found that buying the Presidency was both easier and more effective than they had imagined.

The Shareholders finally figured out that Kate O'Connor made her returns through her unprecedented access to global executives through her Global Leadership Circle – an exclusive club of newly minted super-wealthy who preferred her Colorado ranches and Caribbean island getaways to the glitz of Davos. Under the light of day, she would foster dialogues with business leaders, politicians, and 'experts', and under the cloak of darkness, she'd sell information to trading desks across the globe, picking up a small commission on each trade which would be deposited in one of the myriad of charitable trusts she operated.

Steve's plan to make sure that some of the Shareholders' businesses were targeted by hackers was a nice decoy. It would have been better if he would have included Kate's clientele in the target list rather than giving them immunity. If anyone wanted to know who was on Kate's friends and family list, all one needed to do was observe who wasn't announcing security threats or breaches.

Emilie's birthday party was a quiet affair. Cyrus had watched Horus nearly collapse and saw an exodus of former colleagues turn their back on the enterprise he'd worked to build. The family went to dinner with a couple of friends who were in from Belgium and retired home.

"Come to bed with me, Emilie," Cyrus enticed his birthday girl.

"Not yet, babe," she replied. "We just got copies of pictures from the trip. Fredric just sent them today."

"O.K. I'll take a quick look but then I've got plans for a real birthday celebration – a present that only I can give to only you."

She smiled and flicked on the computer in the study. He came up behind her, pulled her hair back and kissed her neck.

"Hey, silly," she flirted, "this will only take a minute. And then, you can have your way with me."

"So you're not even going to play hard to get?" he replied.

The computer screen lit the room and she opened her e-mail. There was the e-mail from Fredric with about 30 attachments.

"I can't believe that he sent them all in one e-mail," Cyrus said. "I'm surprised a file that size made it through."

"Whatever," Emilie could care less about the technicalities of technology. As long as it worked, she was happy and if it didn't, she had Sorin to help her.

The pictures were breathtaking and with them, the flood of beautiful memories. The trip had been fantastic. In fact, but for the shock that had met them when they returned home, this trip had been a turning point for their marriage. In the mystery of ancient temples, they had found something that they both loved and, having drunk from the fountain for a few weeks, longed to drink deeply again.

"Go back," Cyrus blurted when he saw the group picture on Wayna Picchu.

"What is it, babe?" Emilie looked up to see his gaze sharpen on the image before them.

"Let me zoom in on that group in the background," Cyrus said as he grabbed the mouse from Emilie's hand.

"What are you looking for, Cyrus?" she asked.

"Look at those three people right there," he said, pointing at the screen. "You remember the woman I told you about in Zurich years ago – the one that I met at dinner? Well that's her. What the hell would she have been doing in Peru when we were there?"

"Did they follow us there?" Emilie asked incredulously.

"I don't know but it makes tons of sense about a conversation I overheard when I was down at the resort," he started drifting away.

"What conversation?" Emilie pressed.

"I don't know, really," he started. "I overheard a rather interesting conversation coming from the dining room above the room we were in down by the river during our last night. And if they were there..." he didn't finish his thought.

"Can I look at the last images?" Emilie asked, taking the mouse back.

"Sure thing."

⊠

When a President comes from the same political party that controls both the House and Senate, he is typically not given to pining impotence. Courtesy of constant reminders of the lack of a veto-proof majority – the new standard for domination under the Obama administration – and with the incessant AFN pundits berating him for ineffectiveness, not a single campaign pledge had a chance of survival. More appropriations for the wars. More renditions. More justification for more bailouts. More money ringing in the coffers of the Enterprise. And it came as no surprise that, the first 14 months of the Enterprise's Administration paved the way for even greater comedy in Washington. If casual observers thought that Sarah Palin was out of touch, they were in for a shock when a tidal wave of tea swept the midterms. Fiscal responsibility at all costs – except, of course for self-serving constituents – was the battle cry taken up by pensioners who took over town hall meetings from Portland, Maine to San Diego, California. These mindless throngs had the audacity to demand that the government turn Social Security and pensions over to private accounts at the very moment when the equity markets were fully in control of quant traders who made their returns preying on the stupidity of uninformed traders. In short, the Tea Party whipped millions into a frenzy in which they called on the robber barons to steal their money under the guise of 'no big government'. Privatize Social Security and Medicare through personal savings vouchers – the stupidity was blinding. Billions of dollars under professional management were sitting on the sidelines with nowhere to invest. What level of insanity was required to think that the average American could find a way to invest private accounts in a manner that wouldn't subject their entire savings to the volatility of a market that had lost all of its moorings?

Bank failures, insolvency of pensions, functional bankruptcies of municipalities all provided suitable distractions to insure that no one would discover warnings on Page 4 of the GAO's December 2001 memo.

*"A contingency or disaster recovery plan specifies emergency response, backup operations, and post-disaster recovery procedures to ensure the availability of critical resources and facilitate the continuity of operations in an emergency situation. It addresses how an organization will deal with a full range of contingencies, from electrical power failures to catastrophic events, such as earthquakes, floods, and fires. The plan also identifies essential business functions and ranks resources in order of criticality. To be most effective, a contingency plan should be periodically tested in disaster simulation exercises and employees should be trained in and familiar with its use."*

Earthquakes, floods, and fires sounds so Wizard of Oz-esque. "Lions and tigers and bears, oh my." Huge risks for New Jersey, Virginia and Texas, right? This memo, and the audits and tests that followed were lucrative consulting business for Henri and his firm. In the name of 'continuity of government' and 'resilience scenarios' the firm was raking in millions of dollars for consulting on a topic about which they had no credentialing save the last five illusory reports done for other agencies.   Patrick got a tidy contract for security access, physical data security, and credentialing.   RFID was the ubiquitous form of access into every office building, every parking garage, every college campus since the Virginia Tech shootings and, as a result, tracking the movement of citizens – long construed to be a violation of civil liberties – was the order of the day.  He didn't make a lot in each sale but he sure made it up in volume.

The Commission to Assess the Threat to the United States from Electromagnetic Pulse (EMP) Attack issued its Critical National Infrastructures Report in 2008.   Since Starfish, Starfish Prime and Operation Fishbowl in the 1960's the U.S. government was fully aware that the greatest single point failure of the civilian and military infrastructure of the country is vulnerability to high altitude EMP (HEMP) and certain advances in non nuclear EMP (NNEMP).  The specter of these threats was useful in burying EMP hardening appropriations into the Department of Defense budgets during the late Bush years, a phenomenon that was expanded in scope and price by President Obama.  For all the hardening in defense infrastructure and weapons systems, however, the Enterprise had endorsed a strategy of promoting increased vulnerability for civilian infrastructure – particularly infrastructure supporting the Federal Reserve Banks and Treasury.   The "CC" strategy had been implemented in the name of efficiency to combine Treasury, Federal

Reserve and other government financial data. But like the counterintuitive Senator Byrd-sponsored naval appropriations for landlocked West Virginia, these data centers were selected for political pork expediency rather than strategic risk management considerations.

"This one reminds me of a little sea snail – *Conus gloriamaris* – that lives in the shallow waters off the coast of the Philippines. It looks quite harmless and rather pretty but if it shoots its tiny barb into your foot, the toxin kills you in a few minutes," Chan Siew said after Steve briefed the Shareholders on Phase III. "I made a nice little piece of change investing in a project that was done in partnership with the University of Utah and some researchers in the Philippines making pain killers for medicine and human killers for a few agencies."

"I already hate walking in the sea at night," Kate said. "Now I've got another thing to worry about."

"Oh Kate," Jerry interjected, "you don't want to be in the water, you need to be on the *Genesis* with me ABOVE the water."

"Speaking of the *Genesis*," Lord Haverford chimed in, "I heard that you had some comm trouble on her a few months back. Did you ever sort out what buggered up the systems?"

"Damnedest thing," Jerry replied, "it seems that there was a massive electrical burst that fried everything. However, now that I've been listening to Steve explain what we're about to do, I have to wonder if he's got a pocket-sized EMP device that he used on my lady."

"How are we going to sequence the erasure?" Darius tried to bring the subject back to something that he could get his arms around.

"Well, now that we've got the White House, we need to make sure that one hell of a lot of money starts moving around because we've got to get all our assets in safe jurisdictions before we pull off the events," Steve explained. "It'll take 18 months or so to get enough froth in the system that tracking our asset movements will be next to impossible. We've got your wonderful support, Darius, on the nuclear power projects and the uranium stockpiles. Gabriela's got us access to a bunch of South American oil leases. And, bless her heart, Connie has invited us into land and resource deals ranging from Congo to Chile to Mongolia. While the Chinese government is getting the credit and the blame, they've generously given us a corner of their brocade to ride on and we've got to use it wisely."

"Reminds me of the great old days in Afghanistan when we told the world that we cared about freedom but, in truth, both we and our American cousins needed the poppies and the drug trade to keep our expediencies operational. Covert operations are well nigh impossible if you don't have the scourge of drugs. As long as two bit investment bankers in New York and London are spending a quarter of their bonuses on drugs, you'd be amazed at how many operations we can sustain," Lord Haverford said with an air of nostalgia.

"Yeah," Jonas chimed in, "we're just expanding the addiction to include Nigerian oil, Pacific gold, Mongolian coal and copper and African agriculture – same business model, broader base of addiction."

"Bottom line friends, is that we need to be in hard assets, means of production, you know, rather than in electronic balance sheets. Ayman's going to help us move exposure in untraceable units – keep the transactions varied in size and timing – so that we can move our money without triggering any of the nuts at FinCEN. We haven't been able to get Freis to look the other way on anything and Lord knows we've tried," Steve explained.

"We've got the Operators in on Patrick's contract to do the multi-tiered security access at all the CC locations," Jonas added. "When the Chinese SAFE auditors come through to inspect security, Connie's going to insure that there are a few personnel on the visit who have signal emitters that we'll monitor from the security vehicles just to make sure there's no shielding that we don't know about."

"When we do the erasure, are we going to have anybody on the inside to confirm completion?" Kate asked.

"No need for that Kate, my darling," Steve said. "There will be no question that everything's gone and, given the power failures that will happen at the same time, by the time anyone could get on site for an inspection, we'll have the places obliterated."

"The only thing that is a concern for us," Connie began, her voice evidencing a bit of emotion, "is the fact that we think that China is going to get blamed for launching an attack."

"You think you're worried," Darius interrupted. "What about Iran? After all, for the past 8 years the U.S. and Israel keep threatening us over the weapons that we don't have. For the longest time, we've had a deal with our neighbors in Pakistan and, should it ever come to it, we'll lease theirs. But something like a massive infrastructure strike on the U.S. There's no question that we'll be blamed."

"Friends," Steve jumped in, trying to reassure his investors, "we're not necessarily going to use a nuclear device. We do have several options on the table. We've got a number of physicists who have come in from the cold to help us. The money we've offered is good but far and away, what they like is the thrill of playing with the toys they'd designed back in the Cold War. For them, it's the science."

"How are we going to make sure that our records are preserved – you know all our transactions?" Ayman broke his silence.

"Look to the heavens my dear brother," Jerry fell into his signature southern accent. "AFN's allocated a bit of its constellation to serve as a back up for all of our little secrets. We figured if we used our commercial birds in orbit, they'd be far enough out of harms way to make erasure a non-event and it's a real bitch to go up to a satellite and read it's hard drive if you don't know which bird is chirping."

"Can anyone figure out our back up plan?" Kate asked, feeling like she had suddenly entered an episode of Star Trek.

"Doubtful," Jerry replied. "You'd have to be a master at cryptanalysis and have had experience with satellite communication. Even then, it would be nearly impossible to pick up an encrypted signal when it's time to bring the data back to home after we've wiped the slate clean."

⛊

"If you stand here when the sun sets, Cyrus," Tavita explained, "you're not only seeing the last light of the day but you'll be amazed to see how fast the night falls. Our elders told us that here at the end of Savai'i just past the village of Falealupo, the spirits of our ancestors go after they pass. I don't like being here at night – gives me the creeps."

"It's beautiful," Cyrus said taking in the majestic power of the waves crashing into ancient volcanic cliffs.

From time to time, a wave would hit just right and water would jet out of a lava tube sending water 40 feet into the air in a powerful geyser. Behind them to the east, a large volcanic mountain captured the late afternoon light, clouds flirting around the summit. The village through which they'd come was dotted with small fales. Young children were playing an impromptu rugby game in a small grass field and several elders sat under the shade of the trees.

"You know, this is the place where the mamala healers lived," Tavita explained. "They used various parts of the tree to make a medicine that cured all sorts of diseases – hepatitis, AIDS, all kinds of things."

"Yes," Cyrus replied, "I'm aware of that story courtesy of the work that was done by a group I know in Virginia in the U.S."

"We should head back across the island before the last ferry boat back to Upolu," Tavita said. "If we're going to meet up with the IT engineers, we need to make sure we get to Aggies by no later than 9pm tonight."

"I'd love to come back here sometime," Cyrus said taking a longing last look at the ocean. "Hard to imagine that, of all things, a missionary would have stolen knowledge from a place like this."

"Yes, Cyrus," Tavita said, "it is a shame and, unfortunately, it's not the first though we sure hope that, in time, we'll have more people come here who, like you, want to do real business with us."

Halfway across the channel between to the two islands that make up the majority of the land mass of Samoa, Cyrus looked into the water and saw four giant sea turtles gliding effortlessly through the water. The flying fish shot from the spray off the bow of the boat and flew a meter or so above the water until splashing down 75 feet away. If you were going to pick a place to set up a data communications center, you couldn't pick a more beautiful spot on the globe. And the people of Samoa were as wonderful a community as he'd ever encountered. If the infrastructure could be hosted here, there was a decent chance that Horus could do its data collection locally and nobody would be the wiser for it.

⊠

"Things went well, babe," Cyrus said when he called Emilie after the meeting. "It looks like I'll need to swing through Singapore and then India before I get home."

"I really wish that you'd be here for Anna's recital, Cyrus," Emilie responded.

"I just spoke to her between classes and she understands," Cyrus said.

"She understands because she has to, honey, not because she wants to," Emilie wasn't going to let this one go easily.

"I know."

"Do you need me to book the changed itinerary?" Emilie offered.

"No, I'll take care of it and I'll get home as soon as I can," Cyrus said. "You know that I don't want to have a lot of visibility on my movements back at home until I know who was behind the coup."

"I understand," Emilie replied. "I miss you and love you tons."

"Back at you baby," Cyrus said and hung up the phone.

He looked at his watch. Forty three seconds. Enough time for someone to pick up his call but unlikely that they heard all of it and, even if they had, there wasn't enough detail to trace. Anyone listening in would have no idea what the locations actually meant. Ever since the devastating events around Hank and John's departure, Cyrus and Emilie had an understanding that they'd agree to their own code for places and people so that whenever they spoke on the phone, an observer would be unable to readily decipher the actual meaning of what was being said. Cyrus thought that it made good sense. Oddly enough, Emilie seemed to like the adventure and mystery of it all.

# CHAPTER 11 – WHERE ANGELS FEAR

Sorin had completed his freshman year in university. His childhood dream of running a wildlife shelter had morphed only subtly into biology and environmental sciences but he'd landed an amazing internship working on a habitat assessment in Central Park in New York City. Each morning, well before sunrise, he and several of his fellow interns would walk through grids of the park and identify all of the wildlife they saw. Whenever possible, they'd look for the dens, burrows or nests of the animals to get a sense about how wildlife created their habitats in an urban setting. The second week of June, he was assigned a quadrant that encompassed the southwest corner of the park. At about 4:30 in the morning, he stumbled out of bed and pulled on his not so recently washed polo shirt and baggy shorts. After sending a quick text to his girlfriend, as he did every morning, he grabbed his camera and iPad before heading into the park. As he meandered up West Drive towards the Heckscher Fields, he noticed a raccoon walking under the giant oaks foraging for food that had been discarded by nighttime revelers. He snapped a quick picture and noted the animal on the tracking app he'd programmed for his iPad. He followed the animal, keeping an appropriate distance so as not to disturb it. After about 8 minutes, the animal appeared to have fully sated its hunger and lumbered back towards three large rocks that formed a small crevice into which it disappeared.

He turned to walk away when a tiny glint of gold drew his gaze back to the den. He picked up a stick that had fallen from one of the trees in the thunderstorm the night before and approached the burrow. When he was close enough, he saw that the glint was coming from what appeared to be an embossed letterhead or napkin. He reached the stick into the crack in the rocks and pulled out a damp piece of paper with the letters GLC embossed in gold. He'd seen that logo before but, at this early hour, his mind was not connecting the dots. What was more interesting was the cryptic notes on the page, obviously written in haste.

*- MH-60 – nswdevgru incl. Somali Maersk team – Sun radar jam Rawalpindi*

*...find Cy A...monitor Horus transmission...prepare Lake A strategy...cold winter coming*

*ITU Master Registry – Jerry's birds – BIFROST6-8 – Picasso 101500267*

*Out of fucking cigarettes!!!!*

He read the last line and, there it was. He remembered overhearing a conversation years ago when his dad was talking about a meeting in New York where one of the guys – a chain smoker – got quite angry when he ran out of cigarettes. He grabbed his phone from his pocket and speed-dialed 3 (1 was for his girlfriend, 2 was for Emilie, and 3 was for Dad).

*Damn,* he thought as the phone went to voicemail. *Dad's off in Australia right now. Probably doesn't have his phone on.*

He called Anna next. She answered the phone.

"Hey Anna, it's Sorin," he began.

"I know knucklehead, I saw your name on my caller ID. Do you have any idea what time it is?" she only started to realize that it was before 5 am when the words fell out of her mouth.

"Yes, I'm at work in the Park and just found something that I think may have to do with Dad," he said now fully awake. "Do you have any idea what the GLC is?"

"Yes," she responded. "It's the group that Dad was meeting before his trip to South America. Why?"

"Because I found this piece of paper in a raccoon nest...," he couldn't finish before she interrupted in exasperation.

"You are waking me up at 5 o'clock in the morning because you found some trash in a raccoon's nest?" she said with incredulity. "Let me go back to sleep."

"Anna, just hear me out," Sorin implored. "Let me tell you what's on this paper."

He read the cryptic lines and, once completed, paused.

"Take a picture of it and e-mail it to Dad. He should still be up if he's not in a plane somewhere," she said.

Confirmation hearings for a Secretary of Defense nominee on the heels of the Osama operation are for theatric value alone. Given the loss of the rationale for the nation's collective global war on terror catalyst, and considering that the accolades for the operation were to befall the Navy and Leon Panetta's CIA, the hearing on June 9 was, in a word, fodder for propagandists. Without a clearly defined enemy, in a country like the U.S., you need to come up with a justification for spending vast sums on conflict and, if real enemies don't cooperate the tradition of manufacturing enemies is well established. Anyone listening to his June 9 testimony could readily divine the themes that would replace the Bush-Cheney era Saddam, African yellowcake, Axis-of-Evil, Freedom Fighter turned terrorist-in-chief rhetoric. In the wake of frequent embarrassing revelations at the hands of Julian Assange and others, the predictable public enemy number one necessarily was information and truth. A public that doesn't understand the need for covert and opaque defense must be chastised and agents of information must be marked for their treasonous behavior. However, far more interesting was the emergence of two new arch villains, nefarious threats to our very way of life. The first: hackers. Those slimy, scrawny geeks whose anarchist proclivities threaten to undermine the stability of our antiquated, behemoth dysfunctional government and corporate information technology platforms. And second, electromagnetic weapons built by the Chinese and maybe other bad countries like Iran and North Korea.

The Operators all had bets on how soon they'd hear from someone ever since Carey and Keith had been asked to assist the Director in writing his speech. Karen knew that the Agency's Asia analysts had been tracking a number of Taiwanese scientists who were developing some alarmingly effective EMP devices but she knew that the Chinese collections were analogous to the Valerie Plame African yellowcake fiasco at best. She also knew that Iran and North Korea were being socialized as the pariah states du jour however, with the Chinese partnerships for oil, natural gas and nuclear energy in Iran and with North Korea tottering on the edge of famine again, this was designed for AFN listeners who hadn't been filled with enough fear lately. They also had bets on who they'd hear from first.

"Connie and Darius have requested an audience with Carey and Keith next Tuesday in the Netherlands," Cecil's automated, emotionless voice emanated from the speaker phone. "They have requested that Emma attend for the sake of documentation."

The line clicked dead.

"Pay up suckers," Sun gloated as he gestured around the room with his palm outstretched. "I'm the only one that said that we'd hear from both of them at the same time."

"What kind of bet is it when you take two positions at once?" Keith protested.

"A winning one," Sun shot back.

Emma flew to Copenhagen and rented a car to make her way down to Noordwijk. Carey flew to Brussels and came up on the train. Keith figured that it would be most convenient if he just flew into Amsterdam. After all, he could get to the hotel within two hours max and he'd seen that the hotel had an amazing spa where he could spend some time before the rest of the team arrived.

Hotel van Oranje is a dated, yet glamorous affair perched on the North Sea. Keith checked in around 10 am and, much to his surprise, the room was prepaid including a complimentary welcome massage in the spa. The message at the desk said that he was to arrive at the spa at 3 pm but may wish to take an hour or so to relax in the sauna and steam room prior to the appointment.

"Won't Emma and Carey wish they'd thought ahead like me?" he mused as he rode the lift to the fourth floor.

He placed the card in the door and, with a gentle push, opened the door to a sweeping view of the North Sea beyond his balcony. The wind coming off the sea filled the room and rushed past him as he entered, placing his overnight travel bag on the corner of the bed. He stepped to the balcony doors and leaned out to take in the view of the promenade below and the beach beyond packed with sunbathers in all shapes, sizes and states of dress. Tomorrow, providing that the meeting didn't go too long, he'd spend some time socializing on the beach. It had been far too long since he'd been on a beach in Europe and the flesh was enticing if only to observe.

Quickly unpacking his bags, he put on the robe that was hanging in the room and descended the lift to the Aqua Sauna. Getting off the lift, he was unprepared for the scene that greeted him. Nude bathers were socializing in the pool and, through the steamed glass he saw two naked men and women chatting as they lounged in the Turkish steam room. While he had been around nudity before, his self-consciousness had been too repressive to allow him to shed his clothing in public. Yet, in that moment, he was overwhelmed with a sense that, if he was ever going to cross that emotional Rubicon, now was the time.

He entered the steam room first but immediately realized that his ability to control his level of arousal was best not tested in the company of beautiful European young ladies. Grabbing his towel for discretion, he slipped out before he was entirely embarrassed. He walked further into the room and saw a dry sauna in which two

273

Asian men were sitting. This was a bit safer, he thought, and stepped in, the heat nearly taking his breath away for a moment. He laid down his plush towel and sat on the second row of benches across from the two men who paid him no attention. In about three minutes, the sweat began to pour from his pale skin and he began to relax. A few minutes later, he stretched out and fell into a mindless trance. He would have fallen entirely asleep had it not been for the sound of the door closing as the two Asian men left the sauna. He thought he'd stay in for just a few more minutes.

Once you're sufficiently heated, a sauna goes from being a place of relaxation to hell in short order and the impulse to leave rises quickly. It had been less than a minute since the two men left when he realized that he'd had enough. Wiping his sweat drenched body he hurried toward the door only to find that he couldn't budge it open. Panicking, he looked through the window and saw no one. He tried to look towards the bottom of the door to see if it was jammed. The window was too small to provide an angle accommodating a view to the floor. While not knowing if anyone was around to hear, he called out for help and, when none came, he began banging on the door with his fists. Getting no response, he grabbed the small wooden pallet pillows and used them to attempt to break the glass. Still no luck.

After what seemed an eternity, he saw one of the Asian men returning with what appeared to be a small thermos. Relieved that his calls for help had been heard, he put down the wooden pillow thinking that the door would soon open. Instead, he saw the man lean down and place what appeared to be a small tube on the top of the thermos and thread it under the door. His heart raced as he frantically shouted for help. Looking up at the thermometer in the room, he saw the needle pinned to the right and realized that the room was perceptibly hotter than before. Then, for no apparent reason, he heard the sound of his heart pounding in his chest and moments later was overwhelmed with nausea. He sat back down on the bench, his bare skin burning as it contacted the overheated wood. Exhausted, he glanced up at the window. This time, peering through the glass was not a non-descript Asian man but a woman's face he'd seen many times before. He looked at her, bent over and vomited and all went black.

"I would have thought he would have been here already," Carey said as Emma walked through the doors of the lobby.

"What do you mean?" Emma queried, her voice pleasant as ever.

"Maybe it's the Dutch but I think that the women at the desk said that he left a few hours ago," Carey replied.

"Oh, so he's already checked in?" Emma said lightly.

"No, that's the thing," Carey replied. "When I asked what room he was in, the lady said that he didn't have a room and that he left a few hours ago."

"Have you checked in yet?" Emma inquired.

"Yes, I went down to the beach for a while and I've been waiting here for you," Carey said. "I have my room key but haven't gone up there yet."

"Did you get one key or two?" Emma flirted, pretending to suggest that Carey would have a chance at his unrequited fantasy.

"Only one but you're welcome to it," he played back.

A moment later, she had her key and they both went to the lift together to head up to the fourth floor. Their rooms were beside each other's and in an instant, they were both unlocking their respective doors.

After a few minutes, Carey picked up the phone to call over to Emma's room. An operator answered instead and said that Emma had gone down to the dinner that was being served in the restaurant and that he should go down and join her. He quickly changed his shirt and headed down to the restaurant where he saw Emma sitting at a corner table.

"Do you know anything about this?" she asked as he sat down.

"About what?" Carey replied.

"About a private dinner *arranged in your honor*," she said reading a card that had been on her bed.

"No but I'm sure that Keith is missing out on what will be a lovely night. This place is great."

Moments after he arrived, a young lady came out and filled their glasses with a Shiraz – full bodied with just a hint of pepper. She informed them that their meals had already been ordered and she'd be bringing out the courses as they wished. Salads came out first. Emma was served a green salad and Carey was served a tomato salad with Mozzarella. When they had finished their salads, roast chicken with potatoes were next. Following the entrée, some chilled soup – cucumber for Emma, tomato for Carey. And then desert. They were just finishing their coffees when Carey said that he was feeling a bit tired and thought he'd call it an early night. They both got up from their chairs and left the table. Emma helped Carey to the elevator as he seemed to be a bit wobbly.

Emma slept deeply and was awakened to the sound of sirens from her open window facing the sea. She slipped out of her bed, wrapping a sheet around her naked skin and walked to the balcony door. Down below she saw what appeared to be an ambulance and a number of rescue and police personnel milling about, intermittently pointing up towards her. Ducking back inside, she slipped on some running shorts and a t-shirt and went to knock on Carey's door.

There was no answer. As she turned towards the lifts, she thought she saw a man stepping out and then retreating into the elevator. If she hurried, she thought, she could get to the lift before it went down. The doors were closing just as she arrived and she thrust her hand into the gap to force them open. As they opened she found herself looking in the face of Darius.

"Good morning, Emma," he said coolly.

"Good morning, Sir," she said, not entirely sure of what to make of his tone.

"It's a real shame about your colleagues," he went on, his voice divulging no clue of emotion. "While many of us have suspected that they were lovers for quite some time, none of us could have seen a tragedy like this."

"Darius, what are you talking about?" Emma said, her voice echoed the total incredulity of her response to what she'd just heard.

"Well, according to the police, the two of them were engaging in some sort of sex out on the balcony and the railing gave way. They're both dead."

The lift doors opened as Emma collapsed onto the floor. Her mind was racing as she knew that none of what she had heard could be possible. Could it?

"Come, Emma, let's get some air," he offered her his hand.

She weakly slumped out of the lift and into the lobby where she saw Connie speaking with what appeared to be police officers. Her mind was swirling until she settled in on one thing. She wanted to see Carey and Keith for herself. If they were indeed dead, which she was sure couldn't be possible, she'd want to see it with her own eyes. This was a very bad idea. A human body is not made to fall four floors, hit concrete and steel during the fall and land on pavement. Two of them don't lessen the trauma of the image that she took in. There could be no question that both of them were dead. There was no need to guess at the cause of death as the broken balcony railing seemed to indict itself.

Elizabeth and Steve drove out from the city to meet Emma at JFK the next day when she returned from Amsterdam. She looked terrible. The combination of the events of the past 24 hours and the knowledge that two of her colleagues were dead was bad enough. Trying to figure out what had gone so terribly wrong wracked her brain to no avail. Were Keith and Carey really lovers? Why were the three of them invited over to the Netherlands for a meeting that never happened? And there were a few things that didn't make any sense. Puzzle pieces that became more puzzling every minute. Why did they never see Keith? Why did someone invite them to dinner with only two places set? Why was Darius in the elevator?

Nothing can be more abysmal as an American citizen than to be welcomed home by a Homeland Security Agent at immigration. If first impressions matter to anyone, this vestige of 9-11 has got to be the single worst marketing tool for the American illusion anyone could have concocted. The overweight 50 year old, balding man looked at her and, in entirely too loud a voice, asked if she was bringing anything into the U.S. A wave of emotions rushed over her as her first thought was the fact that she had just lost two of her colleagues and had left their bodies behind in the Netherlands for whatever inquest would be required. She burst into tears.

"Are you alright, Miss?" he said with the sensitivity of course grit sand paper.

"No, you idiot, I'm not alright. Two of my friends were killed in the Netherlands yesterday and I'm not alright."

The Agent reached for the microphone clipped to his shoulder.

"We have a situation, request assistance," he chirped into his radio.

Moments later, three heavily armed security guards descended on the spot as the Agent said, "This lady says she killed two of her friends."

"Put your bags down and your hands behind your head, Ma'am," one of the officers said drawing his gun.

Emma dropped her bags and, as she went to put her hands up, her legs gave out and she collapsed on the floor. She was not given to being overcome and, having it happen twice in 24 hours was not o.k.

Several minutes later, she found herself in a sterile room not much larger than the table inside of it. She blinked her eyes open and saw two police officers and an immigration officer staring at her.

"Ma'am, can you tell us your name?"

"Yes, I'm Kate Winslow."

"Ms. Winslow, can you please tell us what happened out there?" one of the officers inquired in his best made-for-Hollywood voice impression.

"Yes," she composed herself. "I was walking up to the immigration booth when the guard asked me if I was bringing anything back into the U.S. I told him that I wasn't but that two of my friends were killed in the Netherlands yesterday and..." her voice started breaking.

"Ms. Winslow, did you have anything to do with their deaths?" the officer settled into a more humane tone.

"No, officer, they…, well, it seems they fell from a hotel balcony and died." She made it through the sentence and then the tears and sobs rushed back.

"Can you tell us their names?" the officer continued.

She was trained for this moment. But her training didn't include a real situation like this one.

"No Sir, I cannot."

"I'm sorry, Ms. Winslow, I don't think that I understand," the officer took a step back and resumed his tougher image.

"You wouldn't understand, Sir but you are free to inquire of the person who answers this phone," she said as she handed him a laminated card that looked quite official.

"Excuse me," he said as he stepped towards the door. "Keep her here until I come back."

He wasn't out of the room for more than 90 seconds when he returned.

"Ms. Winslow, please accept my deepest apologies and my sincerest regrets. It appears that your associates died in the line of duty and I am deeply sorry for the inconvenience we have caused you. Can we assist you in finding your way home?" his voice was entirely middle aged Brooklyn.

"No, I'd like to get myself home."

"Yes Ma'am."

With that, he escorted Emma through the Diplomat and Crew immigration line and followed her all the way to the curb where Steven and Elizabeth were waiting.

"I'm so sorry baby," Elizabeth ran to embrace Emma.

They held each other for a few moments and then got in the back seat of the Lincoln Town Car.

"You'll understand that we need to know what happened," Steve interrupted the long, awkward silence. "We're going to Control because we need a full debrief before any of your recollections slip."

"I understand," Emma replied as she melted on Elizabeth's shoulder.

Dan greeted them at the door where the whole group had assembled. The office reeked of cigarettes as Jonas and Fengming were apparently seeing who could calm their nerves the most. Munkhbat took Elizabeth's arm as they entered the room and Karen asked if Emma needed anything.

"I'll take a coffee," she replied without a thought.

"Are you up for this?" Steve asked.

"As much as I'll ever be," Emma responded through the haze that was settling in on her.

She recounted every detail of what happened. She was good, partially due to her training and partially due to her remarkable intellect. Sun clattered away on his keyboard as he tried to transcribe notes. Jonas was doodling on a small pad of paper, jotting down one word here and there. Dan was pacing like a caged predator.

"I don't believe it for a goddamn minute," he finally burst out, his brain incapable of seeing reality in the tale that was unfolding. "First of all, Carey would have never gone for Keith. Gay or not, that's not fucking possible."

"Cool it, Dan," Steve interrupted. "We're in collection mode, not analysis. Get yourself together. Now Emma, go back to the lobby. You said that you saw Carey but you never saw Keith. Is that right?"

"Yes."

"And you said that Carey told you that Keith had left or checked out by the time he got there?"

"Yes. He said that the lady at the desk told him that Keith had left – that he didn't have a room anymore," she was now part of the team's forensic investigation and for the moment, her emotions were in check.

"Did either of you see him at all? Any of his things? Anything that indicated that he'd been there?"

"No."

"O.K.," Jonas chimed in, "tell me about the note inviting you to dinner."

"It said that there was a dinner in my honor and that I was supposed to go down to the restaurant," Emma repeated what she'd already told them.

"No, tell me about it. Was it hand-written? On stationery? Christ, do you have it?" he was a bit agitated.

"It was on hotel stationery – maybe a 4x6 card – and, no I don't have it. I think I left it at the table at dinner when I was trying to help Carey back to his room."

"Something's bothering me about your dinner," Karen interjected. "You weren't served the same dishes?"

285

"No, not entirely. I thought it was strange at the time but the aesthetic was beautiful – me with a lot of greens and Carey with reds," Emma reflected on the dinner.

"No, it's not the colors – it's what Carey had in most of his dishes... tomatoes. Did you have any?" Karen went on.

"No."

"Hold on a second," Steve stood up and pulled a file from his briefcase. "Was there anything particularly noteworthy about the tomatoes?"

"Not really. Although now that I think about it, every one of the slices looked identical as though they had come from a perfect fruit. I think Carey even commented on how they looked like perfection," she added.

Steve started moving towards the phone when it rang. He picked it up. He held the receiver to his ear for an extended period of time and then replaced it.

"Karen, may I have a word with you in private?" he asked.

The two of them stepped into the shielded briefing room – Sun's playground they called it – and were there for almost 5 minutes.

When they emerged they both had distracted looks on their faces. Karen headed for the door and disappeared. Steve turned to face the group.

"It appears that we all would be well advised to mourn our friends' passing and move on. The information I have just received indicates that further inquiry would be counter-productive. Carey and Keith will be missed. But we have a job to do so let's get moving."

"Still bullshit," Dan retorted. "I don't believe a word of this story. No offense, Emma. I'm not saying that you're not telling the truth. I'm just saying that I don't believe that what meets the eye is the truth."

"Dan," Jonas intervened, "you, of all people, should know by now that the truth is what will be the story most repeated. In time, it will become the truth. You need to clear your head and get on with what we need to do."

"Emma, can I drive you home?" Steve offered.

"Thanks. I think I'll walk." And without picking up her suitcase, she walked out into the Park and headed down West Drive. A group of young men were playing Frisbee on the grassy field. She sat down on a bench and watched them until they were done. She liked young, athletic men. Their bodies were intriguing. The way their shoulders were so wide and their backs were so long. Glistening with the summer's humidity and sweat, watching these beautiful, lively beings it dawned on her that she'd been so caught up with work that she hadn't indulged romance for a while. And then, as if a specter from hell, the image of Keith and Carey's mangled bodies flooded back only to be exorcised when a young man came by, stopped, asked her if she was o.k. The young man had a camera and an iPad.

"Would you sit with me for a moment?" she asked the young man.

"Certainly," he replied, sitting down not too close. "Sorry, I've been working all day so I'm pretty fresh," he said with a slight smile.

"Oh, that's o.k.," she replied, "I've just flown in from Europe where two of my friends just died."

"I'm so sorry," he said. "What happened?"

"They were killed," she replied trying to get used to reconciling her sense of truth with the events she saw.

"Where did it happen?" he continued.

"At a beautiful hotel on the North Sea – a place called Hotel van Oranje."

"That's interesting," the young man said. "That's one of my Dad's favorite hotels."

"Well, I doubt I'll ever go back there again. I'd never be able to go without thinking about what happened there. Sorry for keeping you and thanks for stopping. Have a good evening."

## CHAPTER 12 – ONE HOT SUMMER

The heat wave across the country couldn't have come at a better time. Forty days above 100 degrees with nighttime temperatures stuck in the 80s was taking its toll across the South and East. Elderly, homeless, the newly unemployed all found themselves suffering under the oppressive heat and humidity. Two-a-day football practices were already being tragically punctuated with 17 year olds dying from heat stroke. Steve and the Operators were collecting a staggering amount of data and they weren't having to lift a finger. Mother Nature was doing their work for them. This time, the response modeling was much easier than it had been in 2003.

Thankfully, the joint U.S. and Canadian task force led by then-Canadian Natural Resource Minister Herb Dhaliwal and U.S. Energy Secretary Spencer Abraham had thrown FirstEnergy under the bus and had glossed over the GE Unix platform collapse when the signal had fried the unshielded computers across the Northeastern grid. The lads at HAARP had cooperated with a power up and system test at 4:04 pm ET – enough lead time to distract all the conspiracy theorists to conclude that the ionospheric weapon caused the August 14, 2003 fun. Their small EMP test targeting GE's vulnerability in Ohio actually got the ball rolling and HAARP simply amplified the confusion. So, while not catalyzing the first system failure, it had been very effective in confounding all investigators with communications and IT failures across the effected region.

Best of all, the entirety of essential data on the Distraction had, in fact, been erased from all terrestrial servers. All of the sensitive AIG files were corrupted during a post-bell back-up and were irreparably damaged. All of the computers that held any of the Operators' communications were irradiated so as to make their final incineration an unnecessary precaution. All the best forensic experts at Kroll couldn't have lifted a single fingerprint off of any hard drive. Steve had seen to it that there were no back up files anywhere and, with the burst on August 14, there was no chance that posterity would ever find what could not be found.

This summer's experiments were different. Sun was monitoring peak load data to see how the grid responded to load balancing and conveniently, Virginia and Texas were roasting and New Jersey wasn't far behind. The Richmond FRIT facility at the West Creek Operations Center seemed to be most stable given the fact that the nuclear power source was relatively close and the urban power demand in Richmond was declining with the decreasing industrial activity in the city and surrounding counties. The East Rutherford Facility (CC2) was a bit more problematic due to the growing demand for air conditioning resulting from the massive server cooling requirements demanded by the quant and derivative traders. CC3 in Dallas was a nightmare. The consumer demand for basic air conditioning and cooling was overloading all power production and CC3 was firing up their generators so often that the emergency diesel supply was constant. With the 42nd day of temperatures soaring over 100 degrees and with the growing threat of water crises from the unrelenting draught, climate expediency was playing into the Enterprise plan well beyond their wildest dreams.

"Make sure that West Creek becomes the citadel," Cecil had remotely instructed the Operators during the briefing scheduled for the first week of July. "The more resilience testing shows it to be the favored location for the backbone of the systems, the more we can confirm our targeting."

Sun was doing his magic on mapping systemic susceptibilities and response times. Meanwhile Munkhbat was finally proving himself a worthy member of the team as Dan took him through Special Forces and demolition training. Much to Dan's surprise – and, essential for the erasure – Munkhbat was particularly adept at aquatic operations. He was capable of intrusion and extraction reminiscent of some of Dan's old Singaporean buddies. While Dan still carried a deep-seated suspicion and anger about losing Carey at this critical point, Munkhbat was looking like he'd make a suitable replacement. The Arab Spring had mercifully extended into the summer so lethal force training could be done under the cover of sectarian and faction violence in Libya and Syria. Munkhbat had some major jitters after his first close-combat kill. Watching a human being die when you're close enough to hear their gurgling last breaths is so much more difficult than their early assassination sniper training. The warmth of the blood from another human being, when you know that its evacuation is due to your blade, takes some getting used to. Watching his student, Dan decided that he'd keep the lethal training to adults only. Killing kids would be too high a risk for his young student.

Karen had spent the past month in D.C. getting people back on script. The Transportation Secretary, turned Director of the CIA, turned Secretary of Defense – the perfect cocktail for the Enterprise's bidding with his understanding of air travel vulnerabilities back in the Disruption all the way to the present EMF hardening – was advised to back off the vitriol about China and Iran. The episode in the Netherlands had cost the Enterprise two extremely talented resources and, just before the bodies were cremated at the families' requests, an enthusiastic pathologist noted that there was a curious anomaly. Traces of anthrax had been found in one of the corpses and there were some indications that one of the bodies fell from the balcony already deceased. As he left the lab in the evening, the forensic pathologist on the inquest was unfortunately struck by a passing motorist. Luckily the accident was not fatal but the blow to his head had mercifully erased all short term memory of the day. When he was fully recovered, he would be transferred to a government post and his cases would be assumed by someone else. The account of his accident was on the third page of the paper in Amsterdam. Nobody knew him and no one would care.

Elizabeth and Emma made the mistake of pulling Interpol records and found that Darius had traveled with two of his former bio-engineers, advisors to the National Center for Research on Biological Engineering. Connie had been accompanied by a security detail however the only credentials they could find ran into dry wells. The names that came back matched with slightly under 13 million Chinese current passports. Trying to run them to ground was as helpful as looking for 'John Smith' in the States. Notwithstanding the paucity of information, Emma was convinced that Darius and Connie had arranged for her colleagues' deaths. Elizabeth was equally convinced but spent her time talking Emma out of confronting Steve with the 'evidence'.

"Nothing good will come of this," Elizabeth admonished Emma.

"If they're capable of killing Carey and Keith, what's to stop them from taking us out?" Emma protested.

"Listen, from a conversation I had with Karen, it sounds like they blamed Carey and Keith for Panetta's fingering of Iran and China on the EMP front. While it made great theater, there are lines even we can't cross," Elizabeth continued. "If you remember back to Control, Cecil specifically asked for you to observe the event so somebody trusts you. You're probably the safest one of us all."

"When's Karen coming back?" Emma inquired.

"She'll be back at the end of the week. With the musical chairs in D.C. between the DoD and CIA, she has been making sure that we don't have any distractions – keeping everyone singing from the same song sheet."

"I haven't seen Jonas for a few weeks," Emma changed the subject. "Do you know what he's been up to?"

"The last I heard he was heading down to Rio to meet up with Lord Haverford and Gabriela. Seems that something's moving with the on-line entertainment play and, from the recent news reports, it appears that the account information is almost fully transferred. Once they get a user profile on the gamers, gamblers and porn addicts, they'll start using user surcharges to start moving the last of the cash. A few dollars here and there times millions of users and, before long, we should be ready to roll."

✉

The antenna array tucked away in the steppes to the east of Ulaanbaatar served a vital role during the Russian occupation. The ability to detect radio signals bounced off the atmosphere gave the Kremlin eyes and ears on a world bristling with perceived threats. In a landscape dotted with gers, flocks of sheep, yak, and horses, to say it has a 'conspicuous presence' is the understatement. Surrounding the array, the collapsing brick and concrete barracks provided ideal camouflage for a massive installation of small satellite dishes. Given that all the lads at NGIC knew that these installations were long abandoned, low resolution surveillance monotonously confirmed the legacy archeology and paid no attention to the deposition of high tech signal detection which now read the skies with impunity. As long as the Orca Mission transmitted no signal, it could collect signals from about 950 satellites without anyone being the wiser. For the past 18 months, signal profiles had been correlated with equatorial and southern hemisphere sites ranging from southern Canada to Chile, from Mongolia to Hobart and from Iceland to Cape Town. Two equatorial 'floaters' powered by wave-action power generators were deployed each time there was a tsunami threat and, as fate would have it, several 7.1 or greater coastal quakes had made the proliferation of these antennae much more rapid than the plan had modeled. Orca tsunami warning buoys would be placed as far north as California and as far south as Sydney. Using the old Cobra orbital model, the combination of inter-satellite transmission combined with terrestrial bounces made Orca's detection sweep invisible.

Two decades earlier, Cyrus had been involved with a cryptography project which pushed the technical and mathematical skills of defense signal intelligence. In addition to the child's play of dynamic fractal ciphers – a process in which failure to correctly input a key would unleash unspeakable damage on the intruding technology – he had come up with an ingenious encryption tool. Using the tritium decay unique to each clock on each satellite, one could integrate the satellite transmission sequence on bounced signals to dynamically encrypt information during transmission. This allowed the U.S. Navy to deploy virtually untraceable signal transmission options using their aircraft carrier communications infrastructure and provided best in class detection evasion. The tritium decay transmission cipher was never officially deployed but, Cyrus never forgot the key. He figured one day it might come in handy.

Data transmission from collection points had been downright ingenious. The cipher for each collection point was comprised of ancient symbols or languages of the indigenous peoples that once occupied the coordinates of collection. Given the Occidental bias of current communications, this antiquities-based signal transmission was like the Navajo Wind Talkers on steroids.

Data storage was even more inconceivable. For years, genetic researchers had marveled at what they described as excessive 'junk DNA' – amino acid sequences which appear to play no significant role in the manufacture of essential proteins. Into this 'junk', researchers began to experiment with encoding messages. Craig Ventner and his team of scientists playfully encoded Shakespearean sonnets into DNA and then had the sonnets reproduce in off-spring demonstrating the capacity for generational, organic data storage. Certain species were more amenable to data replication than others making the race for living data storage barely a glimmer on the horizon. Horus had quietly sponsored two independent laboratories – one in the West and one in Asia – to work on a variation of the theme.

Using flora and fauna that were commonly found in ancient hieroglyphs and symbols, their teams had found that ancient civilizations may have left clues in their art for something far more profound than animistic rituals and symbols as had been popularly believed by historians. In fact, one particular fish that seemed to show up in hieroglyphs from Continental Europe, to the Americas, to North Africa to Asia and India not only was a phenomenal data repository and reproducer but, more importantly, there was another attribute to these creatures that they found noteworthy. When swimming in schools, these fish move in giant flashes of singular, luminous turns. What triggered these instantaneous, collective movements had been a puzzle for as long as humans have observed the phenomenon. The Horus team had solved the signaling and movement puzzle and with it, had the ability to control this latent, organic optical signal. The best news for the Orca Mission was that, not only was the principle of living, generational data storage thought to be too outlandish to be considered, the notion that animal behavior could be a controlled technology was beyond the imaginations of everyone. Well, almost everyone.

There are a few things that you can count on in life. One of the safest bets you can make is that, when a group of people elect to engage in a nefarious set of acts together, mistrust will be a cancer that, in time will grow into a malignancy. Cyrus' bet was that, if Orca could extract information from Jerry's satellites, it would be likely that considerable data would be persistent. Why Jerry? Because, he figured, of all the people who would want to insure that his ego was eternal, the best person to pick is someone who had already trafficked eternity and ego.

The bet paid out beyond his wildest dreams. Chirping high above the Earth in his angels of darkness, Jerry had backed up the communications surrounding the Disruption, the Enterprise's capital structure and financials, and, an unexpected gem. The 'pearl of great price' was a most unexpected window into the place to look for the last clues. Inside a file named "Heavenly Hosts" was a poorly encrypted file labeled "Tishman". And in that file was the design specifications for an ingenious antennae array that had been built into the Petronas Towers in Malaysia, One Canada Square in London and the mother-lode found in the detailed specifications of the Goldman Sachs tower in Jersey City. In each of these files, the Horus team found countless records of discussions that had taken place with Chan Siew, Lord Haverford, Steve, Jonas, and Kate during every step of the construction of these megalithic buildings. What was of particular note was the absence of certain Shareholders' names from any of the minutes or correspondence. Was it possible that a subset of the Enterprise had, or was planning to go rogue?

Embedded within the steel, glass and concrete buildings was one of the most sophisticated antennae arrays ever constructed. These buildings were either designed to receive or transmit information without detection and, within six weeks, Orca's ears were on to every signal emitted. As it happened, the Enterprise had decided to deploy Ayman's asset movement strategy using signals that were processed by zombie terminals in these structures. Tapping into the information was simple once you knew where the antennae fed the beast. Horus had leased office space in close proximity to all three towers and, the collection was on. All relevant data was transmitted to Orca Mission headquarters, analyzed and then encoded into fish.

With the S&P downgrade of U.S. Treasuries – a harbinger of negative economic forces to come – the Enterprise needed to move quickly to finish their asset reallocation. For this, they turned to one of their old associates – Bart Ivanhoe. For the past four years, he had assisted China, Singapore and Myanmar with a shadow gold stock-piling exercise. His past four mines had been announced with a short bit of fanfare but quickly vanished from his signature self-aggrandizing promotion modus operandi. No public company. No pump and dump racket on the exchanges in London, Toronto, New York, or Sydney. No Goldman Sachs underwriters. Uncharacteristic silence. However, the geospatial data told a very different story. Massive mines were being built and considerable processing and pouring infrastructure was visible. It's just that the gold didn't seem to show up on any market. Why would a greedy, self-serving metals cowboy diverge from his usual strategy? The answer was simple. He had a better value proposition. He would mine the gold and pour it for reserve stock-piling. At the appropriate time, China would lead an eight nation consensus to announce the end of Bretton Woods – the end of the dollar's hegemony – and replace gold as the anchor for a commodity-based currency standard. After this audacious move they would announce gold holdings far in excess of two times the official Foreign Reserve data. And in exchange for enabling this strategy, he would be given carte blanche to any metals he wanted up to ten percent of gross production.

Steve arranged a meeting hosted by Patrick in Singapore and the new Wynn property. They were joined by Connie, Jonas, Chan Siew and Lord Haverford.

"We've got about $5 billion left to move into gold," Chan Siew said over dinner in the private dining room perched atop the magnificent boat-shaped signature structure of the casino.

"You and everybody else," sneered Bart slurping down vibrantly red tuna sashimi. "Why don't you get in line with every other latecomer?"

"So, mate, it's going to be one of those nights?" Lord Haverford snapped withholding none of the disdain he felt for this brash tycoon.

"When gold crossed $1,400 per ounce, we knew that it could hit $2,500 – God bless the emotions of people living in the past illusion about having an inflation hedge," Bart softened a bit.

"We bought about $3 billion before the run," Jonas began, "but we had to buy in small enough increments to avoid too much attention."

"Now, my friend," Bart slumped in his seat a bit, bringing his towering torso low enough to establish eye contact, "you have MY attention. Who are you running from?"

"Not running from," Jonas continued. "Embracing in an anaconda-like hug."

"I don't know what you think you could possibly offer me that would be more valuable than what I've already received from my current business partners," Bart said.

"How about a chance to travel without restrictions and free of all your arrest warrants? How about having your name cleared of all charges?" Steve tossed the comment into the conversation with a dismissive nonchalance designed precisely to put the bait in the clear view of the predator.

"And how, pray tell, do you think that the IRS, the SEC and others will turn away when they see me coming?" Bart inquired, his voice clearly evidencing that the hook was setting.

"We have a seat at the table of a proposition which we think you'll find quite compelling – the seat's been cold for over ten years as one of our number met an untimely demise. And, we'll sell you that seat for $5 billion in bullion," Steve deflected the question.

"No!" Bart retorted. "Answer my damn question before you make any goddamn ask."

"Are you familiar with EMP?" Lord Haverford inquired, his English accent calming the tension in the room.

"Yeah, I've read a bit here and there," Bart offered.

"Well, let me tell you what's going to happen to all your IRS and SEC records in a few more months..." Jonas' voice dropped into a professorial aloofness that transfixed everyone in the room. He detailed Phase III and could watch Bart's eyes brighten with every new piece of the plan. The idea of purging a past that had haunted ever since the EPA nonsense in the early days, of seeing his form of justice meted out to those who had made his life so miserable was intoxicating. By the end of the monologue, he was drunk.

"Where do you need the gold?" he asked when Jonas had finished his explanation.

"Precisely where it is right now," Steve replied.

"How the hell do you know where it is – if it is even really there?" Bart shot back.

Connie smiled. "Really?" she asked. "Do you really think that we don't know where it is? Oh, Bart, you sometimes underestimate your partners. This is not good for you or for them."

For a country that could hide platoons of terracotta warriors for centuries, the idea of stealth takes on meaning that mystifies the Occidental mind. Ever since the Olympic traffic had eased the tourist loads at famous sights around the country, renovation had commenced on everything from the Temple of Heaven to the Great Wall at Badaling. The removal of each brick held the promise of another secret passage or chamber sealed by long forgotten masters and shrouded by three generations of cultural amnesia. With each uncovering, a new option for warehousing gold, data, even people, became ever more expansive.

"We know where the SAFE really is my dear Bart. We know and it's best if you are with us. Do you understand?" Connie was impossible to resist oozing her elegant, Chinese charm.

The other Shareholders were dumb-founded when they heard Steve's announcement that a 1/12 fractional interest in the Enterprise had just been sold for $5 billion in gold bullion. The funny thing about the valuation of a closely held private company is that news like this is an elixir: that is, if you're not estimating taxes. While they knew that Bart's inclusion in the Enterprise would be essential to insure their wealth after Phase III concluded, Darius and Ayman were less than thrilled with the moral character of the man that had now joined them. Surely there could have been someone else who would represent the elegance and decorum they ascribed to themselves.

Gabriela, on the other hand, had always found Bart's larger than life outlaw bravado a turn-on and, while age had dampened his youthful zeal, her invitation to a weekend in Florianopolis was every bit the hedonistic erotic fantasy she needed for a bit of spice. His bleached white skin amplified the beauty of her bronzed skin unblemished by unsightly tan lines. One weekend served as ample fuel to fire a mutually selfish ecstasy in which they both reveled and for which their maturity held ample room for discretion.

Henri invited Steve to dinner in the meat-packing district in New York City. He hadn't been around for the Bart announcement and wanted to have a face-to-face with Steve. In his assessment, Steve had lost sight of the fact that while they all had trusted his leadership and his plan, a decision the size of an ownership stake in the Enterprise should have been done in consultation with all the Shareholders.

"It's not that I don't see his value," Henri said as they ordered martinis from a statuesque cocktail waitress whose cleavage and sculpted thighs should have been worth a break in their concentration. "It's the principle of the magnitude of this decision. After all, we have all built a relationship on absolute trust and confidence and I don't know how you think you can control one of America's baddest bad boys."

"Henri, I hear what you're saying and I understand your concern," Steve began. "It's just that we had to make a move and, given how much we need to have the State Council placated, this appeared to be the only way forward."

"How do we know that we can trust Connie, the State Council or any of the Chinese at a moment like we're in? Europe's finances are a mess. Our banks are about to follow Lehman into hell. Greece, Spain and Italy are racing each other over the cliff. And the U.S. is moribund until at least 2013. How do we know that we're going to be able to harvest the fruits of our labors when we fry Richmond?" his voice was serious and concerned.

"What would you want me to do, Henri?" Steve asked, knowing that there was no 'best-practices' mumbo jumbo that Henri could pull out of his consulting repertoire.

"I feel like I'd like to find a way to take some money off the table," he offered. "I would like to diversify. You know, maybe buy some land; get in on some South American oil, something else."

"Sorry pal," Steve felt a twinge of rage coming on. You could question his judgment up to a certain point but, this sounded like a no-confidence vote and he was not favorably disposed. "Until we conclude Phase III, our fortunes rise and fall together."

Henri outranked Steve in his ability to influence the world's most powerful corporate giants. He was friends with countless politicians across the globe. Being dismissed by Steve was not an easy pill to swallow but he knew that, at the end of the day, there was no way he could find a means of redress for his concerns.

"You should try the ribeye here," Steve said looking up from the menu. "They rub it with Mongolian salt mined in the Gobi Desert."

"I can't say that I've had Mongolian salt rubbed into anything before," he glowered, still seething about Steve's unwillingness to show the slightest empathy.

✦

Sun took a walk in the Park with Emma. For the past few weeks he had taken her under his wing as he knew that she was covering up deep seated hostility for the events in Holland. She was a valuable resource, the glue that held the team together, and he didn't want to see her bolt. At the same time, he didn't blame her. After all, she had been the one that Cecil had ordered to witness the execution. That had to be a heavy burden.

"How are the peak load models coming?" Emma asked as they rounded the west side of the lake.

"We're pretty sure that we know enough to create a decoy event," he began. "But you know me and remote simulations. I still can't get the Ambassador and his family out of my mind."

"Seriously?" she asked with incredulity. "It's been a decade and you're still holding onto that?"

"Emma," he was speaking softly, "you never get things like that out of your head."

"Some consolation for what I'm dealing with buddy," she slapped his shoulder playfully.

"I don't know how Dan and Munkhbat do it," Sun continued. "The idea of actually being the one to pull the trigger is inconceivable to me. Hell, my actions have killed a lot of people but I don't have to see them die. I don't have to see those who are immediately impacted – the families, friends, you know. I've never figured out how to exorcise my dreams. Sure hope you have better luck."

"I'm not sure what I am having a harder time with," Emma mused. "I miss Carey every day… yeah, I miss him. Not so much Keith. But I can't seem to shake my conviction that Darius and Connie were directly involved – who knows, maybe even did the killing themselves. And worst of all, there's no way to know what actually happened because no one will ever be allowed to ask."

"That's where you have to just let it go, girl," Sun tried to be as empathetic as he could. "Until we're done in another 18 months, you need to focus on what you've got to do. After that, you better find a great man, settle down and put this life behind you."

"Speaking of what I have to do," she probed, "I can't say I know what the hell I'm supposed to be doing. Ever since I got back I feel like everyone's working but me. It's giving me the creeps. If I'm not focused on something, I've got too much time to think."

"Why don't you bring that up with Jonas and Steve?" Sun replied. "If you tell them that you're ready to be operational again, I'm sure they'll put you on something. Hell, it's been months since we've had anyone officially tracking Horus. That little shit Cyrus just refuses to die but it seems that he's off our trail, at least for now."

"Not so fast," Emma blurted. "From the moment I met him in Switzerland, there was something about him that didn't settle well with me. It wouldn't surprise me if he's just gone deep. Unless somebody takes him out, there's no sanctuary and even then, according to the guys that left, he's planted poison pills that detonate if he doesn't contact certain people on a frequency no one has figured out. According to Hank, he said Cyrus told him that critical data on 'perpetrators and their actions' was stored off-site and that if anything happened to him, he'd take down a wide swath of those in power...including us."

"Why didn't he come onside with the Enterprise? After all, Steve must have made him an amazing offer," Sun inquired.

"You're asking a question that I don't think has an answer that any of us would understand," Emma answered. "The only thing that I'm fairly certain will seduce him is the thrill of the hunt. Once he's got it in his mind that he's going to settle scores, I would hate to be in his way."

"Any chance that he had a hand in the events in Holland?" Sun mused.

"No." Emma said reflexively. "That one was an inside job."

⚑

The phone at Control hadn't rung in weeks. Nobody really noticed it until it did.

"Asset transfers are complete – we're operational," crackled the voice through the speaker.

"I'm assuming that this means that we're going gaming?" Dan said, not as much to the phone as to his colleagues.

"You will all be transferred to Auckland – that is, all but Emma," the voice continued without divulging any change in meter or tone.

"Auckland?" Jonas said looking surprised.

"When you get there, you'll meet up with Jerry's boat and, for the next few weeks, we're going to turn into a naval operation," Cecil said.

At 3:37 in the morning, flames started flickering on the second story of the building. By the time a Park patrol saw the fire and smoke, three floors were engulfed. The NYFD response was slowed slightly by the traffic control for the President's visit to New York that morning. He was going to make a speech on Wall Street in an attempt to shore up confidence in the flagging U.S. stock market. By the time they got to the building, there was no saving it. The fire fighters needed to do what they could to contain the collateral damage to adjacent buildings.

When she went out for her morning run, Emma instinctively looked over her left shoulder towards Control. At first glance, she didn't register that the entire façade was blackened in the pre-dawn light. Two more steps and the image seared back into her brain and she looked again. Control was gone.

## *CHAPTER 13 – TOO BIG TO FAIL*

"You look lovely tonight, my Lady," Cyrus said as Emilie emerged from around the corner of the expansive bathroom in their suite at the InterContinental Hotel in Alexandria.

She was wearing a breathtaking Nicole Miller dress – deep emerald green – and an exquisite necklace with matching earrings made from South Sea black pearls. Over the past few months, her new fitness routine was paying huge dividends and tonight, at the event at the Biblioteca Alexandrina, she would be turning the heads of everyone with any testosterone swirling in their bloodstream. Cyrus had been invited to speak to an audience on strategies for renewed vitality in the post-transition Egyptian economy. The event had been sponsored by a number of his long-time friends in the region and was the first international forum held since the uprising that ousted Hosni Mubarak.

"You're not hard on the eyes yourself, silly," she giggled as she stopped to inspect herself in the full length mirror.

"I do the best with what nature has given me," he said as he walked over and ran his hand down her back with just enough finger tips to get a little scratch on her skin.

"Do that and we'll never leave the room," she chided.

He grabbed her, held her tightly to his chest and planted a kiss on her forehead.

"Thanks for coming on this trip," he whispered. "I'm always better with you around."

"I wouldn't miss it for the world. Not your speech, of course, but our Nile cruise," she teased.

"Are you ready?" he asked her.

"Do I really look alright?" she pleaded with her signature, imploring tone.

"Which part of 'beautiful' do I need to explain?" he said the same way he'd said it a thousand times before.

"Thanks," she beamed and reached for the door.

The event was a spectacle to behold. Close to 700 guests assembled around sumptuous tables overflowing with the most amazing cuisine. On the way in, metal detectors scanned everyone and, inside the reception hall, sharply appointed security guards wanded all the guests to make doubly sure that there was no disruption. The security did nothing to dampen the festive mood within the hall and, by the time Cyrus was done with his speech, the sense of national pride and identity was evident in the boisterous conversations echoing through the building. The idea that Egypt could serve as a proof-of-concept for taking the best of Islamic financial and social models and integrating them with a re-discovery of the country's long history as being a trading center for the world's cultures was a message that energized the crowd. Against the cacophony of economic failures across Europe and America, the notion that a new normal was emerging which included previously side-lined countries and economies actually sounded like it just might work. At least for the evening, there was hope.

They got back to the hotel at 12:30 in the morning, a waxing moon lighting the promenade and the sea beyond.

"It's beautiful isn't it Cyrus?" Emilie said, her arm tightening around his.

"I told you you'd love it here," he smiled back.

"I never imagined that I'd ever get a chance to see Egypt and I feel like it's all a dream," she went on, her voice drifting in the light breeze that played with her flowing hair.

She was brushing her teeth when Cyrus got a text on his phone. Four tsunami sensors had triggered in the Southern Pacific.

"Hey babe, I'm going to switch on the news for a second," he called to her.

"You'll regret it, my little Pharaoh," she called back. "Tonight I'm going to be your Cleopatra."

He laughed as he switched on the news. BBC already was reporting the breaking news. A series of four 7.1 magnitude earthquakes had occurred within a few minutes of each other. One epicenter was just outside Christchurch – still reeling from the seismic actions early that year. The second was in Japan and, while communications were quite disrupted, the reports were suggesting that Fukishima had gone from disaster to apocalypse. The third was off the Aleutians. But it was the fourth that drew his attention the most. The New Madrid fault in the middle of the U.S. had slipped and the devastation from Arkansas through Missouri and into Illinois was unfathomable. Dams and levies all along the Mississippi and Arkansas Rivers had been breached. Three interstates were impassable due to collapsed bridges. In a word, the earth had heaved with a severity the likes of which defied hyperbole.

They stood next to each other as images of devastation raced across the screens.

"My God, Cyrus, this is unbelievable," Emilie said as she took in the flood of information.

"You know what's so weird?" he said sinking into his analytic sobriety. "They all had the same magnitude and they all happened within minutes of each other. It's as though they were triggered."

"You can't trigger an earthquake, can you?" Emilie asked. "I know that they tried to do it in James Bond's *A View to A Kill* but that was Hollywood."

"There are technologies that have been suggested to have the capacity to do this kind of thing," he provided little specificity because his mind was racing.

"I hope our friends in Samoa and Fiji are o.k.," Emilie continued.

"They should be fine," he replied. "I've got our buoys sending updates and the islands should just see big waves like super high tides. It shouldn't do too much damage."

"Should I call the kids?" Emilie always wanted to ask permission for something that Cyrus knew she'd do anyhow.

"Why don't you," he said.

She reached for her phone and dialed Anna. There was no connection. She tried Sorin next.

"All circuits are busy do to increased traffic," the automated voice said.

"Where are the kids now, Cyrus?" Emilie asked rhetorically.

She knew that they had taken the weekend to go to see the NY Giants play up at the new stadium in East Rutherford.

"I think I have the number of the Embassy Suites at the Meadowlands," he offered looking in his phone.

He dialed it and got the operator.

"Could I speak to Sorin or Anna Alexander please?" he asked the young man who answered the phone.

"Let me connect you now," the young man said.

Sorin answered the phone.

"Hey Dad," he said, "we were just getting ready to go out to dinner at the Outback Steakhouse."

"Great, brother," Cyrus said. "Are you and Anna having a good time?"

"Yes," he said. "How about you and Mom?"

"We're having a great time. We just wanted to check on you guys with what just happened in Arkansas."

"What happened?" Sorin replied.

"A major earthquake. Turn on the News."

"Holy shit," Sorin exclaimed as the TV flicked to life. "This looks terrible."

"Yeah, there were four big ones – three in the Pacific and one in the middle of the U.S. Make sure you get home safe after the game tomorrow and why don't you and your sister stay at the house until things clear up…," Cyrus didn't finish because Anna got on the other line.

"Dad," she said, "the TV has just flashed an emergency alert saying that all phone lines are being prioritized for emergency communications so we may…"

The line went dead.

"They're doing great, Love," Cyrus said to Emilie.

"Thanks for calling them. Now, any chance that you can take me to bed or are you too distracted?"

"If by distracted, you mean that I can't take my eyes and hands off you, yes," he said grabbing her around the waist and hoisting her onto the tall bed.

The economy was worsening on both sides of the Atlantic. The earthquakes insured that millions of people would be both economically and physically displaced. Infrastructure failures ground transportation to a halt. No east west railroad or highway from Arkansas north to Illinois was passable. Within 24 hours, the damage assessments started rolling in. Pipelines for gas, oil, water, sewer – everything was leaking, gushing, or destroyed. Power outages left over 35 million Americans in the dark. Hospitals were given priority for back-up generator fuel if it could reach them at all. The National Guard was deployed to provide some sense of order and preserve businesses from anticipated looting. Any hope of seeing the economy turn out of its death spiral trajectory towards recession or depression was dashed in the 50 seconds of the quaking earth.

On Sunday afternoon, President Obama gave a nationally televised address. In it he announced that, due to the extraordinary events that had just unfolded, only essential government services would be operational for the immediate future. The President's Cabinet had convened and had elected to temporarily close all non-essential financial institutions including all U.S. stock and commodities exchanges. This closure would persist until a basic assessment could be made regarding the extent of the devastation of everything from power to communications to the projected fall harvest abundance of wheat, soybeans, corn and other agriculture commodities, all of which now couldn't be accounted for at all. Since the midpoint in his first campaign for the White House, his oratory skills had been cowed behind a teleprompter. Given the degree to which every word he chose to utter was, in fact, a carefully market-tested signal architected by a Los Angeles marketing and media agency for precise effect, his impulse to empathy came across as disingenuous.

"America was, is, and always will be the strongest nation on earth," the puppet mouthed, unconscious of the ventriloquist's intrusive hand. "While we have been shaken in this moment of trial, our nation will show the world that we are resilient, united, and free."

At a moment when over ten percent of the population was without water, power or food, appealing to some nostalgic ideology may have sounded good to the Californian script writer who was just glad the San Andreas hadn't blown. But if you were in touch with the suffering across America's heartland, a bit more empathy and acknowledgement of loss may have been more appropriate.

During the Disruption, the world came to the aid of the U.S. in an unprecedented outpouring of generosity and concern. In return, Homeland Security treated all citizens of the world to mug-shots, fingerprints, travel restrictions and every other imaginable intrusion on hospitable gratitude. Rather than rising in the light of freedom from the rubble of fallen towers, President Bush led the country into a dusty, fiery hell of torture, renditions, Guantanamo, and endless wars. The world grieved with us and we returned more grief.

"How are things going over there Emma?" Steve inquired when he had raised her on the satellite phone.

"It's a mess," she replied.

"We are three days north of Auckland and, damned if we didn't feel the wave roll under the *Genesis* as it went under us. Nothing serious but I'll bet that some of the Pacific islands had some amazing surfing if they were up for it." His cavalier tone was somewhat unsettling.

"From the reports I've seen, the area from the Rockies to the Ohio River Valley is largely incapacitated. Bridges out, roads destroyed, this one was a real doozie," she said.

"Is anybody talking about the cause?" Jonas took the phone from Steve and inquired.

"Not a word anywhere," Emma replied.

"Let us know the minute you hear anyone suggesting that this could have been a triggered event," he instructed her. "We're monitoring all the news feeds we can from here and we need you to do the same."

"Well, that's a bit difficult given the fact that all signals have been pre-empted for emergency broadcasts," Emma said dryly.

"Yeah, don't look to the TV – we're already controlling all of that. I'm more interested in what comes up on the social media crawlers. Since we got Goldman to grab the control of Facebook, what we've got them doing is some sentiment analysis and I've already got their crawlers sweeping for any whispers. As soon as they come up, we're taking them down but we need to track everyone who may be on to unauthorized inquiries," Jonas said with a foreboding tone.

"Who all's with you down there?" Emma inquired. "Are the Shareholders all together?"

"No. A few of us are in the general vicinity but everyone's gone mobile for now," he replied.

"Without Control operational, how is Cecil going to be communicating with us? Or, more importantly, me?" Emma sounded very conscious of how alone she was.

"You know your favorite bench on the Heckscher Fields side of West Drive – the one where you go to visit your ghosts? Well, on the left arm rest, there's a small latch that opens to reveal a matchbox-sized drawer.  Check it each afternoon and, should you have a message, it will be there.  And it will be from Cecil."

"How did you know about 'my' bench?" she inquired.

"Oh Emma, ever since Carey and Keith died, you've worn a hole in it.  We saw you speaking with a young man there right after you got back and it seems that you return everyday hoping to find something that you've lost," Jonas actually was genuinely compassionate this time.

✉

When the markets opened six days later, the Dow, S&P and NASDAQ all fell so dramatically that trading was stopped intermittently in an attempt to stave off complete collapse.  European and Asian markets, all holding their breath during the suspension of trading followed suit.  Trillions of dollars of value was erased in the first week and there would be trillions more to go.  With no Chinese U.S. treasury buyers, it was now up to the banks, insurance companies and pensions – all required to buy fixed income products even when everyone now had long known that these 'investments' would never pay out – to buy the nonsense sold as Quantitative Easing III.  Bank of America was looking like it would hold.  Citi, with its princely patron unable to admit defeat, would persist in name as the cost of failure would be more damaging to ego than the money that was being thrown away.  J.P. Morgan Chase was excessively vulnerable given their reserve management strategy.  But most troubling was Goldman. They had sailed through 2008 looking like they were invincible given the fact that they had been given the privilege of picking the pockets of the taxpayers by running the funny money that the Treasury was printing. AIG's Maiden Lane securities, bailouts in every form, all were brokered both going and coming by Goldman and their fees were usurious. This time around, however, the same racket would draw too much scrutiny. They'd have to make it on their own.

"Goldman cannot collapse," Steve said during his call with the President on Tuesday morning.

"We let Lehman go and who even remembers Bear Stearns?" the President replied. "So why can't we kill off Goldman. The public hates them and they've been worthless in supporting me through the summer."

"Goldman is an AIG," Lord Haverford chimed in. "It's not that they have done anything to earn our sympathy, God knows. The problem is that Goldman is sitting on too much information to ever fall into the hands of a bankruptcy trustee. AIG couldn't be allowed to fail because it held too much classified data about the Disruption and a number of our covert funding programs since the Clinton Administration. Hell, Greece couldn't fail because without control of their intelligence services, all of our Near East operations would be at risk of exposure. When we've been using U.S. defense contractors to run money to our enemies to keep the 'War on Terror' simmering, we couldn't have some lefty from Brussels uncover that! Without Greece, we wouldn't have the IEDs that keep Americans fearful. And Goldman? Mr. President, you have no idea how far they've reached. From Somali pirates, to the Lord's Resistance Army, to resource conflicts across the globe – you lose control of Goldman's data and, well, Sir, you'd have to erase every computer from D.C. to New York to London not to risk an unrecoverable PR disaster."

"So, if I hear you correctly, gentlemen," the President lowered his voice slightly, "you're saying that we have to prop up Goldman again?"

"Sir," Jonas went into lecture mode again, "you have two options. Either you prop them up or you have to authorize an intervention that will wipe out any trace of any of their information."

"How would we go about the latter?" he asked innocently.

"Well, Sir," Steve replied, "we've got an expert here who can walk you through what could be done. He's been working with us from the beginning. His name is Sun."

"It's an honor, Sir," Sun stammered as he began to speak. He'd never spoken to the President of the United States before and, while he knew the President wasn't what the public assumed, he still was conscious of the office. "As you know, the Goldman Tower's construction included some highly classified security systems –

particularly given the proximity of the PATH to the building. We could use an underground electromagnetic pulse device on one of the trains to neutralize the building and its contents."

He paused to allow anyone to step in. Hearing nothing, he looked at Steve and Jonas and then continued.

"Sir, you would need to authorize such an action because it would take a high degree of coordination."

"What kind of casualty count would something like this entail?" the President asked, his voice slightly more engaged.

"Sir," Sun replied, "there should be little to no direct casualties. To be clear, the level of impulse we'd require could take out pacemakers, medical equipment, you know. So if anyone was in the neighborhood walking their dog, they'd probably keel over..."

"So we're talking about an acceptable risk?" the President interrupted.

"Yes Sir," Jonas snapped.

✄

Their Nile cruise had been magical. For seven days, Cyrus and Emilie had taken in the amazing hospitality of the Abercrombie & Kent staff. They had spent their nights topside on the boat in the company of a Cairo businessman and his wife and with another couple visiting Egypt from Vancouver. Tourism had taken an enormous hit from the Spring's uprisings and so every pyramid and temple offered a sumptuous, exclusive venue for exploration with their young Egyptian guide. She was an elegant young Muslim woman with impeccable English and her command of antiquities was legendary. Each cavernous tomb's former occupant came to life in her narrative. She wove a tapestry of history that seemed to include three punctuations with millennial amnesia. She could transit between 1500 BCE to European occupiers in the 19th century as though nothing but a coffee break separated these epochal shifts. But, despite the British motif of her delivery, the stories were captivating.

This was the first time Emilie had slept in a moving cabin on any mode of transportation without having some claustrophobic fit. Years earlier, trips on trains and boats, while magical during the days, were anything but during compartmented nights. In part, the stateroom that Cyrus had arranged aided in the illusion of a more terrestrial abode. In part, the waters of the Nile plied more easily than the Caribbean seas or the rail beds across Europe. The dividends this confidence paid were magnificent as, for the first time, Cyrus got to play out his Arabian Nights fantasies with a very willing co-star. During the days, the sun warmed their affections without creating oppressive heat or discomfort.

When they flew out of Cairo for an indigenous elder gathering in Cairns, they were so obviously affectionate that, at the airport, three complete strangers had inquired if this was their honeymoon.

"No," Emilie playfully smiled when asked by a rather uptight looking American woman who had been clearly disapproving of their public display of romance, "I'm having an affair with this married man."

The woman looked away in disgust as Emilie jumped up and gave Cyrus a squeeze around the neck.

The gathering in Cairns included elders from across the Pacific, shamanic practitioners from Arizona, Peru, Mexico, West Africa, and spiritual voyeurs from across the globe. With the growing enthusiasm around the much-heralded, yet deeply confused Mayan calendar punctuation in 2012, the line between cultural practice, wisdom, and charlatanism was, at best blurry and was compounded with every sacred plant and sweat lodge that attended the blooming serious experiences and cults. Emilie and Cyrus had been invited to attend as they were asked to sit on a panel discussing the intersection of Post-Industrial Social Orders with Indigenous Community Frameworks.

Flying through Singapore, they became immediately aware of how deeply out of touch they'd been in Egypt. They hadn't made a conscious effort to have a week away from the news but they certainly hadn't realized the magnitude of the devastation from the simultaneous earthquakes a few days prior. Japan's nuclear reactors were devastated and the radioactivity escaping into the seas, the air, and land was rendering massive areas uninhabitable. The Christchurch quake from earlier in the year had brought down far more than this one – in part because what was prone to fall had already collapsed. The only tsunami of any consequence had been in Alaska and, thankfully, it had hit no populated coastal areas to speak of. But the mess in the United States was monumental. Sitting in the Silver Kris lounge at Changai airport, the AFN and BBC broadcasts were indistinguishable. It was as though the news anchors were reading from the same script, Cyrus had commented to Emilie.

"I wonder how the kids are doing?" Cyrus asked, squeezing her hand.

"I spoke to Anna while you were getting our boarding passes," Emilie replied. "She and Sorin made it home without any trouble. She said that there were a lot of National Guard convoys on the highways and that some of the New York and New Jersey exits were closed but, by the time they got through the tunnel in Baltimore, everything seemed to be pretty normal."

"Did Sorin get back to campus?" Cyrus inquired.

"Yes, classes started on Tuesday evening and so he went back in the afternoon."

While they were sitting in the lounge, Cyrus' phone rang.

"How are things on the home front, Edward?" Cyrus started.

He didn't speak for a full five minutes as he was getting a download from Edward on updates from a week off the grid. He interrupted Edward only twice to remind him that he was in Singapore and the capacity for truly private conversations in a place like this was tenuous at best.

"I'll call you from Cairns," he said at the end of the briefing. "Should have a little bit of time there where I can step away."

"By the way, Cyrus," Edward said as he was getting ready to head to bed, "I just heard that my friend, Gray Wolf is coming to the event with a delegation of American elders. He has your picture and he'll find you when you're there."

"That's amazing," Cyrus said. "I'll make sure we connect."

The conference was not a traditional international conference by any stretch of the imagination. No cavernous halls. No PowerPoint presentations. No podiums, microphones, or amplifiers. In the hills just south of Cairns, a group of aboriginal elders had found a grove of trees whose sweeping branches formed shaded gathering areas for a comfortable seating of over 500 people. Attendees gathered at 8:30

in the morning, greeted with the sounds of drums, didgeridoos, and a variety of wind instruments. An observer would have thought they'd fallen through a time portal into the archives of the *National Geographic* as each delegation came in their customary dress. The colors included earth tones, brightly colored feathers and beads, gems, metals and flesh. It was an immense gathering.

The plenary session – if one were to ascribe labels to this event – was comprised exclusively of blessing and invocation rituals. And while there was no printed agenda or proscribed program per se, it was clear to see that each contributor held considerable grace around making a contribution without usurping too much time. After the opening, an elder from the Amazon got up.

"My Sisters and Brothers," he began. "One week ago we saw great lights in the sky – aurora of colors danced before the great shaking. In our circle, we knew that the movement of the earth was not part of the ordinary dance of mountains."

"Yes," an elder from Peru arose on the opposite side of the grove. "Our condors flew in a pattern that we've never known before. The nests that they return to each evening no longer called them."

"In our reef, the Red Emperor usually tells us when the earth will quake," said a short, dark-skinned man from one of the Pacific islands. "This time, the deep rolling sound that we hear did not happen. The birds circled the volcano but did not roost in their normal trees. In the past week, their nests have held no eggs."

One after another, story upon story painted a poetic, terrifying global consensus that whatever happened last week was not part of any natural order contained in a legacy wisdom metaphor. Cyrus and Emilie sat transfixed at the dance of speakers who shared their experience with the group. After thirty or forty minutes, what was abundantly clear was that whatever triggered the quakes fell outside of a convention on any plane. Cyrus wondered if it would be appropriate to introduce a possible, very human, very technological explanation for what could have unleashed the devastation. For communities of long-preserved cosmology, would it be appropriate to suggest that there are technologies which have been designed to turn the Earth itself into a weapon? What type of humanity – or inhumanity – would be required to think about using the ionosphere as an elastic weapon to target seismic effects on the land?

"A strange group of people came to our shores on the day I left New Caledonia," a rather stout woman spoke, her voice as lyrical as a tropical bird. "On their boat, they had all manner of devices – big metal kava bowls – and their souls were black. They came looking for food and water which we were happy to give them. But they had no manners, no gratitude. At night, they were very loud and very rude."

At the first break, Cyrus made his way across the crowd to the New Caledonian woman. After exchanging greetings Cyrus eagerly inquired about the boat. Her description was rife with metaphors through which he could discern that this was a luxury yacht of some sort. He continued to gently prod for information, attempting to remain respectful. After three or four minutes of questions, the woman stopped him.

"Would you like to see some pictures I took of the boat?" she said pulling out a brand new Canon DSLR. "I used my telephoto lenses on this one because I thought it may be helpful to have decent pictures of the boat and her occupants."

Cyrus could feel the cultural bigotry burn on his face. He had worked for years to maintain room for asymmetries like a woman in grass skirts and barefoot having a better digital camera than he owned. But, experience and all, old patterns of discrimination still have their way of manifesting regardless of how sensitive you think you've become.

"I don't suppose you could e-mail them to me?" he asked, pulling out all the stops.

"No worries," she said, "I've got a great 4G signal here so I'll send them right away."

After thanking her profusely, he walked back to Emilie who was holding court with a number of new found friends.

"I just made a complete ass out of myself," he said when she turned her attention to him.

"Stop the presses!" she playfully exclaimed. "Now that's the most amazing revelation I've heard all morning. You mean to tell me that somebody actually let you take a good look at yourself?"

"Thanks for the vote of confidence," he feigned being hurt.

"On this conclusion of our first day together, let us be reminded of the wisdom we know from our Sisters and Brothers of Qunsop Mountain – the great monument to human achievement. If we bring all of our people together and seek to achieve anything in this journey of life, so long as we work together, our combined energies cannot fail," concluded the same man who had opened the day.

"Why does it sound so much more believable coming from him than coming from a politician or banking executive?" Emilie mused rhetorically.

Sitting at his computer in the hotel room that night, he opened up the eleven high resolution images he'd received from Margaret. He didn't have to make it past the second image which showed the stern of the boat. In bright gold outlined blue letters was the name *Genesis*

2:25. What was an interesting anecdote was the number of faces he recognized – including one that used to be in his office on a daily basis.

## CHAPTER 14 – LIGHTNING STRIKES TWICE

"There's not much left for the team to review," Edward said during his morning briefing at the Horus offices. "We've got three scenarios fairly well detailed and, from everything I can see, we're not going to stop what they're calling Phase III."

Andrew chuckled. "Bizarre segue, I know, but what you just said reminded me of a story Lisa's dad told me. When he was a young man, he was working in a machine shop. One of the things he had to do was to wire several three phase motors in series to run a larger conveyor belt. As I recall, he said that these motors need to be wired identically – that while polarity doesn't matter – insuring that every motor is wired exactly the same does. Anyhow, he apparently wired one motor in the series wrong and when the conveyor belt fired up, everything worked fine except for the one motor that was wired with opposing polarity. It blew up and nearly took the whole machine shop with it. When his boss asked him if he had wired every motor the same, he insisted that he had. Only trouble was that the only remaining piece of the motor that blew up was the wiring plate with red, black and white still visible. And wrong."

"Hold on a second, Andrew," Cyrus jumped in. "That's brilliant."

"No," Andrew said, "Edward just said Phase III and my brain went down a rabbit hole about three phase motors...no brilliance save the explosion."

"Let's say, for the sake of argument," Cyrus continued, "that they erase the dollar. What that means is that a whole bunch of people lose a whole bunch of investments and savings. But what if, when they do this, we could use their EMP burst to trigger something that bites back?"

"How, pray tell, would you do that?" Andrew asked.

"Well," Edward interrupted, "we could turn their satellites on each other and, rather than backing up their files, we could corrupt them essentially leading to the erasure of all their asset transfers."

"Even better," Cyrus said, "we could move their assets to the accounts of others so that when they went to make a claim, there'd be nothing in their accounts."

"That's a bit too cliché – sounds like a modern day Robin Hood," Andrew protested. "I think having them wipe out their own assets would be a ton of fun. Kind of like the U.S. and Israel threatening to nuke Iran's reactors only to find out that China's secured the financing for these projects with U.S. dollar guarantees."

Without the glue of regular communication, the Shareholders' anxiety mounted. Henri, Lord Haverford and Gabriela arranged a meeting in London at Haverford's flat. Since Kate was in town for an

African famine benefit in the West End, she said that she'd drop by after 11pm. None of them were happy about how events were unfolding. While Henri and Gabriela suspected that Lord Haverford knew more than he let on, they needed a chance to air their concerns and this seemed to be the best place to do so. Since the earthquakes, they had heard nothing from Chan Siew or Patrick. Ever since the events in the Netherlands neither Connie nor Darius had been seen or heard from. And, none of them could recall the last time they'd actually spoke to Ayman.

"I've still got a bee in my bonnet over the Bart situation," Henri huffed as he took a sip of scotch.

"There was no other way to get off our currency risk, Henri," Lord Haverford replied. "I don't like that buffoon anymore than you do but no one else has curried enough favor with the Chinese to pull off what only Bart can do."

"Doesn't change for one minute the fact that I don't trust him, and frankly, with him, Steve, Connie and the rest of the lot," Henri wouldn't let it go.

"What have you gentlemen done to make sure that you're not fully dependent on the Enterprise?" Gabriela asked. She knew that no one else cared for Bart but talking about him made her uncomfortable even though she knew that their secrets were safe.

"Well, I know that Ayman's been purchasing an awful lot of real estate over the past 18 months and, from all I can tell, at least some of that is coming from our fees. Jerry's rolling in so much profit from his media business that I don't think he even cares. And our little Persian lion – who knows about what he's been up to," Henri evaded answering her question.

"There's no question that Connie's big win comes at the grand finale. In fact, I suspect that she may very well be the only one that actually wins in the end," Gabriela mused. "But what about you guys?"

"We moved all of our on-line gaming to Macau and Singapore now so we're feeling quite good that, come what may, we won't be destitute," Lord Haverford replied. "I'm sure you're finding that the demographics in Indonesia, China, and India are making your multi-gamer products much more lucrative. Nothing like having the one-child-policy one hundred million men who will never have a woman to marry spending money insatiably on video games to make you a handsome piece of change."

"Yes, it's working out quite nicely," she said, her voice halting. "But I have this nagging feeling that, if the quakes were not an accident, we could wind up as casualties if the erasure doesn't stay as precisely targeted as Steve and Jonas think it will be. And then what? Where do we go if it goes wrong?"

"That kind of thinking doesn't belong in this Enterprise, Gabriela," Henri cautioned.

"I know," she replied. "I just want to know where I can put my money so that it doesn't disappear."

Watching their responses, she knew that they'd swallowed the bait. She and Bart had already worked out their own plan – gold, platinum and zeolite. But by pretending to be helpless and worried, she'd flush out how long it would take for her expressions of mistrust to get to Steve and back to her. Her intuition was right. Lord Haverford was on the phone that night to Steve.

⌗

"When is the last New Moon before the November elections?" Karen asked looking up across her new bifocals.

"October 15th, of course," Elizabeth shot back. "Why do you wonder?"

"Because Sun says that we need to have as much darkness working in our favor as possible for the erasure and we can't do it after the elections," Karen responded.

"What about Steve's idea of having it happen on December 21, 2012? After all, with so many people thinking that an old stone in Mexico has prophesied the end of times, why not give everybody what they're waiting for?" Dan said putting down the Glock that he was cleaning.

"Jonas and Steve have been back and forth on when to pull the trigger. If they do it before the elections, they'll have the President declare martial law and suspend Constitutional transition of power. If they do it after the elections and the electorate doesn't hand us another marketing victory, it would look unsightly," Karen said matter-of-factly.

"If I was Quetzalcoatl, I'd be seriously pissed," Dan said sliding a clip into the stock with a loud clack.

"You know, when I think of a plumed serpent deity, I don't think of a strapping Jewish killer," Elizabeth laughed.

"Well maybe you should, little Lizzy," he poked her in the side with his unarmed hand.

"October the fifteenth, two thousand and twelve," Karen said looking back down at her notes. "The first strike will happen at 8:12pm and we'll do the clean up operation by 10:15pm. That ought to make Lord Haverford happy with his obsession for symmetry and all his wacko numerological compulsions."

"Do you really think that we need two hours and three minutes to execute our mission?" Dan said, his voice laden with condescension.

"I've got Munkhbat trained to blow the targets from a safe distance in under 45 minutes."

"Yeah, so long as you don't get too cold to help me," Munkhbat jousted.

"Hey, just because I didn't grow up on a Siberian yak farm doesn't mean I can't handle the cold, my little Khan," Dan snapped.

"Yeah, well tell that to your delicate fingers that can't work unless the water temperature is like the beach at Ibiza," he reminded Dan with this reference of a night the two of them spent with four actresses a few months back.

With Elizabeth in the room, Dan elected not to utter the words that reflexively entered his mind. After all, once you've trained a killer, giving him a reason to kill you, no matter how superficial, is a bad idea. And Munkhbat wouldn't take kindly to anything coming between him and Elizabeth – at least nothing that she would ever know about.

One more day and they'd finally be back on land. Spending this much time at sea was wearing on everyone. Steve, Jonas and Karen were the only ones to chopper off for a day or two. They'd disappear and then reappear. The durations of their trips seemed to indicate that some stops had been on land and others had to be on some form of vessel. No one talked about the trips. But no one trusted them either. And, in the final analysis, it's the malignancy of mistrust that wears relationships thin far more than the simple not knowing of things. Karen was going to find Emma and make sure that the several months without contact hadn't created any operational issues. Dan, Elizabeth and Munkhbat were going to move to Richmond as they had all been assigned to the West Creek Operations Center disaster response simulation team contracted through Henri's firm – complete with his gratuitous RFID subcontract to Patrick. Sun was going to be stationed in East Rutherford. After he confirmed operational readiness for the White House, he would set up the relays for Kuala Lumpur and London. They had debated long and hard about going back to Cleveland. The Key Tower had been a helpful utility in 2003 and creating an apparent redundancy to the past made sense on one hand. After all, if the same disaster befell the same place twice, it was conceivable that it would throw investigators down a self-fulfilling path. The downside risk, however, was that if Cleveland was seen as a ground zero again, people would look for the Tishman and César Pelli link and, if that were to happen, it could have undesired consequence. In the end, Cleveland, it was determined, was too high a risk.

⊠

When Mak Khan came out of his briefing with Darius, his mind was reeling. Since the drone attacks across the border from Afghanistan, the mounting anti-American sentiment was growing but, the opportunity to settle the score for the national sovereignty embarrassment of the Osama raid sounded too good to be true.

Given all that ISI had done for the CIA, DIA and other intelligence operations over the years, this reputational blight was an offense for which recompense couldn't come fast enough. Since the French had delivered the quiet drive submarines to the undersea base on the coast, a select few within ISI knew what could be done with these silent fish. Their experiment off the coast of San Diego – the one that had been used to test the burst on the unsuspecting *Genesis 2:25* – had proven that they could move into American waters and scurry back to base without being detected. Given the visit from the Chinese a few months later, they had some indication that, while not knowing the vessel, the Chinese Pacific listening array had detected something going and coming but they didn't know the precise nature of the vessel nor its payload.

Darius called Connie.

"Let the State Council know that we'll have one boat in the Hudson for the delivery of the package," he said.

"Wonderful, Darius. This is spectacular news. What did they want in return?" she asked knowing that the Pakistani government was not going to do this just as an act of retribution.

"They want to have an equal seat to India at the table when the basket currency replaces the dollar," he said.

"Well, I'm sure that can be arranged my dear friend," Connie said.

"They have made a special request, though," he continued. "While they're happy to see the EMP wipe out Manhattan and Goldman, they'd like the Goldman Tower to be a kinetic event."

"I'm sure that, too, can be accommodated," she said, reassuringly.

"When Tishman talks about their properties achieving greater asset value than simply the real estate, I can't imagine that they could ever envision how valuable their properties will be when this all happens. So many people around the world will celebrate the undoing," his voice was pitched with excitement.

"Yes," Connie agreed. "Given the state of affairs in the U.S., having one more illusion fall will solidify America's psyche as a fallen super-power. And won't it be ironic that the much heralded Cold War victory of capitalism over communism will end with the only powerful communist state on earth owning the entirety of the capitalist superpower?"

Darius paused for a moment. "Regrettably few Americans will take the time to reflect on that irony," he mused.

Emma had saved all of the notes from Cecil. They had come intermittently but the last one was the first that contained a request for information.

"Confirm date," was the sole words on the card. She knew it was from Cecil because it had the signature embossed GLC logo at the top. It was noteworthy, she thought, but it made sense given the fact that Karen had arrived at the official date while at sea. She replaced the slip of paper into the hidden compartment and decided that, on this occasion, she'd stick around to see who Cecil was – or at least who was carrying messages for Cecil. She perched herself on a rock outcropping shielded by enough of the stubborn leaves that had not yet relented to the chilling Fall air. Dressed in three layers of wool with an outer insulated jacket and pants combination, she looked more like an abandoned sleeping bag than a person. Much to her chagrin, the bench was occupied briefly in the late afternoon by an elderly couple whose matching white poodles socialized for about 30 minutes before they moved on. As darkness seeped into the park, a group of young people milled about the bench – a few of the young men sitting on the back while others milled around. She kept her focus on the left arm and, while occluded from time to time, nothing seemed to be out of the ordinary when the group raced off across the lawn kicking leaves as they ran. At about 1am, she saw what looked like a raccoon meander past the bench slowly shuffling through the frigid night air. And, as she'd been trained to do years ago, she kept her vigil into the first light of dawn, eyes focused on the bench.

A couple, he wearing black, silver and blue running pants that extended just below the knees and a black thermal fleece and she, wearing skinny black leggings with pink and white accents with a bright pink running jacket entered the park walking at a brisk pace. They arrived at the bench and stopped to stretch. The woman alternated putting her heels up on the left arm of the bench and stretching her hamstrings. The man did push ups with his feet hooked over the back. "What a great looking couple," she thought as she watched them. She heard a noise coming from below her; a rustling in the leaves, and glanced down to see a raccoon crawling into the crevice below her perch. When she looked up, the couple was rounding the corner heading north on West Drive. Conscious that she had diverted her gaze, she decided that one of these two could have been Cecil so she crawled off the rocks and, after carefully inspecting the perimeter to see if anyone had been observing her, walked over to the bench. Draping her tired body across the armrest, she inconspicuously triggered the release and the container opened. Rolled up in a tiny piece of paper were an old cigarette butt and a note. Scrawled on the note was the word, 'THANKS' in rough strokes. At the bottom of the paper, it was signed, "SOUR ROACH".

"Karen," she said when she got to her apartment, "we've got a problem."

Karen took a moment to collect her thoughts as she woke from a deep sleep. "What is it?" she said.

"Meet me at Le Pain just south of the park in 15 minutes," Emma's voice was earnest.

Moments later, staring across the table at Emma, Karen said, "Are you sure you know who left the note?"

"I'm pretty sure it was one of the runners. The woman was constantly hovering around the armrest so I'm pretty sure it was her."

"Cecil is a woman?" Karen asked with incredulity. For a decade all of the Operators were sure that it was a man. Some of them thought that Jonas may be Cecil with a remote triggered recorded voice.

"The only other possibility is that one of the kids last night could have done the drop. I couldn't recognize them but it did strike me as a bit strange that they congregated around that bench for a full five minutes and then ran off across the lawn," Emma reached into her memory but the lack of sleep was still vanquishing the second cup of steaming coffee she was nursing in her hands.

"Cecil couldn't be a kid," Karen dismissed. "He... or she... has been giving us orders for nearly 11 years."

"Yeah, so it must have been one of the runners. And if I had to bet, I would bet that it was the woman," Emma grew more confident in the recounting of the events.

"You're going to have to take all of this to the lab to see what they can lift off of this," Karen said in a serious tone. "I would recommend that you meet Steve down in Bethesda and make sure that they look at everything – paper, cigarette butt, the whole 9 yards."

Cyrus was beaming. Though the fruits of this day would be months away, he reveled in the fact that Anna and Sorin had successfully executed their mission in the Park. His run in the Park that morning with Emilie was worth the comedy of watching Emma react to what the kids had placed there the night before. The fact that they got another cold weather run in for their marathon training was just an added bonus. The only puzzle piece the Horus team had been missing was the date and, with that, all the triggers could be set. The AFN satellites would have one last broadcast before they'd initiate a deorbiting sequence and, as they burned in the Earth's atmosphere they'd take with them the last vestige of Jerry's empire. At that moment, all the data from the Enterprise – including all of their gold records – would bounce through Picasso 101500267 and then transmit a bifurcated signal. The historical communications file would be fed into the Biblioteca Alexandrina. After all, what a more suitable place to house the records of one of the greatest perverse fetes of modernity than in the monument to the supremacy of knowledge of antiquity? The Biblioteca team would see to it that the files were distributed to news organizations around the world. The financial accounts would be transferred to an irrevocable trust domiciled in the Maldives for the establishment of an institution to support the repatriation of sovereign resources usurped by the World Bank, IMF and the rest of the multi-lateral cabal which spent 50 years perpetuating poverty under the guise of development. There was one catch. The trust would expire the moment that the last of the land mass of the Maldives slipped below the surface of the sea. At this expiration, the assets of the trust would be allocated to all nations in reverse proportion to their current per capita income.

Edward and Andrew called the team together to lay out the chain of events. All systems would be on standby mode beginning on October 1, 2012. Each of the towers would be wired to confirm that the EMP burst had hit them which would initiate the deorbit sequence. The asset transfer would follow the satellite decommission but its timing would be up to Poseidon. Each Orca buoy was fitted with an optical sensor which would activate the Picasso bounce when one of the schools of fish flashed in unison. Since it was clear that someone in the Enterprise knew about Picasso, if they ever desired to deconstruct the events that unraveled their plan, the fingerprints would be on that satellite. However, what would be a complete mystery would be why the signal had transferred from a tsunami warning buoy.

"When the towers get hit, AFN will go dark, right?" Melissa said at the end of the briefing.

"Not before one last transmission," Edward said. "For one minute, we're going to switch the signals and AFN's content will stream to Jerry's porn subscribers and, well let's just say that there will be a generation of conversations around the one minute that will be pre-empting the news."

"Do you think that's a good idea?" she pressed.

"You know, Melissa," Edward continued, "parents who have been letting the propaganda machine infect their homes for the past 15 years have done more harm than 60 seconds of sex could ever do to corrupt their children. And the FCC fines that Jerry will pay will insure that he's never licensed again."

"No one goes near West Creek from here on in," Andrew said sternly. "From the recent contracting records, we've identified at least two members of the Enterprise who are contractors there which means that place is a hornet's nest. It wouldn't surprise me to find out they're running their entire operation right from inside the Center."

"Do we know how they're going to take it out?" Melissa inquired.

Pulling up an image of Google Earth, Edward drew a series of concentric rings and then turned back to the team. "Our guess is that they'll hit the Lake Anna nuclear power facility. That will take down the main power supply throughout much of Virginia – definitely take all the Richmond grid dark. That gives them the cover story that it was a power outage – kind of like 2003. Given the fact that we've got all of the blueprints from the building contractor in the files, I suspect that they'll take the building down as well. We have no idea how that'll happen but, with the river right there, there are a host of options."

Dr. Sheldon looked at Steve and Emma with a blank stare. "It's Jonas." The words just hung in the air. "The paper is from Kate O'Conner's stationery supply, the DNA on the cigarette butt and on the scrap of paper is from Jonas. But there are a couple of anomalies. The paper appears to be stock from an order she made some time ago and there appears to be traces of some type of rodent urine on one corner – obviously weathered a bit. Emma could have contaminated the sample when she picked it up but it would appear that this paper's been outside for quite some time. The other thing is that the ink on the paper doesn't match any of Jonas' typical writing choices. We can't match the handwriting at all but the ink has got us stumped."

Emma pulled Steve aside. "There's no way this could be Jonas, could it?"

"No, he flew to China from San Diego and is working on ironing out our immigration logistics," Steve whispered.

"Is there any chance that it could be Karen? After all, she did get into the City early enough yesterday afternoon," Emma probed.

"Not a prayer," Steve replied too quickly. He had been at Karen's apartment last night where the two of them had finally given in to the passions that their proximity at sea had fanned. Her afternoon sunbathing was unbearable for Steve – that amazing, mature woman uninhibited at sea consumed every waking and sleeping thought and had broken his concentration for weeks.

"Steve, you have got to tell me who Cecil is – he or she is our last possible explanation and, this message looks like we may have a rogue," Emma's pleadings were insistent.

Steve looked at her for a moment and then replied, "You know I can't do that. But what I can tell you is that you, me, and Karen are the only ones to know about this right now. Do you understand?"

"I understand the words that you're saying but, Steve, ever since Carey, I've been afraid that we've reached too far and we're running too great a risk."

"Well, that may be true," he replied, "and for that reason, I'm going to suggest that you go deep – disappear – and when all this dust settles, I'll come find you."

"Are you firing me?" she said, her voice raising a bit.

"Eau contraire! I am saving your life. Leave this mystery to me." It looked like he was getting ready to walk out. "Oh, but what do you make of "SOUR ROACH"?"

She looked at him and mused for a moment. "Somebody's playing games with us... or maybe with Jonas since it's his roach in the paper."

As she left the lab, she kept writing the words on her notebook. Nothing. Exhausted, she looked out the window as the car sped north on I-95.

"Driver," she inquired, "do you know if the airport in Little Rock has reopened?"

"Yes Ma'am," he replied, "flights getting to Little Rock and St. Louis are now departing from Baltimore and Philadelphia."

"Would you drop me off at BWI please? I think my plans have just changed." In an instant, she decided that her temporary unemployment would give her an opportunity to do something that she'd wanted to do since the quake. With millions of people living in temporary shelters, she wanted to head out to the heartland and see if there would be something she could do to help. Who knows, maybe even meet someone out there who would help her forget the past 12 years.

Ayman, Darius and Connie assembled at the location Jonas had requested on the expansive inner courtyard of the Forbidden City. They each were outfitted with tourist gear complete with obnoxious cameras around their neck and floppy hats. Jonas chugged up to them slightly out of breath. Exchanging pleasantries they walked across the marble pavement bridge to approach the great hall that was directly in front of them.

"You know during the war, invaders stripped the gold leaf off these giant vessels," Connie said as they approached the staircase.

"They would have been magnificent in the sunlight," Ayman commented as he surveyed the great structures.

"Amazing how much is lost when people see the short term value of a thing but fail to appreciate its historical significance," she added.

"That almost sounds like a fucking fortune cookie," Jonas huffed. "I suppose that you're trying to warn me... no us... that we should be circumspect."

"Oh no, my dear Jonas," Connie giggled, "no warning. No, the government is totally behind our October surprise – in fact they'd like to move it up so that they don't have to wait for such a long time. After all, when the Treasury is erased, they'll have a way to calm down our citizens who are angry at how much we invested in the U.S. economy. No, I just think that it's a good idea to visit places like this and make sure that what we're doing matters in the long term."

Jonas was tired and not in the mood for philosophical reflection. "You Confucians can do whatever long march nonsense you wish, and I'm fine with that. I just want to know that we're all going to land on our feet in the end."

Ayman, Darius and Connie shot quick glances amongst themselves. Jonas would be helpful after the fact which is why they were willing to meet with him. As for the others, they saw little utility post the erasure. Bart and Gabriela would be fine and probably wind up getting married and spending their latter years rather peacefully. Kate, Henri, and Lord Haverford were so self-absorbed that they didn't even figure into the picture. By this time, no one cared for Jerry. Patrick and Chan Siew would be wealthier than had the Enterprise never existed and would retire in the same anonymity with which they entered the world.

"Do we neutralize the Operators when this is over?" Ayman asked Darius as they walked past the concubine's chambers.

"There shouldn't be many left," Darius said with an icy tone.

"It's an EMP, not kinetic so there should be inconveniences but not fatalities," Ayman pressed.

"Right," Darius dismissed.

"We'll have Fengming back here in a few weeks to handle all of our logistics," Connie offered.

"And what about Steve?"

Jonas' question hung in the air. No one answered.

>🏴<

Simon arranged for Habbib al Nassar and Amal Assad to meet Munkhbat and Dan in March. Several of Syria's Eastern European suppliers had volunteered to be part of the supply team when they heard that the target was going to be U.S. banks. Ironic, in that while they hated the U.S., all their deals were done in dollars and they lived off the fat of covert operations for generations. Mercenaries are to be trusted for their greed and tenacity – not for their intellectual aptitude. In blowing up the dollar, they'd actually be harming themselves but, like other exoskeletal creatures, they'd find a new conflict on which to feed before long.

The idea was rather simple. They'd send explosives into the cold water intake at the plant on tethers which would insure their placement without risking premature detonation. A few charges around the reactor building would create significant distraction and, the fire, with any luck, would be such a huge distraction that the intrusion into the core would be undetected. The Chechen demolition experts had worked out the details and had tested it on a couple of old sewer treatment facilities. The fluid dynamics worked and the fragmenting explosives could get through all of the filters to get close enough to the core to blow it.

"You are having one single target, yes?" Habbib asked Dan. "Just like you Jews to be too focused."

"We love precision, you guys love mayhem," Dan mused.

"Do you need any shooters?" Amal inquired. "We've got some amazing capabilities at range. Thanks to our President, we've gotten a lot of practice these days – you know, keeping the peace and all."

Munkhbat looked at him and recalled his first sniper detail with Amal. "No, this time around, we're going to be long gone when the fireworks start. All we'll need is close contact if someone disrupts are installation."

"That's truly unfortunate," Amal lamented.

"Simon, what do you get out of all of this?" Habbib inquired.

"I am a simple Greek shipping merchant, my friend. I'll pick up a few things in China, come across to Yemen to grab your containers and then I'll be off to Norfolk and New York."

"Sometimes I wonder who you work for, Simon," Amal leaned into the conversation.

"Anyone who pays, my friend. Anyone who pays."

"Where's the rest of the team that you'll use?" Habbib came back to the erasure event.

"You're looking at the team, Habbib," Munkhbat proudly replied.

"Just the two of you?" Amal said incredulously.

"We're the kinetic team – the rest of the attack, well, you'll see..." Dan's voice drifted off. He knew that after this event, every Lord of War would want to get an option to lease their arrays but for now, he'd stay focused on explosives.

✄

Tim Simpson and Hugh McGrath invited Senator Simpson onto the show they now co-hosted. AFN's Prayer-a-thon had raised close to $25 million for disaster relief following the quakes and the President had awarded his arch nemesis in media, Jerry Robertson, with a Medal of Freedom for all his efforts around the earthquake. For a few weeks, these two caricatures had talked about America coming together but things were getting back to business. With the Republican and Democratic tickets battling for the real estate on

Pennsylvania Avenue, Jerry's Prayer for America segment – co-hosted by former Presidential candidate and Texas Governor Steve Perry – had migrated from unified to partisan before mold could grow on a flooded house in the bayou.

Tim's perfectly coiffed hair, it had been decided, needed to convey a bit more maturity so, over the past several weeks, the AFN hairstylist had discontinued the coloring so that some grey appeared. "Hugh, tell me what kind of chatter we're hearing these days."

By 'these days' he was referring to the months of physical and economic hardship that had swept the nation. The constant drone of bank failures and home mortgage foreclosures had ceased to be news. People didn't want to hear about their neighbors losing jobs, homes, and futures. Depressing news, the editorial board had decided, was un-American. If the economy was going to grow, news had to be positive. This was a delicate balance for AFN as they loved to prey on fear but, unfortunately, when Americans are hungry and homeless, the line between maintaining fear and irritating a festering sore was making their job nearly impossible. While the candidates were out-spending all previous Presidential campaigns, Obama clearly had the incumbent advantage as he'd done all he could in brokering foreign investment in rebuilding American infrastructure. When every citizen was looking for assistance, the 'no big government' message wasn't polling as well as it had at the mid-terms.

"North Africa and the Middle East have reverted to sectarian violence so, for the moment, there are more enemies at home than targets here," Hugh said with his reassuring, suave delivery.

"In our Committee, we are being briefed about the situation in Venezuela and Cuba with ailing leaders watching their successors vying for power. We're seeing border conflicts in Central Africa building on the back of the persistent famine. And, as you know, there are major parts of Afghanistan that have fallen into extremist hands since our withdrawal commenced several months back," Senator Simpson added.

"Should we be concerned about the Chinese investment in our interstate and rail infrastructure given their high speed rail disaster back in the summer?" Tim asked.

"The President had no other path on that one, Tim," Senator Simpson replied. "The Treasury was tapped on all fronts and we simply had to come up with a way to finance critical infrastructure. Given their appetite to diversify into transportation and logistics to support commodity trade, they were a willing source of capital and, Lord knows, we needed it."

"Yes, but doesn't their financing essentially give them most favored treatment to control tolls, rail traffic, and the like?" Tim's off-camera producer wanted him to wedge open a campaign tool for the Republicans.

"That's a tough one," Hugh jumped in. "Yes, it's far from ideal but, on the other hand, if we had waited to have our economy to support the rebuilding through tax revenue, we would have had a physically divided country for 5 to 10 years."

This line of questioning was a dry well.

"How about the Chinese Navy?" Tim changed the subject. "With their aircraft carrier practicing maneuvers in the Straits and with their recent flare up with the Vietnamese again, should we be concerned with them becoming a hostile force in the region?"

Hugh had a morsel that he couldn't resist throwing into the mix. "Until they have full battle groups complete with destroyers, frigates, and submarines, they're not capable of mounting a serious threat. The real concern that we'll have on the China military front is the conflict over the clean water supplies from the Himalayan watershed. I wouldn't be surprised to see a land conflict with India in the coming months as they continue to divert water from the south to the north." There, he had said it. Nobody was talking about this but it was a great way to create fear of China without making it hit the average American's consciousness – just a slow burn of fear… the best kind.

"Wow, Hugh," Tim said, genuinely surprised, "you never cease to amaze me with your reach of foreign intelligence and we're blessed to have you here as part of the AFN family."

"SOUR ROACH," Emma scrawled onto a napkin in the Habitat for Humanity tent after everyone had gone to bed.

"What's that about?" a voice from behind asked her.

"Oh nothing," she said, turning to look at the tall, tanned young man standing behind her. "You have an interesting accent. Where are you from?"

"I grew up in Switzerland. Do you know Zurich? But after I came over to the U.S. for school, I decided to stay on and volunteer with Habitat," he replied.

"Where did you go to school?" she inquired.

"George Washington University class of '01," he replied.

Maybe this meeting, she thought, would end very differently than the mirror of it she'd had a decade ago in Zurich. She sure hoped so.

David E. Martin

# CHAPTER 15 – THE LADY IN THE LAKE

Coal fired electrical generation was the mainstay for powering the mid-Atlantic region for decades with copious reserves in Southwestern Virginia, West Virginia and Kentucky. With the economic arguments for alternative fuel power generation weak at best, the placement of a nuclear power facility at Lake Anna, a reservoir to the northwest of Richmond Virginia was justified on the basis of the critical classified industries that required reliable power. The National Ground Intelligence Center in Charlottesville was a vital asset for processing geospatial intelligence and foreign intelligence collections for all the alphabet soup agencies. The CIA and FBI both used the nuclear power infrastructure for countless anonymous facilities from Orange Virginia all the way to the beltway. And, given Richmond's tobacco, filters, and pharmaceutical manufacturing and banking industries, cheap, reliable power was a boom for retaining businesses until out-sourcing made power impotent against the cost of cheaper, more qualified labor in Asia and India. For the blue collar and coal baron aristocracy for whom the Outer Banks was too liberal – girls in bikinis distracting prep school sons – lake front real estate provided water skiing, fishing, and wake-boarding amusements in the long, humid summers. Perimeter security was adequate but not impregnable. After all, this was gentrified Virginia, not activist-filled California.

Civilian casualty from a full meltdown would be minimal and, while the pine forests would be contaminated for decades, collateral damage would be minimal. Within a 60 mile radius – an arc large enough to hit the NGIC, Orange County residents, and the West Creek Operations Center – movement would be restricted to a point that operational disruption was inevitable. If you were to pick a ground zero target, this one was about as counter-intuitive as they come. Which made it perfect.

Vice President Joe Biden had visited China on several occasions since the controversial summer 2011 Combined Forces Command exercises – a war game designed to intimidate Pyongyang despite all of General Thurman's cover story rhetoric about readiness. With over a half million troops deployed for the exercise in August, the Navy was baffled at what appeared to be an inordinate amount of transparency afforded by the usually secretive People's Liberation Army. In addition to an invitation to the new carrier for a full capabilities inspection, the Chinese had invited Navy flight instructors into the carrier deck flight simulation zone – a mock-up for practicing deck landings. With all the financial dependency that the Administration had on the State Council, no invitation – no matter how improbable – was to be turned down. Backing away from the F-16 sales to Taiwan had been a bitter pill but the Department of Defense found a way to keep the jobs by liberalizing sales to private buyers.

"The carrier is a decoy," Edward exclaimed as Cyrus walked into the office in late September. "Ever since she was unveiled last summer, all NATO capabilities assessments have been seduced by this iconic behemoth. When the Titanic would-be casino of Macau went up to Liaoning, we thought that this Mississippi riverboat was a PLA ruse but, given the statements made by Geng Yansheng over at the Defense Ministry, our bet is the *Varyag* is a whole different sort of bet altogether. While everybody's watching above the waterline – particularly intrigued by the Shark's deck operations practice – all eyes will be distracted on this Soviet, Ukrainian, Macau casino *cum* Chinese 'capability'. Until the official commissioning, scheduled for October 2012, she won't have a name or an official mission. The date is intriguing. Why October, 2012? May have something to do with the Zheng He fleet and some anniversary of the fifteenth century missions. Who knows? But, far more importantly, what no one's been watching is what's below the water. We just picked up a report that Attack 98, one of the PLA's UUV assembly facilities, just put several shipping containers on board a ship registered to a Greek shipping company. If that carrier could be armed with undersea capabilities, all the Sharks circling above would be serving as camouflage for the real assets flying in the waters below."

"Did you ever get a briefing on the folks at Tsinghua after Dr. Yuri Sandrikov demonstrated his supercavitation propulsion systems?" Cyrus asked.

"Yes. Apparently the prototyping went well and they've achieved Mach 0.8 in preliminary runs," Edward looked up from his briefing. "There's an interesting wrinkle in the attendee list, however, Cyrus and I thought you'd find this rather fascinating. It seems that several Pakistanis were invited under a cooperative technology transfer deal structured two months ago between Islamabad and Beijing. Our reports out of the horseman of Pamir indicate that at least twenty Pakistani naval brass went down to Liaoning for about five days. Nobody knows where they went or what they're movements were – all closely guarded."

Cyrus was processing the information but, in the interest of not having an awkward pause, he asked a question the answer for which he already knew. "What type of payload are these fish capable of?" he mused, his voice drifting off.

"We're not entirely sure," Melissa jumped in, "but we're looking into it."

"We have two Orca buoys to the north and two to the south of Japan and they should be able to pick up any large scale deployment," Cyrus was returning to participation in the conversation.

"We have some models of what a single supercavitation device would look like on our hydro sensors. It would be one hell of a sight to see a squadron of the fish launched at once. Even at depth, there'd be some serious surface signatures. From all we can find, they have a range of about 300 miles one way so it would be tough for any of the devices to impact any U.S. assets," Edward continued.

Cyrus looked at him and, after a long pause, added, "Unless they're delivered by a carrier."

Andrew was listening too literally. "I didn't think that the Chinese carrier was operational with a battle group," he said.

"Not an aircraft carrier, Andrew – a third party long range sub," Cyrus' words were measured. "If the Greek ship stops in Singapore, I'd be surprised. Too much scrutiny by the Port Security apparatus. But I bet it will hit Malaysia at KL, sail on to Pakistan, on through the Mediterranean to Britain and then New York."

"So you think that the EMP will be delivered by UUVs?" Andrew asked.

"No, not just UUVs but I do think that they're going to keep all their options open," Cyrus was back into his distracted thought.

※

The Petronas Towers in Kuala Lumpur have foundations that reach over 100 meters below the surface of the Earth giving them the deepest foundations of any building. Dwarfing the base of One Canada, the Goldman Tower, the World Financial Center and other Pelli masterpieces, the Haitian concrete engineers required an unprecedented amount of reinforcing iron to provide structural integrity for the towers above. As a result, while not the tallest building measured by height above ground, its capacity as an antenna made it the likely master signal. The Japanese and Korean firms that managed the visible construction were oblivious to the dual purpose designed into the soaring steel and glass monoliths joined far above the ground by the Kukdong Engineering & Construction skybridge. In the daylight of the 16th of October, tourists snapping photos would likely notice the signature aurora just before the EMP burst would take out the communications and wipe their camera drives of all their photos.

Lost in the London mists fed by the neighboring Thames, the pyramid signature of One Canada was illusive to the average London visitor. But for the conspicuous flashing aircraft warning light perched at 240 meters above the river, during the early morning hours of October 16, few would notice as the beacon would be the first indication that the world had changed. A few cabbies would be looking in the right direction in time to see the light go out just before the rest of the Tower, and then most of London would go dark.

Under the official plan, the Goldman Tower would be hit from below via a subterranean burst. The 180 meters from the PATH station to the riverfront would provide no attenuation of the magnetic burst. Sun and Karen's frequent visits to the Cosi café on the ground floor provided perfect opportunities to do the conductivity tests that confirmed the susceptibility of the Towers and, with their frequent service calls on the Provident Bank ATMs, they had more than adequately confirmed their ability to confirm erasure before communications were entirely lost. The optical network that Sun had designed ran right under the noses of unsuspecting bank customers. Darius and Connie knew that there would be more fireworks but by this time, there was no more need for discussions which could be intercepted. They were in execution mode.

The only high altitude burst would be directly above Interstate 64 about 25 miles west of Richmond. The missile would be launched from a Pakistani submarine which would surface just long enough for the launch and then immediately dive deep. One of its sister vessels would deliver the kinetic ordinance to the Hudson. Technically, it would go as far as the 40 miles due east of Trenton and then release the Tsinghua fish. They'd do the rest of the work on the Goldman Tower. And, to make sure that none of the Shareholders would ever doubt that Connie had done her job, Jerry's birds would actually image one sub releasing several UUVs just beyond the Naval perimeter at the mouth of the James River. From there, the fish would swim up to Richmond and using their gyroscopic stabilization robotics climb their way to the West Creek. They'd be in position no later than October 10th. Munkhbat and Dan would confirm their presence with a visual inspection on the 12th and Sun would ping them to activate their detonators to blow during the critical darkness following the Lake Anna action.

⌦

Steve attempted to convene a meeting of the Shareholders at the Admiral Lord Nelson guest house in Simon's Bay on the way from Cape Town down to the Point. The fact that only Gabriela and Bart

370

responded affirmatively was annoying. Kate and Lord Haverford were otherwise engaged in a trip they were making to visit clinics for radiation poisoning victims in Kazakhstan. They wouldn't be back until the 20th of October as they wanted to be well outside of New York and London, respectively, when the excitement happened.

"What do you make of this, Jonas?" he asked his old friend as they sat on the Maid of the Mist deck watching the mighty Niagara Falls.

"Nothing."

"Do you mean to tell me that, on the eve of our final act, everyone's got opening night jitters?" Steve pressed.

"You know, Steve, it's a funny thing. Sitting down here looking up into the cataract I'm reminded about how fragile we are. Just a bag of carbon, water, and a couple minerals – the same things that we go to war over, the same things that we spend our humanity to control – nothing more. And, but for a tiny bit of electricity in our heads, we'd be worse off than the rocks that create these awesome mists."

Taken aback by this uncharacteristically philosophical musing, Steve asked, "Where the hell did that come from? You of all people have made fortunes using your math to rob from those emotional impulses in your fellow man. Now that we're on the verge of achieving greatness, you're getting all Buddhist. It's as though you don't care about what we've built."

371

"See, that's the thing – it's not what we've built. It's what you've imagined, Steve. You've done one hell of a job – nobody has balls to take on what you've done – but the thing is, your bet requires that you're the smartest and the brightest. If you're wrong, we're all dead and you don't seem to get that."

"What's got you concerned?" Steve probed.

"Silence."

"You'll have to do better than that my mysterious philosopher," Steve was slightly irritated.

"When Karen got back to New York, she tried to get in touch with Emma but she'd disappeared. I contacted my friends at SABRE and they told me that she'd boarded a plane for Little Rock after charging a car service from the lab in Bethesda. Now you know that Horus is in Bethesda and I'm afraid that she may have talked," Jonas was clearly concerned.

Steve was eager to reassure his colleague. "Oh no, she was with me all day. I saw her get into the car and followed her north. She turned off 95 towards BWI and I know she flew out of town that day. There's no chance that she had any contact with Horus."

"What were you doing at the lab?" Jonas pried.

"We had a few jitters around a note we found – a practical joke from Cecil. She'd put one of your cigarettes and a note in Emma's drop – kind of freaked her out."

"Why didn't you tell us?" Jonas insisted, his voice more agitated than he'd heard in months.

"Because it wasn't material," Steve replied.

"There was no practical joke from Cecil, Steve," Jonas was now intently looking at Steve with an almost accusatory stare. "Cecil doesn't communicate anything without me and she stopped communicating with Emma three days before we returned."

"That's not possible," Steve replied. "I saw her communications leading up to the last note."

"What was on the last note?" Jonas asked.

*It couldn't hurt to tell him now,* Steve thought. "It just said, 'Thanks' and was signed 'sour roach' – you see meaningless."

"Does 'sour roach' mean anything to you, Steve?" Jonas now was condescending.

"No, does it to you?" Steve responded reflexively.

"No, goddamn it, Steve. That's precisely why you should have told us. Did you see if it was a code for something – did you run any crypts on it?"

"No."

They didn't speak for five minutes or more. Steve was furious with his friend and colleague. Few things were more disturbing to him than having his judgment questioned. Jonas was trying to unravel the cipher but his frustration with Steve invaded his typically analytical mind. Nothing was coming. Some of the best ciphers are relatively simple once you know them, he pondered, but the problem was that, when they were most simple, the temptation to find acrostics or jumbled words was too easy. And even if you got across the first finish line and guessed it right, you still need to find the lock for the key. Fragments of memories jumped ahead of every thought. Did the cipher include all the words on the page, a combination of them, none of them?

"Your aft lights are out," the Virginia Fisheries and Wildlife warden called out to Munkhbat and Dan as they were coming back to the marina on the northeast side of the lake.

"Sorry, Sir. We'll get that fixed. Have a good evening," they called back.

"Ya'll didn't see anyone swimming out there did you?" the warden inquired.

They had been underwater for almost four hours setting the charges but had changed into dry clothes and covered their hair with caps so they couldn't be suspected. "No. We were just out shooting some sunset images of the migratory birds," Dan said holding up his Canon with a massive telephoto lens.

"They're sure thick on the water this Fall," the warden commented, pleased that someone wasn't trying to shoot the birds. "We got a report of an Asian woman who was diving over near the plant early this afternoon. No boat, but what looked like some pretty fancy gear. Some of our locals called it in but by the time I got to the area to check things out, there was nothing. None of the alarms were triggered."

Dan and Munkhbat knew that there could have been no alarms. They had disabled them all over a week ago and, with some magic that Sun had coded for them, no one in the control room at the plant was any wiser for it. The breach would be detected during routine scheduled systems tests on the 17th of October. "If we see anything, we'll let you know."

When they were out of range of the warden's boat, they looked at each other and, without exchanging a word, decided that any unscripted movement would attract too much attention. Whoever the diver was, it was none of their business. Probably one of the Shareholders checking up on the preparations.

Steve arrived at the Oval Office early on the morning of the 14th. Secretary Geithner had been with the President late into the evening trying to work out a strategy to pump enough business to Goldman to avert what they all feared to be the inevitable. With assurances that the public would respond favorably to the visible collapse of the now vilified bank, the down-side risk of going through with the EMP strategy was far less damaging than letting them be forced into liquidation. By making their collapse an 'attack', the public would rally to the President this close to the election. Afterwards, they could do a mop up operation – move all essential professionals into the pre-determined posts in the other banks – and, no one would be worse for wear. Best of all, despite that fact that he was polling dead even with his Republican opponent, the President knew that his approval numbers could use a boost from a series of courageous acts in the wake of an attack he could blame on an enemy state. They had settled in on pinning this one on Iran because, with the public behind the President rattling the sabers of revenge against Iran, the conservatives would have to fall in line and support the President and, with that, he'd be re-elected.

"The Joint Chiefs just left, Steve and I've authorized Alaska to be standing by," the President said dryly.

"I don't think that will be necessary, Sir," Steve said in a re-assuring tone. "You're doing the right thing."

"I never thought I'd live to see the day when I authorize something akin to what you guys pulled off with W," the President added. "I guess there's some bizarre symmetry in the fact that we're hitting the opposite side of the river. If you'd have been standing at the World Trade Center, you'd have had a great view of what we're doing tomorrow."

"Yes, Mr. President. The irony has not been lost on me. The cost of being the last super-power is that, to catalyze public responses, if an enemy doesn't act, you have to target yourself."

"Sounds like a Shakespearean drama," he mused.

"I would recommend," Steve offered, "that you relocate to Camp David tomorrow, just for precaution. While we doubt that there will be any significant response, being out of the District would make good sense."

"Tomorrow night will be a New Moon so the stars will be beautiful, Steve. Would you care to join us?"

"Sir, I'm going to be otherwise occupied," he said with a chuckle. "Maybe a rain check after the dust settles?"

"Certainly," the President replied.

✉

"The heavens are telling the glory of us," Jerry said as he joined Steve, Gabriela and Bart on the *Genesis 2:25*. The four of them had taken Jerry's plane out to San Diego and, true to form, Melissa and Sam – still striking their too good to be true Barbie and Ken – had their drinks ready to be served before they settled into the new upholstered deck lounge seats. "We're waiting for Silas and Congressman Conway – I've enticed them to come with photos of some of our newest crew," he said pointing to the sun deck where four young ladies lay sunning themselves.

Thirty minutes later, the two arrived in a white Range Rover. Sam grabbed their overnight bags and escorted them to the gangway leading onto the teak aft deck.

"Afternoon, gentlemen," Jerry called, standing as he reached out his hand to shake theirs.

"To what do we owe the pleasure?" Congressman Conway asked. He'd gained a lot of weight over the past several months. He was constantly out of breath even when he had no exertion.

"Just a little thank you gift, that's all," Jerry said as he sent Sam to the bridge to set out. "We'll be dining off of Ensenada tonight, friends. I

378

hear the whales are on their way to the Gulf and with any luck we'll see a few."

After 50 minutes, the coastline of Southern California dipped into the haze. The ocean was beautiful; temperature perfect, sun bright.

"What kind of buoy is out here?" Bart asked as they passed an elaborate piece of technology floating well beyond the shipping lane markers. "It's got the logo of what looks like a killer whale on the side."

"Probably some damn tree-hugger environmentalist measuring global warming or some such nonsense," Jerry scoffed.

"Looks a bit rich for that ilk," Gabriela said.

"You've got some explaining to do, Steve-o," Silas said squinting his eyes at Steve.

"About what, Silas?" he asked.

"My sources tell me that you hired Simon to do some shipping for your little escapade. Wouldn't bother me if you hadn't spent so damn much time in Pakistan. Ever since the raid on OBL, we've had trouble getting any details but we hear that you guys are right friendly with our Islamic Indians."

"I've got no idea what you're talking about," Steve was genuine in his denial. He had been told that Dan and Munkhbat had been outfitted via a humanitarian container sent from the Green Crescent as a goodwill gesture for earthquake relief. Their shipment was to be delivered in Norfolk.

"With what I was told you ordered, I think we're on the wrong coast to see the fireworks, you lying sack of shit," Silas knew Steve was deflecting what he knew.

"Silas, I'm dead serious. I've got no idea what the hell you're talking about."

"You arm Pakistani subs with Chinese UUVs, send them packing to at least two known destinations and you're telling me you don't know what I'm talking about. Steve, I wasn't born yesterday. Sure wish I was with the ladies you brought along but I'm too old for your bullshit. Now, tell me what's going down."

Steve was getting so visibly disturbed that Jerry stepped in. "We've got a little New York surprise tonight – a little nudge to take Goldman down."

"You're taking a lot more than Goldman down with what I saw on the manifest. You've got underwater explosives enough to level the Financial District in Manhattan and, from the looks of things, you've got at least one hot submarine off the coast of Virginia."

"Oh," Jerry jumped in. "That fish is standing by just to give us some back up if we need it. I've got the satellite images of it surfacing. Care to see them?"

As the *Genesis* turned due south, they passed another buoy.

"Hey Sam," Steve shouted, happy to have a momentary distraction. "Circle back and come up alongside that thing so we can have a closer look."

Sam brought the *Genesis* about and came up within 15 feet of the buoy. It was bristling with more communication hardware than any of them had ever seen. Under the Orca logo, there was a series of ITU reference numbers. Jerry was enough of a hands-on manager that he knew that this floater must be some sort of beacon. He ran up to the bridge and came back down holding a paper-back book filled with tables. "Read the numbers off to me," he said as his feet hit the deck.

Gabriela looked over the edge and started reciting the nonsense that was printed on the side. Jerry's face paled.

"Those are our birds," he stammered. "Who the fuck would be broadcasting to or listening to our birds out here in the ocean?" his face was growing red. "Get closer to this thing so I can climb on board to see what's on this bobber, Sam," he growled.

Two of the deckhands were running to drop the bumpers over the side when the buoy contacted the side of the boat. There was a giant arc that flashed through all the metal on the deck knocking one of the young men into the water. In an instant, the engines died and the boat was silently rocking next to this mysterious object.

"Sir, the bridge is dead," Sam called down.

Jerry was rushing up the ladder to the bridge when Steve's satellite phone started chirping. "Thank God this is still functional," he said putting the receiver to his ear.

His face went ashen when whatever was on the other end got done speaking. The phone dropped out of his hand. Everyone on board could hear a woman's voice calling, "Steve, Steve, are you there?" as it fell to the floor and smashed.

Steve was shaking.

"What was that about?" the Congressman asked now starting to realize that he was in the middle of something other than another hedonistic party on Jerry's boat.

"We're dead," Steve voice croaked as he slumped into his chair.

He was staring at the logo on the buoy and slowly raised his hand. "Orca," he mumbled.

"What's the big deal?" Bart said, not given to this kind of dramatics. He'd been all over the world – seen every manner of evil – and he wasn't a big fan of people who didn't handle stress well.

"That was Emma," he said. "The message was not 'sour roach' – it was HORUS ORCA."

"Are you telling me," Jerry said, measuring each word, "that Horus has taken us down? That little shit that you couldn't buy has played us?"

"Sir," Sam called. "You'd better come up here. It looks like we've got company."

It started with what looked like water boiling only different in the size of the singular wave bearing down on them. Flying at the *Genesis,* just below the surface of the water at about 600 yards, were what looked like three objects that appeared to be moving through the water faster than anything Sam had ever seen. They were closing so fast that Jerry got to the bridge when they made contact with the bow.

A school of fish that had been swimming about 200 yards behind the boat suddenly turned in unison and swam away.

⚏

"Dive seven degrees down bubble and set heading for 2-9-3," the voice echoed in the vessel.

"You know, we have a Persian saying that the haughty hunter scorns the wounded stag, but the hungry hunter gives thanks to the Almighty and is fed," Darius said turning to XO. "We'll join our Atlantic brothers soon, In Shaa Allah."

"There's a whole new world coming with those little Tsinghua piranhas," the Commander replied, "A whole new world."

⚏

"The 7:55pm PATH train is closed for service. Please board the next train for New Jersey," came the voice over the loudspeaker as the last of the commuters were making their way home. Moments later a five car train slowed as it passed the platform and then resumed speed as it sank down the grade to pass under the Hudson River. Next stop would be in New Jersey just north of the Goldman Tower. In the bar next to the platform a large crowd was gathering around a set of TV monitors. Tim and Hugh were just talking about the latest release of classified documents on WikiLeaks when suddenly the monitors flashed and the screens were awash with hardcore images having been switched signals in the middle of a graphic porno.

"Now that's some quality entertainment," hollered a young investment banker upon which the crowd broke into spontaneous applause.

Moments later, an explosion rocked the cavernous station and alarms sounded. The sound of water rushing in the tunnel was only stifled momentarily by the screams of people running for the stairs as the Hudson River began swallowing those who couldn't make their way out of the plunging darkness.

〰️

Sitting atop Qunsop Mountain in East New Britain the Alexander family sat at Naski with Clement, Damian, Mamma and Boniface. Just a few days earlier, Edward had called Cyrus to let him know that events had played out as planned with respect to the target selection. The damage had been far worse than any of them had imagined. On October 16th, China had demanded redemption of its Treasury holdings and, without the capacity to do so (or even confirm their existence), together with Saudi Arabia, Pakistan, Brazil, Australia, Norway, Canada and Switzerland, a new economic G-8 monetary convention was established. In an act of desperation, an emergency session of the Congress had mindlessly assembled to ratify President Obama's declaration of martial law and with it, postponed the elections indefinitely.

Long after the sun set across the Bismarck Sea, Cyrus laid back on the ground and looked at the canopy of light spread across the heavens.

One by one, first Emilie, then Anna, and finally Sorin laid their heads on each other's abdomens and, in silence took in the beauty above them. Mamma looked over.

"You know, Cyrus, we're awfully glad you brought the whole family along on this trip. Having you all here means so much to all of your big family here."

Damian smiled, his few remaining teeth visible in contrast to his deep black skin. "Cyrus, you always have a home here with my people."

"Thank you, Damian," he said.

"Our people remember a time when the islands of the Earth were all one and when people lived in peace with each other and the world. On this mountain, they built a tower that reached the skies so that they could climb up to heaven and back. And then, after a long time, the people became greedy and wanted to own the tower – each for his own family. The Earth was sad and one day, the land parted. Our elders say that on the day that the Bird of Paradise and the Hornbill Toucan fly across this mountain top, this will signal the time when the land will come back together and the people will work together again," Clement's voice was melodic and low and hung in the cool air with an intermittent breeze.

"I don't know about the birds, my brother," Cyrus said, "but shortly you should see something equally amazing in the sky above. Just lay back and look up."

Everyone lay in silence. The sounds of the forest joined in the subtle chorus of their breathing. In the distance, the Tavurvur caldera rumbled with a low boiling growl and then fell silent again.

Far above them, a light passed across the star field with a constant magnitude.

"Cyrus," Damian asked, "do you know what that is?"

"Yes, it's a satellite."

He'd scarcely uttered the words when a brilliant flash lit the sky. At first it looked like a meteor but, as it fell, it was clearly fragmenting into the Earth's gravitational embrace. About 20 minutes later, about 60 degrees from the first, a second distant meteor fell.

"Cyrus," Damian's voice came softly, "were those satellites too?"

"No," replied Cyrus. "Those were a Bird of Paradise and a Hornbill Toucan."

## About the Author

Dr. David E. Martin is a business founder, public policy advisor, and foresight communicator. From his pioneering work in unstructured data analysis and linguistic genomics to his ground-breaking work in global finance and ethics, his life experience obtained in over 120 countries is woven into his first novel, Coup d'Twelve. Dr. Martin gained international notoriety for his data analysis in disclosure prior to the global financial crisis in 2008. His foresight work has been deployed in several international conflicts. He has been a guest on Bloomberg and NPR's This American Life; has been invited to testify in Congressional and EU Parliamentary hearings and roundtables; and has made numerous additional domestic and international media appearances. He shares his life with his wife Colleen and his two children, Katie and Zachary, along with a host of friends and colleagues around the world.

Made in the USA
Columbia, SC
09 May 2023

16294119R00212